MURDER FOR NOTHING

MURDER FOR NOTHING

An Ellie Quicke Mystery

Veronica Heley

This first world edition published 2017
in Great Britain and the USA by
SEVERN HOUSE PUBLISHERS LTD of
19 Cedar Road, Sutton, Surrey, England, SM2 5DA.
Trade paperback edition first published
in Great Britain and the USA 2017 by
SEVERN HOUSE PUBLISHERS LTD

British Library Cataloguing in Publication Data
A CIP catalogue record for this title is available from the British Library.

ISBN-13: 978-0-7278-8727-6 (cased)
ISBN-13: 978-1-84751-843-9 (trade paper)
ISBN-13: 978-1-78010-903-9 (e-book)

This is a work of fiction. Names, characters, places and incidents
are either the product of the author's imagination or are used fictitiously.
Except where actual historical events and characters are being described
for the storyline of this novel, all situations in this publication are
fictitious and any resemblance to actual persons, living or dead,
business establishments, events or locales is purely coincidental.

All Severn House titles are printed on acid-free paper.

Severn House Publishers support the Forest Stewardship Council™ [FSC™],
the leading international forest certification organisation.
All our titles that are printed on FSC certified paper carry the FSC logo.

MIX
Paper from
responsible sources
FSC
www.fsc.org   FSC® C013056

Typeset by Palimpsest Book Production Ltd.,
Falkirk, Stirlingshire, Scotland.
Printed and bound in Great Britain by
TJ International, Padstow, Cornwall.

ONE

*N*o good deed goes unpunished.
*Ellie Quicke, happily married and the head of a chari-
table trust fund, believed in helping people in trouble. And
none of her good deeds had returned to bite her until she took in
a weeping girl who needed somewhere to stay. The consequences
were mayhem and moneylending. Oh, and murder, of course.*

Monday morning

Ellie's three-year-old grandson had inherited his mother Diana's
determination, demanding his granny's attention with the relent-
lessness of a road drill. 'Biccy, biccy, biccy! I want biccy!'

The two agency cleaners were amused but they were poised to
leave, having completed their weekly assault on the house. 'Bye,
Mrs Quicke!' they said.

Ellie chased her grandson down the corridor and into the kitchen,
calling out, 'See you next week!' to the cleaners as she went. Evan
wasn't supposed to have a biscuit till lunchtime, and there was
another hour to go. She managed to catch him and turn him away
from the cupboards as the phone rang in the hall.

'Biccy!'

'Come on, lovey, let's get the phone first.' He'd dropped his
favourite soft toy on the floor. She picked it up and thrust it at him,
which almost diverted him from his pursuit for food, and did soften
his next demand.

'Biccy, Granny?' Ellie walked him back to the hall to answer the
phone. It didn't do to leave him alone or he'd have the contents of
the biscuit tin on the floor. She usually closed the doors to all the
ground-floor rooms before he arrived but sometimes the cleaners
left a door open as they moved through the house, and then Evan
would get in and create chaos. Tidying up after him could take
hours.

As Ellie went to pick up the phone, he slipped out of her grasp.

Horrors! He'd spotted Midge, the cat, who'd been having a nap on the hall chair. If he tried to tease Midge, if he went for the cat's tail . . . 'No, Evan, no!'

A thin scream announced that she was too late.

She swooped on Evan who, yelling fit to bring the roof down, slid out from between her arms and crumpled to the floor. Bother!

The phone continued to ring . . . and now the doorbell ditto . . . and the clock struck eleven.

Ellie opened her mouth to call on her husband for assistance, and then shut it again. He'd been called away on some emergency or other, hadn't he? Oh, dear.

With some difficulty, she managed to pick Evan up off the floor . . . phew! He was getting heavy and she wasn't getting any younger. Blood shot from his finger where Midge had scratched him and tears pearled on his fat cheeks. He bawled his grief into her ear, half deafening her. Where was his soft toy? He'd dropped it somewhere . . .

The phone continued to ring. As did the doorbell.

The only way to stop Evan was to distract him with a biscuit, even if it wasn't time for him to have a snack yet. But the biscuit tin was in the kitchen and the phone was ringing.

Balancing Evan on her hip, Ellie reached for the phone. 'Yes . . .?'

A tinny voice, which Ellie could hardly hear.

She said, 'Who? Can you speak up, please?'

'Ellie, are you in? Could I . . .? May we . . .? I need to . . .'

Ellie concentrated. The racket that Evan was making! 'Lesley? Is that you?' Lesley, her friend from the police, was on honeymoon, wasn't she? Not due back till the end of the week.

Evan turned puce with rage. His lung capacity was formidable. Ellie didn't normally like offering a bribe, but . . . 'Evan, would you like a biscuit?' That did it. He stopped mid-yell. Ellie returned to the phone. 'Lesley, is that you?'

'It's me,' said Lesley. 'I can't believe it! They say it's murder!'

Evan threw himself backwards. Ellie staggered but managed to hang on to him . . . just. She said into the phone, 'Hold on! I'll be back in a minute!' She dropped the receiver and rushed through into the kitchen, where she found the biscuit tin and, one-handed, managed to open it. Evan grabbed two biscuits, one in each hand. His colour was miraculously restored to normal as Ellie bore him back to the phone in the hall, where she set him down on the floor to pick up the receiver again.

The doorbell continued to ring.

Could she reach the front door while she was on the phone? No. 'Lesley, sorry about that. Are you still there? Where are you?'

Lesley and her husband were supposed to be camping somewhere in the north of England, weren't they?

'I'm really sorry to disturb you, Ellie,' said the voice with a crackle in it. Lesley must be on her mobile phone. Was the battery running out? 'May I . . . may we . . . come round? Now?'

Ellie said, 'Yes, of course, but . . . Lesley, what's wrong?'

'Be with you in a minute.' Tension twanged over the line. Lesley cut the call.

Someone was still beating out a rhythm on the front doorbell. Ellie crashed the phone down and hastened to open the door. It was half past eleven in the morning. A parcel delivery?

No. It was her young house guest, Angelica, who had begged for a room for a few days till she could sort herself out, and who had outstayed her welcome in spades. Angelica had described herself as a party girl. Unfortunately that description had proved to be nothing but the truth, as she had twice got Ellie out of bed to answer the door at three in the morning, saying she'd forgotten her key.

Today, Angelica was laden with shopping bags and was wearing a blindingly white smile. 'I've forgotten my key again. Silly me!'

Angelica was a true blonde with a peaches-and-cream complexion and green eyes set below dark eyebrows. She imagined her astonishing good looks would take her to the heights of a modelling career but did nothing to make her dreams come true. Also, she ignored all the rules a house guest normally observed. She played loud music at unsocial hours, expected to be fed at Ellie's expense but left junk food containers around, had failed to offer Ellie any money for rent and hadn't lifted a finger to help in the house. Ellie felt that the sooner the girl left, the better.

Now Angelica swept past Ellie into the hall. 'Can you pay the taxi for me? I'm right out of change.'

'What!' said Ellie, torn between wanting to box the girl's ears and amusement.

'You're a doll!' Angelica batted her eyelashes at Ellie and made for the stairs.

Outside in the drive, someone shouted, 'Oi! Who's paying!' It was the taxi driver, who'd descended from his cab in search of his fare.

Ellie sang out, 'Hold on a mo!' Where had she left her purse?

Evan wandered back into the hall, having raided the biscuit tin – again! He wouldn't be able to manage his lunch, would he? But for the moment, he was Sunny Jim in person.

Ellie said, 'Evan, have you seen my handbag?'

'Why?' Evan's response to all questions was to ask this.

'Because Angelica is in trouble and I'm trying to help her.' Not that Evan would care about that. Ellie pounced on her handbag, which had landed on the floor by the clock for some reason. Also at the foot of the clock was Evan's favourite toy, a pink velvet Hippo. Ellie picked it up and gave it to him to tuck under his arm.

Sorting out some money for the taxi driver, Ellie decided that she really must have a word with Miss Angelica. The thing was, where else was the girl to go? Apparently she'd quarrelled with her mother, who had turned her out some months ago. After that, she'd moved in with Ellie's friend Lesley and her fiancé until, just before their wedding, Angelica had been thrown out of there as well.

The reasons were understandable. Angelica was a spoiled brat who could wind her dear cousin Andy round her little finger. He indulged her as everyone in that family seemed to have done, until Lesley had put her foot down and shot the girl out, which didn't surprise Ellie one bit. What surprised Ellie was that Lesley had put up with the girl's behaviour for as long as she had.

Ellie promised herself a reckoning with Miss Angelica, soon. And she would get a receipt from the taxi driver to present to the girl.

At that moment, Midge the cat made a mistake. He leaped down from the high ledge on which he'd taken refuge out of Evan's reach and sped across the hall with the intention of going upstairs to spend some downtime on Ellie's bed . . . and Evan spotted him.

Dropping Hippo, Evan lunged for the cat. Ellie was just a fraction too slow, but she did manage to grab him from behind and lift him into her arms. He jackknifed in them and shouted, 'No! Down!'

Midge laid back his ears and streaked up the stairs.

Evan wriggled out of Ellie's arms, half fell and half jumped to the floor and set off after Midge. Fortunately or otherwise, he tripped over his own feet and landed on his face, losing the remains of his biscuit. Ellie cringed as Evan drew breath, ready to let out one of his ear-splitting yells.

She scooped him up . . . oh, her back! And staggered out of the house to pay the taxi driver, who was fuming at the delay. Evan kicked and yelled.

'Got a good set of lungs on him!' said the taxi driver as he cleaned Ellie out of cash and wrote her a receipt.

He was no sooner out of the drive than another car drove in. 'Thank God,' said Ellie as her daughter Diana erupted from the car. Diana was dressed all in black, and was in a matching black mood.

'What's the matter, poppet?' Diana didn't wait for an answer but plucked Evan from Ellie's hold, at which he sat up in her arms and smiled. The little . . . rogue!

Diana said, 'What have you been doing to him? And what's that? Have you been feeding him biscuits at this time of day?'

Ellie took a deep breath and prepared to defend herself but Diana wasn't listening.

'Well, I would have thought you could have looked after him better, what with you having nothing else to do all day . . .!' Diana inserted Even into the baby seat in the back of her car and buckled him in with a jerky movement. 'I need to get back.'

'Wait!' Ellie scrambled back to fetch Hippo, without whom Evan refused to go to sleep. She dusted him down and rushed back to the car as Diana was getting herself back into the driver's seat.

Diana said, 'Same time tomorrow, right?' and turned the key in the ignition.

Ellie wanted to say that she didn't think she could look after Evan properly any more. He was exhausting. But, before she could do so, Diana was gone in a swirl of dust, honking as another car tried to enter the driveway. Diana made the other car wait. Of course.

The other car inched its way into the drive and parked. Badly.

Ellie's friend, Lesley Milburn, was driving, with her very new husband in the passenger seat.

Without waiting for his wife, Andy erupted on to the driveway in a flurry of bad language. Ginger hair, rugby-playing build, wearing holiday gear of a black T-shirt and jogging trousers. A charging bull of a man in a shocking temper. He bellowed, 'Where are you hiding her, then?'

'What?' said Ellie. 'Who?' She went round the car to reach Lesley, who hadn't moved from her seat. 'My dear, whatever's happened? Come on in.'

Andy set off for the house, yelling, 'That bitch, Susan! Where is she? I'm going to wring her—'

Ellie blinked. Susan was Lesley's niece, a stocky, ginger-haired, dependable girl in her twenties who was training to be a chef. When she'd first started her training – long before Angelica had turned up – Susan had lodged temporarily with Lesley and Andy. She'd left because the flat really wasn't suitable for three people, but she'd been such an easy person to have around that Lesley had asked if Ellie could give the girl a room in her house.

Susan had proved to be an ideal tenant for Ellie, renting the flat at the top of Ellie's house and becoming a valued member of the household. She didn't just observe the house rules, she paid her rent on time and sometimes cooked for the family. So what did Andy want with Susan?

Ellie opened the driver's door to help Lesley out, but her friend didn't seem to know how to move.

Lesley said, 'Susan and murder. It doesn't sound right, does it?'

'What?' Susan and murder?

No, it certainly didn't sound right. Lesley didn't sound right, either. Or look it. Her colour was bad, more green than peach, and she made no move to leave the car. Ellie wasn't sure she could lift Lesley out of the car, and would have called out to Andy for help if he hadn't already disappeared into the house.

Lesley lifted a tired face to Ellie. A tear leaked from the corner of one eye. 'Oh, Ellie! I don't know what to do.'

'First things first. Let's get you out of there.' Ellie half pulled and half steered Lesley out of the car and steadied her, making sure she could balance on her own two feet. 'Can you walk?'

They could hear the bull roaring inside the house. 'Susan! Get the hell down here! Now!'

Ellie was puzzled. 'What does he want with Susan? She's at college, as usual.'

Lesley shook her head. 'It's not murder. It can't be.'

Ellie forbore to question Lesley further as she looked on the verge of passing out. Lesley was some thirty years younger than Ellie, but she wobbled across the drive and into the hall like an old woman.

Andy and Lesley were supposed to be on honeymoon. Obviously something had happened to disrupt their plans. But not murder! No way!

From the first floor came the sound of doors slamming as Andy explored, shouting, 'Susan! Where the devil are you hiding!' Music assaulted their ears as he opened another door.

A girl screamed. Angelica? 'Andy, do you mind!' Followed by laughter. Angelica obviously didn't really object to Andy bursting in on her. Had she been trying on some of the garments she'd just bought?

'Oh, sorry, Angel.' He moderated his voice. 'Where's Susan, then?'

Giggle, giggle. 'How should I know?'

Actually, Susan and Angelica had never got on. Angelica wasn't kind to anyone whose unfashionable curves attracted attention.

Angelica squealed, 'Andy, please! Can't you see I'm changing?'

'Oh. Well. Sorry.' He shut her door.

Ellie called up the stairs, 'Andy, Susan isn't home yet.'

Either Andy hadn't heard her or he'd chosen to ignore what Ellie said, for he continued to throw open doors along the corridor.

Ellie shrugged and helped Lesley through the hall and into the sitting room at the back. 'Let's get you comfortable.'

Andy's heavy footsteps continued overhead. A moment later, they heard him pounding up the second flight of stairs to Susan's flat on the attic floor. 'Susan! I know you're in there!'

Ellie helped Lesley on to the settee. 'Cup of tea, right? And then you can tell me all about it.' She reflected that it must be something fairly dramatic to have brought the newlyweds back home early. Murder? No, come off it! And Lesley had said it wasn't murder. And anyway, why was Andy in search of Susan?

Ellie would have released her hold on her friend in order to get her some tea, but Lesley clutched her hand.

'Ellie, I'm destroyed.'

Ellie listened to what Lesley was saying without words. Lesley felt she was destroyed. Why and how? Ellie said gently, 'Tell me.'

'The flat. Wrecked. Burgled. We can't stay there.' A tear welled up in each eye.

Ellie shook her head in silent sympathy. A burglary? Bad news.

The bull thundered down the stairs and burst into the room. 'You're hiding her from me and I won't have it. Where have you put her? I'm going to twist her neck round till her eyes pop out of—'

Ellie put as much authority into her voice as she could. 'Andy, stop! I told you, Susan's not here. She's never home at this time of day.'

'What!' His colour was bad. Was he going to have a heart attack? He confronted Ellie, nose to nose. 'So where is she?'

Ellie refused to give way. 'You know where she is. She's at college.'

'But the police must have been round here, looking for her. You'd better come up with some answers, right?'

'What?' Ellie tried to get through to him. 'I haven't seen any police. I've been in all morning, babysitting my grandson. Susan is not here. She's at college. You know that perfectly well. She goes every day. Why would they be looking for her, anyway?'

He didn't shift. 'She's your responsibility. You'd better produce her, right?'

Lesley made a small sound. She was clearly distressed, and so pale that Ellie wondered if she were going to faint.

Lesley tried to speak. 'I'm sure it wasn't—'

'Yes, it was. Of course it was. Deceitful bitch! I never took to her.'

Lesley lifted a hand to her head. 'You were fine about her moving in with us for a while. She paid her way which helped us to save, and I really don't think—'

'That's your trouble, Lesley,' said the bull. 'You don't think!'

Ellie could hardly credit what she heard. How rude! How insensitive! What was the matter with the man? For two pins she'd give him a piece of her mind. He should be looking after Lesley instead of shouting at her. Ellie didn't like his tone and, come to think of it, she'd never really taken to him, either.

But she swallowed the sharp words that had risen to her tongue. It wasn't up to her to intervene between a newly-married couple. Something had clearly upset them, something about the flat. First things first. 'Exactly what has happened?'

Lesley's pallor had taken on a Halloween-green tinge. Was she going to be sick?

Um, yes. Lesley made a convulsive movement out of her seat, and Ellie helped her out of the sitting room and down the corridor into the kitchen. Lesley vanished into the toilet, and yes, she was comprehensively sick.

Ellie put the kettle on, trying to take in the situation. Andy was the deputy head of a primary school, keen on sport and flexing his muscles. Lesley was an old friend of Ellie's, climbing the ladder in the police force. They'd got married ten, no, eleven days ago.

They were not acting like newlyweds.

No, they weren't, were they? Some people said the first year of married life was the hardest as each had to adapt to the other. Usually there was enough love between the couple to see them through the rough patches. What had gone wrong here?

Well, for one thing, Ellie had always wondered whether or not the two were a good match. Lesley had a stressful job in the police and liked to unwind when off-duty by going to the pub or meeting up with friends. He, on the other hand, was something of a fitness fanatic, ultra-neat and tidy in the house. He'd reached the position of deputy head in a primary school in double-quick time, but had so far failed to land a headship. Plus, his temper was uncertain.

One week before the wedding, Lesley had almost called the whole thing off but gone through with it in the end. But now, less than a fortnight later, she was clearly unwell and he was criticizing her in front of other people.

Ellie busied herself with picking up the biscuit tin, which had ended up on the floor, with broken pieces of biscuit strewn around. She thought that Lesley would tell her what had happened in a minute. What should they have for lunch? A sandwich of some sort. Perhaps some home-made soup? More importantly, what would they have for supper tonight? Was this one of the nights when Susan had planned to cook for them? Ellie couldn't remember.

She couldn't stop thinking of what Lesley had said: 'I'm destroyed.'

Ellie wondered if the girl had meant not only that her flat had been wrecked but had also realized she'd made a horrible mistake in marrying Andy . . .? Which Ellie would understand.

It was not a good situation for Lesley to be in.

Lesley had a flat on the ground floor of an old house up by the church, which she'd been sharing with Andy for some six months or so. If they had been burgled . . . but Lesley had said something about murder. Surely that wasn't right.

Ellie checked the fridge. Sliced ham and tomatoes would do for lunch, but what did they have which they could eat tonight? Um. Not much.

Andy charged into the kitchen, mobile phone in hand. 'Give me Susan's phone number. I want her back here, now!'

Ellie disliked confrontation and her first reaction was to do as she was bidden, but no, she didn't like being ordered about and she decided to sidestep his demand. 'Your wife is not well. Wouldn't you like to see to her first?'

'This is all her fault! You do realize, don't you, that everything is on my computer? I told her, "I need to take it with me." She said I'd relax better without it and she took it out of the car and put it back in the flat. Can you believe it! And now, where do you think it is? Down the pawn shop? Sold on through someone in the pub?'

That was bad news indeed. Ellie said, 'What exactly has happened?'

He strode around, waving his mobile phone. 'The flat's been wrecked! It's uninhabitable! Everything of value has gone. It looks as if there was an illegal party there and, to make matters worse, there's a dead girl in the garden!'

TWO

E llie gaped. 'A dead girl in your garden? You mean . . . murdered?'

'I assume so. She's just been dumped there, like so much rubbish.'

'Who was she?'

'How should I know? A party girl, I suppose.'

'You didn't know her?'

'What! Me? No, of course not.'

'Did you see the body?'

'They showed me photos. Ugh. They said she'd been a pretty girl. Lots of red hair. I didn't know her from Adam, and neither did Lesley.'

A key turned in the lock of the front door, and someone called out, 'Hello, I'm home!'

'Susan!' Andy's colour rose. He thumped the table. 'Where have you been?'

'What?' Susan appeared in the doorway. Andy might have a rugby player's build but Susan was also solidly built. She was not conventionally pretty and never bothered with make-up, but her frontage was fabulous and nowadays she did wear low-cut T-shirts to show off her assets.

'Where have I been?' Susan dumped some bags of food on the table. 'We had a couple of hours off so I went shopping for tonight's supper. I heard of this new deli, thought I'd check it out. Salad, cheese, pâté, ham. What's up, Andy? I thought you weren't due back till the weekend. Where's Lesley?'

'I'm here.' Lesley appeared, looking frail. 'Sorry, everyone. Sorry, Andy.' She sank into a chair as if it were too much trouble to stand.

Andy blared at Susan. 'So why aren't you under arrest?'

Susan opened her very blue eyes wide. She decided he was joking. She laughed. 'What? What for?' She began to put her purchases in the fridge. 'The deli is something else. Three shelves of cheeses, right? Some even I'd never heard of.'

Ellie said, 'Let's all calm down. Andy, sit down. Start from the beginning. You and Lesley went off up north. You were called back because burglars got into your flat while you were away, right?'

'Not burglars, no. At least . . .' He gestured widely. 'All I know is that the people in the flat above us were also away this last weekend. They got back late last night, looked out of their sitting-room window when they went to draw the curtains and saw something odd – not in their part of the garden, in ours. They went down to investigate and found a girl lying there, dead. Can you believe it! In the bushes! And that's all Lesley's fault, too.'

Lesley put her head in her hands as Andy ploughed on. 'I told her, I said we want a low-maintenance garden. She should have ripped all those plants out. What do we want with a lot of shrubs and flowers? But she always found some reason why . . . And now look what's happened! A girl, dumped in the bushes. No identification; nothing.'

'That's terrible,' said Ellie.

'Not half as bad as what they found in our place. The entrance to our flat is round the side of the house, so our neighbours hadn't noticed that anything was wrong at first. But when they went down to the garden they found our front door open, lights left on and a trail of destruction. Oh, God! Water leaking from a smashed toilet, the gas still burning! The place wrecked! Everything! The fridge and the freezer left open, the telly tipped on to its back, my laptop, and hers, of course, all gone! Plus most of our wedding presents.'

Lesley covered her mouth with her hands, trying not to choke . . . or to vomit? She waved her hand and rushed off back to the toilet.

Ellie waited to see if Andy would follow his wife but he didn't. Perhaps he knew she'd prefer to be sick by herself? She said, 'So it wasn't just a burglary, then?'

'The police think it was an illegal rave. The flat upstairs hadn't been touched. Our neighbours hadn't been so stupid as to leave a key with anyone else, had they! Anyway, when they found the body they phoned the police, who phoned us. We were way out in the sticks and didn't get the message at first. And when we did, we had to drive back through the night, only to find . . .' He raised his fists in the air.

'Why do the police think it was a party?'

'Noise. They asked the neighbours. There'd been complaints over the weekend. Comings and goings. Susan had advertised a party on the Internet and they went to town on it, didn't they?'

'What? Don't be ridiculous,' said Susan.

Ellie shook her head. 'No, Susan wouldn't do that.'

'Of course she would. Anything for money. She had the key, hadn't she? And why my dear wife thought it was a good idea to entrust the key to our place to you, you lump of lard, I do not know!'

Susan reddened and looked as if she were about to slosh Andy, so Ellie said, 'That's very rude, Andy. And not true, either.' Susan was a well-built girl with an impressive bosom, but she was not a lump of lard.

Andy wasn't to be diverted. 'It's all of a piece! Lesley has no sense at all! Fancy giving the key to a college student! I told her, "You do realize your folly has invalidated our insurance!"'

'But I didn't!' gasped Susan. 'I wouldn't! Honest!'

Lesley fumbled her way back into the kitchen and dropped into a chair. She looked so pale that Ellie was alarmed.

Andy, however, was focused on Susan. 'You had a key!'

'Well, yes, I did. Lesley asked me to look in and see if her pot plants needed a drop of water midweek and I'd planned to go tomorrow, but—'

'Then you advertised a rave party on—'

'No. Never!'

Lesley shook her head. 'No, Andy. I'm sure she didn't.'

Someone sang out from the hall, 'I'm just off. Might be back late. Don't worry if I am. I found my spare key, so I can let myself in.' The front door opened and shut behind the girl.

'Angelica!' said Ellie, understanding that someone other than Susan might well have been responsible for holding a party in her cousin's flat.

Lesley echoed, 'Angelica, of course. Andy, you gave Angelica a key?'

'No, I—'

'But she had one when she was living with you, didn't she?'

said Ellie. 'Did she give it back to you when you threw her out? She does tend to mislay keys. She's done it here, too. Perhaps she had a copy made when she was living with you and kept it when she left?'

'What!' Colour flared in Andy's cheeks. 'How dare you! Just because she's young and beautiful, you've got a downer on her! I've heard that people who are past it can be jealous of the young, but this . . . this takes the biscuit!'

Lesley protested, 'Andy, please!'

Ellie didn't want a shouting match so tried not to react to his offensive language. Yes, she had been knocked off balance by his insinuation that she was 'past it', particularly since life with her dear husband Thomas was full of interest and that included time out in the bedroom. She told herself that she was a grown woman and perfectly able to deal with a short-sighted and delusional idiot like Andy.

She tried for the voice of reason. 'Your cousin Angelica is short of money. She has no job. She complains she hasn't a penny to fly with and yet she's been out on yet another shopping spree today. So I ask you again, did she return her key when she left your place?'

'What are you suggesting? That's slander!'

'No worse than you suggesting that Susan made wrongful use of her key.'

'Angelica would never do that to me. She would never let our flat be wrecked!'

'I don't suppose it ever entered her mind that it might happen,' said Ellie. 'But she's not exactly Brain of Britain, is she?'

Andy reddened. 'How dare you talk like that about my cousin!'

'If she advertised a party on the Internet, a lot of uninvited guests might well turn up and she'd be unable to control what happened.'

He wasn't entertaining that thought for a second. Also, he knew that the best form of defence is attack. He turned on Ellie. 'You only say that because you are a jealous, spiteful old woman who has long since lost any appeal she might have had to men!'

Lesley groaned but, before Ellie could tell him to mind his language, Susan fired up. 'How dare you! Mrs Quicke is the kindest, nicest, most generous . . . Oh, I could do you an injury if it weren't beneath me to do so!'

'Please!' Lesley's voice shook. 'Andy, you don't mean it. Ellie really is not . . . I'm so sorry, everyone. I don't know what's the matter with me.'

Ellie examined a thought which had been hovering at the back of her mind. Was Lesley pregnant? Was she suffering from morning sickness?

Andy either hadn't guessed or was in denial. 'For heaven's sake, Les! Pull yourself together. You got us into this mess and you'll have to deal with it.'

Lesley closed her eyes and quivered.

Ellie put her hand on Lesley's shoulder. 'You are on leave, aren't you? Then let your colleagues at the police deal with it. I assume you've been called back to give them a statement about what you know?'

'Yes, of course,' said Andy, flinging himself into another chair. 'Fancy being dragged back from honeymoon for this! They asked me to provide a list of everything that's been stolen. I can tell you, that's going to take for ever because all the wedding presents went as well. We hadn't even unwrapped some of them. Worse still, I shall have to get another computer first thing, and who's going to pay for that, I ask you!'

Lesley said, 'I've been meaning to tell you that—'

Andy overrode her. 'Everything is on it! My whole life! Wrecked!'

Ellie said, 'Andy, Lesley doesn't look too good to me. Who's her doctor? Is she with the practice in the Avenue?'

He blustered. 'There's nothing wrong with her, just a spot of travel sickness. I told her, she should pull herself together. She brought all this on herself. She said she'd take care of every-thing, that we could leave the flat just as it was. And look what happens!'

Ellie said, 'Lesley, shall I give your doctor a ring?'

Lesley shook her head. She ran her tongue over dry lips. 'No, no.' She even tried to smile. 'Just some water, please?'

'My dear, of course.' Ellie got a glass of water for her friend as the front doorbell rang.

Ellie looked at Susan, who said, 'I'll get it, shall I?' And disappeared while Ellie gave Lesley the water.

Ellie was worried. She put her hand on her friend's forehead to check that she wasn't running a temperature, which she wasn't.

Susan returned, looking somewhat flushed. She said, 'This is Rafael.' Someone she knew?

A stranger. Tall, dark and handsome wasn't sufficient to describe him, though he was all of those. What else? An impression of old money and a sense of entitlement, but a sardonic twist to the mouth hinted that he didn't take himself seriously. If it wasn't a pejorative term nowadays, you'd say he was a gentleman. But that wasn't all of it, either.

Late twenties, maybe? Tall and willowy, he moved with grace. Dark-skinned enough to be of Mediterranean origin. Longish dark hair; thin eyebrows which had possibly been attended to by a beautician. Clean-shaven and lightly scented. Lips on the thin side? Eyes, brown. Contact lenses?

Clothes, all black; a soft-as-air leather jacket over a silk shirt, and trousers which had been made for him. An expensive package.

Attractive? Oh, yes.

Trustworthy? Mm, possibly not.

Susan was unusually brusque. 'Rafael says he was supposed to meet up with Angelica this morning but she didn't show up. He's come round to see if she's all right.'

The newcomer extended his hand to Ellie. 'You,' he turned his smile on Ellie, 'must be the delightful Mrs Quicke, who has been so kind as to take Angelica in. Sorry to intrude. I must have just missed the little puss.'

Ellie was attracted but some part of her brain warned her to beware. The man had brains, but . . . a complex personality?

Rafael moved on to Andy. 'And you must be her wonderful cousin, the one she talks about all the time? Andrew, is that right?'

Andy deflated like a punctured balloon. 'Sure. Her cousin. And you are . . .? I don't think she's mentioned you?'

'Puss hasn't told you about me? Naughty puss. I must have words. I've heard so much about all of you – the wedding, and her being your bridesmaid and all.' He held out his hand to Lesley. 'And you are the clever one of the family? Something in the police? I will have to be careful what I say in front of the constabulary. Correct?'

Lesley let him shake her hand. And said . . . nothing.

Ellie reckoned Lesley wasn't often at a loss for words but she herself wasn't sure what line to take with this man, either.

He seemed perfectly at his ease, looking around, appreciating what he saw. 'I do love these big old houses. They remind me of my childhood. High ceilings, furniture handed down through the generations. Our house was on the river. Chilly in the winter but pleasant in the summer.'

Nobody seemed to know what to say to that, either.

Ellie wondered about offering to make a cuppa for everyone and decided against it.

Rafael said, 'Have I called at a bad time? I sense some tension in the air.'

'Yes,' said Andy.

'We-ell,' said Ellie.

He smiled his thin smile. 'The problem is that I keep missing Puss. She was supposed to meet me yesterday but she said she had the collywobbles and couldn't make it . . .'

Ellie looked at Susan, and Susan looked back at Ellie, frowning. Angelica hadn't said anything to either of them about having a stomach upset, had she?

'Then she promised to meet me this morning without fail, and although the coffee shop in the Avenue is good, I wouldn't wish to drink more than one cup. She didn't answer her phone, so I thought I had better come round to see what was going on.' He looked straight at Ellie.

Ellie didn't know what to say. 'She went out this morning, shopping—'

'Ah.' That seemed to mean something to him?

'And came back a short while ago. She changed and went out again. I don't know where.'

His eyes narrowed, turning his face into a mask.

Andy rushed into speech. 'I don't know who you are, or what you want with my cousin, but—'

'She has something of mine.'

Andy said, 'Well, I'm sure she'll return it to you when she can. Obviously there's been some misunderstanding about—'

He shook his head. 'Twice she's arranged to meet. Twice failed to do so. And there's been innumerable missed phone calls. She tells me she's broke, but this morning she's *been shopping*?' He put so much meaning into this that they all understood that Angelica had some money of his and was in the process of spending it.

Andy reddened. 'You can't just go around accusing—'

'I haven't accused anyone of anything, have I? I see no need to involve the police, yet, as this must be a family matter for you, Andrew, and for your dear wife . . .' Here he ducked his head to Lesley, who didn't seem to be listening.

'My business card,' he said, placing one on the table. 'I would like my property to be returned with the least possible delay. If there is a shortfall, which seems likely in view of Puss's shopping spree, then I expect you to make it up. Understood?'

'What!' Andy was slow on the uptake, wasn't he?

Lesley slapped the table, open-handed. 'You've lent her money and she hasn't returned it?'

Rafael's eyebrows raised. 'You have it in one.'

Lesley wasn't listening. 'She owes you money but has no means of repaying it. Did you know she held a party in our flat at the weekend?'

Something changed at the back of Rafael's eyes. For a second he looked shocked, and then he brought out his smile again. 'Your flat? I understood that it belonged to Puss, an investment on the part of her parents.'

Andy blinked. 'What? You mean . . .? But her father's dead and her mother hasn't two pennies to rub together. That flat is ours. Do you mean that she took you there? Why?'

'It seems I was misinformed.' A silky tone, but it was clear that he was *not* amused. Had Rafael believed that Angelica had moneyed parents who would be only too happy to subsidise her extravagance?

Lesley was pursuing her own line of thought. 'You've seen the flat? Did she invite you in for a business chat over coffee? Or for another reason?'

Ellie considered Rafael's good looks and the thought sneaked into her mind that he might have been visiting Angelica in the flat for sex. Yet was he the sort to pay for it? No. Resoundingly not. This man would never have to pay for it.

Lesley said, 'Was she using our flat as a knocking shop? Ugh!'

'Ridiculous!' said Andy, reddening further. 'She wouldn't do that.'

Rafael swept the suggestion aside. 'Not my scene. Business and pleasure should be kept separate. She did say she'd planned to have a party, true. She invited me, in fact. But I had another engagement.'

Lesley leaped on that. 'How many people did she invite? And how? There are reports from the neighbours of loud music and lots of people coming and going. So, somehow or other, the news must have leaked out that there was a party and people turned up with or without an invitation—'

'I repeat, not my scene.'

Lesley rubbed her forehead. 'The neighbours complained about the noise. It's on police record that they complained.'

'If I had been there, perhaps I would have sympathized with the neighbours,' murmured Rafael.

'But then . . .' Lesley was frowning, trying to concentrate. 'Something happened to turn the mood of the party to destruction. What happened, Rafael?'

He spread his hands. 'I have no idea. I had another, better offer that night.'

'Are you telling us that you were not there that evening? Not at all?'

'Indeed. A friend had tickets to the opera. An international company appearing at the Coliseum. Of slight value, but I do feel one should keep abreast of the latest developments in the arts. I was, I admit, somewhat bored. I even thought of leaving after the first act but decided to stick it out. After all, I was accompanying a beautiful girl and I couldn't abandon her there, could I?'

'Surely you can't have been foolish enough to think Angelica would manage a party without it turning into a riot? What of the girl who died?'

'What?' He took a half step backwards. This time he really was shocked. 'A girl died? Really? How? I suppose I need hardly ask that. Drugs, one assumes? I didn't think Puss was into that scene, but . . . if you invite all and sundry into your house, drugs will follow as night follows day. I do not care for them, myself. Now, I really must be on my way. I have spent far too much time on this affair already. I would suggest that in your dealings with the Plod, you forget my name. I do not wish to be associated with drugs.'

'Can you prove it?' Lesley was being bulldoggish.

'Can you?' His eyebrows rose. 'Even if you are with the police, you are not beyond suspicion. What will your superiors say when they discover you let your flat out for a party which ended in drugs and death?'

Andy was purple in the face. 'We did nothing of the kind!'

Lesley put a hand on his arm. 'Don't, Andy. Can't you see he's winding you up?'

Andy shook her off. 'He's a liar. I don't believe he refused an invitation to a party. He's responsible for our flat being wrecked and my property stolen, and he's trying to get away with it by saying he has an alibi for the evening! Well, the police shall hear about this.'

'I said,' Rafael's voice hardened, 'I can prove I was not there.'

Andy wasn't listening to reason. 'Get out! Out! Before I lose my temper and lay my hands on you.'

'Dear me.' Rafael looked at his watch – a very good, expensive watch. 'How crude! And totally unnecessary. I thought I was dealing with civilized people. Well, one lives and learns. I have another appointment, so I must reluctantly tear myself away. With one last thought. I am a businessman and I have a written contract with Miss Angelica. I cannot afford to let my customers default on payment. You understand? I must therefore hold you all – yes, all of you – responsible for its return. And if I don't get it . . .' A shrug.

'Then what?' said Andy, glowering.

'We don't need to talk about that, do we? Mud does stick so. Even for people with a previously perfect record, such as your dear wife. Even for teachers, in a position of responsibility. Even, I am sorry to say, for elderly ladies who run a charity. When fingers are pointed . . .' He smiled thinly. 'But I am sure there is no need to go as far as that. No, no. We will come to some agreement, right? There's no need to see me out.'

He took his time about leaving, letting his eyes linger on each of them in turn. On Ellie, Andy and Lesley, and finally on Susan, who had very sensibly kept herself out of the conversation. Rafael walked by Susan without looking at her again. She flattened herself against the wall to let him pass.

Rafael drifted off down the corridor and they heard the front door open and close.

Ellie sank on to a chair, thinking that she'd come across some villains in her time but that Rafael was like a poisonous snake. His threats still hung in the air. Poison, yes.

Except that Ellie had to concede that Rafael had reason on his side. He was a businessman working in a shadowy industry. He lent money out and expected a return on it. Possibly he was charging an extortionate rate of interest, but it was up to his customers to agree to it or not. He was a hard man. Yes. But you could see his point of view.

Lesley reached out to touch her husband. 'Andy . . .?'

He shook her off. He said, 'That was blackmail. We must tell the police.'

'No, it's not blackmail. It's business.' Lesley let her hand fall to the table.

Ellie looked at Susan, who hadn't moved since Rafael had left and was now staring into space. Susan had been uncharacteristically quiet during Rafael's visit, hadn't she?

Lesley said, 'Andy, I must tell you . . . Oh, sorry. Excuse me . . .' And vanished to the toilet.

Andy was working himself up into another temper tantrum. 'What a scam artist! Did he expect us to take him seriously?'

Ellie thought it would be wise to take him very, very seriously. 'You must talk to Angelica about it, find out how much she borrowed and at what rate of interest.'

'Poor kid! Why didn't she come to me if she needed money? Then she wouldn't have had to get mixed up with that scumbag.'

Ellie said, 'May I remind you that Angelica is an adult and ought to take responsibility for her actions? Discuss it with your wife.'

'Lesley won't do anything to harm Angelica. Anyway, Lesley's on sick leave. You can see she's not up to working.'

Ellie reminded herself it was never any good interfering between husband and wife and you should never, ever take sides. The two of them must work out their own path in life. She changed tack. 'How long has Lesley been like this? Has she seen a doctor?'

Andy said, 'Oh, she picks up viruses all the time, can never go on an airplane without collecting some kind of bug.'

Susan inserted herself into the conversation. 'Andy, I don't think this is travel sickness.'

'No, well, she must have eaten something. It started a couple of days before we got married and got worse – we had to stop at every service station on the motorway. Honestly, I thought we'd never get there. I can't drive at the moment, with my leg . . .'

The week before the wedding Lesley had had, with good reason, a showdown with Andy over Angelica's behaviour. Instead of throwing something at him, she'd thrown a mug at the wall. The mug had broken and ricocheted, inflicting a cut on Andy's knee. Lesley had driven him to hospital to have the cut stitched up. Lesley had felt guilty and Andy had made the cut an excuse to get out of doing anything physical . . . including the driving, apparently.

Andy rubbed his knee, pulling a face to show it still hurt. 'And what a fuss she made about having to put up the tent and . . . well, it was all her own fault, wasn't it?'

Ellie knew why Lesley had lost her temper and, though of course it wasn't right to throw things, breaking the mug had been an accident and, if Ellie had been in Lesley's place, she was pretty sure she'd have done more than throw a mug at the wall. Andy's behaviour had not been without blame.

'And she kept me awake that night, crawling out to be sick every five minutes. It's enough to make anyone lose their cool. I told her to take something to settle her stomach but she didn't seem to understand how it made it impossible for me to sleep, and when I gave in and we went to a B and B for the rest of the week, she wasn't any better. Even when I'd found this splendid restaurant which cost the earth, she wouldn't eat anything but bread. What a way to start a marriage!'

Ellie tried to count on her fingers. 'How many days has she been vomiting?'

Andy shrugged. 'Too many! I ask you, what sort of honeymoon was that? And then, to be yanked back from Yorkshire to find the flat wrecked and my belongings stolen . . . well!'

Lesley returned, her forehead glistening with sweat. 'Andy, it's no good. I have to lie down for a bit. Ellie, I'm sorry to be such a nuisance. We shouldn't have come here. We'll go to a B and B somewhere.'

'No, you don't,' said Ellie, casting her lot for good or ill. 'You're not fit to go anywhere. You say the flat's uninhabitable. How about dossing down here for the night?'

'Oh, I couldn't.' But her eyes said, *Help me!*

Ellie said, 'Andy, have you booked anywhere for tonight?'

'What do you think I'm made of? All I could think of was—'

'Getting back to London, seeing the police and getting hold of

Susan,' said Ellie. 'I understand. 'But now you know it wasn't Susan who started all this—'

'Well, it certainly wasn't Angelica!'

Ellie, Susan and Lesley looked at him, each asking themselves how he could be so blind and coming to approximately the same conclusion, which was that men were not to be trusted to use their common sense when beauty was involved.

Andy seemed to be reconsidering his boorish behaviour. A bed for the night? He bit his lip and his colour rose. Was he ashamed of his former behaviour? Yes, but he wasn't going so far as to apologize for it. Ellie could see him calculating the cost of going to a hotel against the offer of free accommodation. It was too much to expect him to apologize. Or was it? Yes, apparently it was. But, he did manage to say, 'Well, that's, if you're offering . . . well, thank you. That would be helpful. Just for tonight.'

Lesley said, 'Ellie, I'd love it, but won't it be too much for you?'

Susan squared her shoulders. 'How can I help? Mrs Quicke, do you want me to move out of the top flat for them?'

'No, my dear. That's your space, and anyway, there are only single beds up there.' Ellie strongly believed that if husband and wife had had a difference of opinion, a cuddle in bed would smooth the way to a reconciliation. Andy and Lesley might not be getting on particularly well – an understatement? – but if they were tucked up in bed together tonight they would, surely, find comfort in one another's arms?

Ellie calculated this and that. 'Angelica must move out of the main guest room, which has a double bed in it and is en suite. Andy and Lesley can go in there and there'll be room for their luggage as well, though their camping gear had better go in the garden shed. Angelica can move into the small guest room opposite. Yes, Susan – if you'll help me put clean sheets on the bed and find some towels, that would be good. I think Lesley ought to be put to bed straight away.'

'No, no. I'm perfectly all right.' Lesley made a convulsive movement, put her hands over her mouth and fled for the toilet again.

Silence. Andy shrugged and started for the door. 'I suppose I'd better make a start on bringing the luggage in.'

Did he expect Ellie or Susan to help him? Well, they weren't going to do so.

Susan said, 'Mrs Quicke, Rafael has the right to demand his money back, hasn't he?'

'I'm not sure what the legal position is, but I believe so.'

Susan was troubled. 'I think Angelica's spent it, don't you? If so, can he really ask us to repay him?'

'No, I don't think so. He can sue her in a small claims court, though. She might have to declare for bankruptcy, with all that that entails.'

'I can't afford to help her out.' She rubbed her forehead. Susan was a student and had no money to spare. 'Look, I know Angelica's a bit of a fool and all that, but . . . Do you really think she was so stupid as to pretend she owned Lesley's flat in order to borrow money?'

'You heard him. She told him the flat was hers. I suspect she also told him that Andy and Lesley earn good money and that I'm a generous, rich old lady. I think she gave him the impression that she was a wealthy girl with a solid background.'

Susan fidgeted. 'Rafael hangs around with the crowd in the pub sometimes. I had heard he lent money out now and then but he's not really a moneylender.'

Ellie sighed. 'Be that as it may, we've all been forgetting something. 'A girl died.'

THREE

S usan said, 'Yes, you're right. I keep forgetting that someone died. No matter how awkward it's going to be for us, we have to tell the police that Angelica arranged a party and invited lots of people. They'll want to know names. We'll have to try to sort Angelica's finances out later.'

'Good girl. Lesley will know who we should tell. Now, I'll just see if she wants anything before we tackle the bedrooms.'

Ellie tapped on the toilet door. Lesley's voice, muffled, said she would be all right in a minute and please, not to worry about her, so Ellie led the way up the stairs and threw open the door into the main guest bedroom. And blanched.

Chaos ruled OK.

Apparently Angelica didn't believe in hanging clothes up or putting underwear in drawers. Clothing was strewn on the unmade bed, the chairs and the chest of drawers. Drawers gaped open, as did the doors of the wardrobe. Much of the clothing was brand new, tangled in tissue paper with the labels still on. Bags marked with the names of expensive high street shops had been thrown into one corner. The dressing-table unit was covered with jars and aids to beauty while face powder lightly dusted every surface. A strong, flowery scent attacked their nostrils.

Susan put her hands on her capacious hips. 'I suppose the bathroom will be even worse.' Susan was disgusted. She was responsible for cleaning her own quarters and kept them in immaculate condition.

Ellie was outraged. 'No wonder she told my cleaners not to bother about doing this room when they came this morning. They would have had something to say about this.' Ellie picked up a sequined boob tube which was on the floor at her feet. 'These clothes. How much money has she spent on them, do you think?'

Susan said, in a flat voice, 'We're looking at hundreds of

pounds. Maybe a thousand. How much do you think she borrowed from Rafael? Although I think he was stupid to think she could repay.'

Ellie looked and felt grim. 'Not if he thought the girl owned that flat. Not if he was told that her relations had good jobs, that Lesley was with the police and Andy was a deputy head. And not if he thought I might come up with funds from my charitable trust. Do you think she's spent everything she borrowed from him?'

'Mrs Quicke, I hate to sound unsympathetic, but no matter what Rafael says about us all chipping in, I don't have money to spare for Angelica's debts.'

'Neither do I,' said Ellie. 'The trust fund is for charity, not for silly girls who borrow without being able to repay. Phew! What a fug!' She threw up the windows looking on to the garden and breathed in some clean air. 'I suggest we pack the brand-new clothes back into the bags they came in. Perhaps we can get the shops to give us a refund. The stuff she's worn already will have to stay.'

'Mrs Quicke, about Lesley—'

'Yes, I'm worried about her, too. Do you know who her doctor is?'

'I think it might be the practice in the Avenue, but I can't remember Lesley ever being off sick before so I'm not sure.'

It took them both nearly an hour to pick up, sort out and stash Angelica's new clothes into the bags they'd arrived in and to transfer the used clothing into the less-capacious fitments in the small guest room opposite. This room was only occupied occasionally by one of Ellie's grandsons and consequently was somewhat Spartan in its furnishings, although it did have a *Star Wars* poster on one wall.

When Ellie and Susan had finished transferring Angelica's belongings, there were still two carrier bags full of oddments which wouldn't go anywhere. They tried putting them under the bed in the spare room but it was too low. Eventually they dumped them beside the chest of drawers.

Susan cleaned the bathroom and replaced the towels, while Ellie bundled the cosmetics into a cardboard box and put it in the small bedroom. Together they turned the mattress and made up the bed with clean sheets. Every now and then they heard Andy grunting up the stairs and dropping luggage in the corridor.

After Susan had vacuumed the carpet and Ellie had dusted every surface, they invited Andy to enter the newly cleaned big guest room.

He looked around.

Ellie thought he might say 'thank you' but of course he didn't. He said, 'No television?'

Ellie wanted to hit him but the doorbell rang at that point, so she muttered an excuse and brushed past him to go downstairs and answer the door.

There stood Angelica, in a pretty shower of tears. 'Oh, Mrs Quicke! Thank goodness you're in. I know you'll help me. I'm in such trouble!'

Susan, halfway down the stairs, said, 'Don't tell me! She's lost her key again, has she?'

Tears running down her cheeks, Angelica sobbed, 'I was mugged. He took my purse with all my cards and the key in it! And I can't pay the taxi, either.'

'You were robbed?' Ellie's forgot her first impulse to box the girl's ears and drew her into the hall. 'Now, now. No need for tears. I'll pay the taxi while you phone the police.'

Susan said, 'Hah! She's done it again!'

Ellie was torn between slapping Susan or Angelica. Or possibly both. Her good nature won the day. Just. But she did feel cross. That was the second taxi she'd had to pay for that day. Where had she put her handbag?

Susan said, 'Angelica, where did this happen? In the town centre? Why didn't you go to the police there? And what's happened to your legs? Why didn't you walk back?'

'You don't understand! I wasn't thinking straight. All I could think of was getting back here to Mrs Quicke and to safety.' She turned her pretty face up to Ellie, all puppy-like and adoring.

Susan made a noise as if she were about to be sick, and Ellie's temper veered back from sympathy for Angelica to wanting to shake the girl. 'All right. I'll pay the taxi for you, Angelica, but I expect you to refund the money.'

Angelica's tears vanished in miraculous fashion. 'Oh, thank you, thank you! I knew I could rely on you. I promise to repay you when my ship comes in.'

'Your ship, Angelica,' said Ellie, 'has run on to a sandbank. You've got some explaining to do, young lady.' She wondered at herself for taking such a harsh tone. It wasn't like her.

Angelica started for the stairs. 'Oh, thank you, Mrs Quicke. You're a star!' With a sunny smile: 'I'll just get out of these old clothes and—'

'You stop right there, young lady,' said Ellie. 'I want you to ring the police and report the mugging while I pay your cab.' She darted outside, paid what was on the meter, then returned to find Susan sitting, arms folded, on the stairs, blocking Angelica's way up.

Angelica dithered. 'Oh, go on! Don't be such a pain. Let me pass.'

Susan said to Ellie, 'She hasn't rung the police. Did you really expect her to do so?'

'No,' said Ellie, realizing what had really happened. 'She's no intention of doing so, has she? Well, now, Angelica. I think you'd better start talking. Something's happened to Andy and Lesley's flat and you're going to tell us all about it. They can't go back there, so they're moving in here for a couple of nights, which means we've transferred your things into the smaller guest room.'

A pretty pout. 'You can't! Well, I mean, obviously you can, but . . . I mean, you've been so kind to me and naturally I fully intend to repay you one day when—'

With her eyes on Angelica, Susan gestured to the pile of Angelica's shopping, which they'd left at the top of the stairs. 'Yes, Angelica? Mrs Quicke and I are wondering what we should do with these? Sell them on eBay, perhaps?'

Angelica gasped, 'You can't! They're mine!'

Ellie said, 'Angelica, did you have enough money in your account to pay for them? Did you have *any* money in your account when you bought them? You say you've just been mugged, but the truth is that Rafael caught up with you, right? It was he who took your cards, wasn't it? Did you give him the pin numbers for them, too?'

'I . . .' Angelica looked stricken. Tears rose to her eyes again. She really was quite some actress. 'He stopped me in the street and I tried to get away but he hung on to my arm till . . .' She held her wrist out for them to see. 'Oh, how it hurts! I just know there's going to be an awful bruise. I do bruise so easily!'

Andy appeared on the landing. 'What's going on? Hello, Angelica, are you all right?'

'No, I'm not!' Yes, tears fell. 'Oh, Andy! Thank God you're here! I'm in the most awful mess!'

'There, there, puss.' Andy's tone was indulgent. 'We've just been hearing all about it. Why didn't you come to me if you were short of cash? How much was it? A couple of hundred?'

'Before she comes clean about that,' said Ellie, 'she has to ring the police and report that she's been robbed—'

'What?' said Andy.

'No, I . . .' Angelica floundered, unable think quickly enough to explain why she couldn't do that. 'I gave Rafael what I have, of my own accord. There's no need for the police.'

Susan said, 'The clothes you've just bought are going back to the shops, right? Mrs Quicke, I've got a lockable cupboard upstairs in my flat. Shall I shove them in there for now? Or shall I make a start on returning the goods to the shops?'

Angelica shrieked, 'You can't do that! They're mine.'

Ellie said grimly, 'Bought but not paid for, right?' She beckoned to Andy. 'Come on down. We have to talk. Susan, bring those bags. They can go into Thomas's office for the time being.'

Angelica looked at her bare left wrist. 'Oh, I can't stay to talk just now. I promised to meet a friend in half an hour.'

Ellie grasped the girl by her upper arm and led her into the sitting room. 'You can ring them and say you've been delayed. Unless . . . did Rafael take your mobile phone as well as your watch and your purse? He did? Hm, he does appear to have a practical turn of mind, doesn't he? Sit down, everyone. Now, Angelica, start talking. How much did you borrow from Rafael and what interest does he charge?'

A toss of the curls. 'I don't know what you're talking about.'

Andy looked worried. 'I've heard that some of these moneylenders charge up to a hundred per cent a month. She wouldn't have been so stupid as to do that, though. Would you, Angelica?' He smiled fondly at Angelica, who turned pink.

'Sit down, Andy,' said Ellie. 'You, too, Susan. Those bags can wait. Now, Andy, Angelica really is in deep trouble. I'm not sure that we *can* help her . . . or even if we *should* help her. Let me tell you what I think has been going on, and then you must decide what, if anything, we can do about it.'

'Oh, yes!' said Angelica. 'All I want is for it to go away and you're so good to me, I'm sure you'll understand how it all happened and help me out. I promise never, ever to do it again.'

Andy failed to grasp the seriousness of the situation. 'Of course we'll help. How much are you in for?'

Angelica looked at him adoringly. 'Oh, would you? I'm afraid it is rather a lot.'

Ellie said, 'I suspect it's thousands, not hundreds. Andy, be careful what you promise. Angelica has no job. When her mother threw her out, she moved in with you and Lesley for a while but that didn't work out, either, did it?' Ellie forbore to add that it had been Andy's overindulgent attitude to his cousin that had caused Lesley to throw the girl out, upon which the girl had arrived on Ellie's doorstep with a plea for accommodation.

Ellie continued, 'Angelica asked me if she might stay here for a couple of nights till she got herself sorted out. Like a fool, I assumed she meant exactly that and let her in.'

'Well, that's understandable, I suppose.' Andy was as indulgent as ever towards Angelica. 'I mean, you have money and this big house, so why shouldn't you offer her a place to stay?'

Susan sniffed richly. 'Huh!'

Ellie puffed out a sigh. 'This house costs a mint to run. Susan pays her way, so why shouldn't Angelica? Look, let's work it out. Angelica has no job and is short of money. She got Rafael to advance her a considerable sum with promises to repay. She makes promises easily, doesn't she? From what I've heard, she's always been indulged by her family. She probably assumed someone would come to her rescue if she couldn't come up with the readies. Isn't that right, Angelica?'

Angelica produced a tissue and blotted the tears that were threatening to ruin her make-up. 'You don't understand. I fell in love!'

'What!' said Andy, showing signs of shock. He hadn't expected that. Nor, to be honest, had Ellie.

Angelica brightened. 'He's so wonderful! He's so . . . so . . . everything! But his family is so . . . They have property everywhere, and a yacht, and businesses all over, but I didn't have the right handbag or shoes or, well, anything! He wanted me to be with him, at his side, and of course I wanted that, too. He said he'd take me on the red carpet to a film premiere, and to Ascot and everything. I had nothing to wear and the family expected him to marry this girl who looked at me as if I were dirt. I had to show him I was just as good as her, didn't I? I had no choice. I had to keep up or lose him.'

Ellie looked across at Andy, whose mouth had fallen open. She'd wondered for some time how deep his affection for his little cousin ran. Had he, consciously or otherwise, become overfond of her?

Andy reddened. So, he was in denial about his feelings for the girl and was going to go for anger instead of acknowledging his jealousy? Oh, dear. He was going to explode, wasn't he?

Andy said, 'I've never heard anything so ridiculous! Angelica, you don't know what you're saying! You're far too young to fall in love.'

Ellie looked across at Susan, who rolled her eyes.

Angelica squealed, 'You don't understand. You can't stop me loving him! I'd give my life for him. Nothing else matters. I shall go mad and jump in the Thames if I can't have him!' She gulped, tears at the ready. 'I'd walk through fire for him. I think of him all the time. If he dumps me, I'll cut my wrists—'

Ellie broke in: 'You borrowed money in order to have the clothes needed to go out with him. How much?'

'Rafael said there was no hurry about returning it at first, he was all nice and easy until last week when he turned nasty and said I had to make some sort of effort to repay him. He was on and on at me to take a job but I couldn't do that because Jake might ring up and want me to be available, and if I wasn't, he'd go out with his old girlfriend. Then I heard on the grapevine that I could make some money by holding a party in my flat.'

Andy choked with rage. 'How were you supposed to do that? And it's not your flat, anyway!'

'Well, no.' She reddened. 'But I'd kept a key, of course, and everyone *thought* it was my flat, and it was convenient to meet Rafael there when you went away because I didn't want him coming here and finding I was only living in one room. It was only two thousand at first, but then I had to ask for some more.'

Someone hissed out a long breath. Susan?

Ellie observed, 'It seems that Angelica collects keys. She's already had a duplicate made of our front door key here, hasn't she?'

Angelica cringed. 'Don't look like that, Andy. I knew the people in the flat above you were away at weekends and it sounded such a great opportunity to make some money just for inviting a certain person, and I wanted to show Jake what a nice place I had. I invited some of my friends, too, and one of them must have put it on Facebook and, well, I suppose it did get a bit out of hand. Then it all went wrong because Jake walked out on me anyway!'

Andy said, 'You mean you invited lots of people, some of them you didn't even know, to a party at our flat?'

Angelica turned imploring, tear-filled eyes to her cousin. 'Andy, you know I wouldn't ever have done anything to upset you!'

Andy's face indicated that he didn't know whether to be angry or register understanding of her plight.

Ellie said, 'I suppose a lot more people came than you'd anticipated? Some had been drinking heavily before they arrived? Pushing and shoving became crashing and bashing. Furniture got broken. The place was wrecked. And someone died. Who was she, Angelica?'

Andy's mouth dropped open. 'I'd forgotten about her. Angelica, tell them you had nothing to do with the girl who died.'

Angelica sobbed, 'I only wanted a bit of fun. What's wrong with that? It's what's supposed to happen when you're young and pretty. I've been to so many other parties and I wanted to hold one myself. My friends came, and then they brought others, and there seemed to be lots of drink, and then two men started to fight in the kitchen, and a girl was sick, and I was screaming and screaming at them to stop it, and they didn't! They didn't take any notice of me, and I begged my friends to help me get them out, but they didn't, and so I . . .' Her voice trailed away.

Ellie said, 'So you left them to it?'

'No!' Andy protested. 'Angelica, you didn't, did you?'

'Don't look like that! What else was I to do?'

Andy said, 'Well, you could have rung the police.'

Angelica wailed and bent over, hiding her face in her hands.

'You mean,' said Susan, who was visibly shocked, 'that Angelica just walked out of a rowdy party she'd set up in Lesley's flat? Walked out and left them to it?'

Angelica whimpered, 'What else could I do? I was so frightened. I'm sure your insurance will cover the damage.'

Ellie said, 'Let's hope the insurance people see it that way. Now, back to basics. How much money have you borrowed from Rafael in total? And how much have you spent?'

'I don't know! I only bought the merest necessities. I meant to pay it back, I really did. But when I told Rafael I needed more time, he was really horrid to me and threatened me, so I said he could take what I had in my handbag and he did! He took my watch and my cell phone and my purse which has all my cards in it and . . . Andy, you've got to help me!'

Andy gaped. He was in shock.

Susan eyed Angelica with dislike. 'I think Rafael ought to have taken more than her purse. I think he should put her in a greasy spoon café and make her work for him as a waitress till she's paid him in full.'

Angelica wailed, 'Oh, no! I couldn't work as a waitress! I'm worth more than that!'

'Hang about,' said Andy, recovering his wits. 'It's illegal to charge a lot of interest, isn't it? He can't force her to pay him.'

Ellie said, 'Use your common sense, Andy. If she signed a contract – which he says she did – then it's not illegal. She can't go to the police about it. She had a business arrangement with him and she's cheated him out of his money.'

'I was desperate,' wailed Angelica. 'I had to have some new clothes! You ought to have looked after me better, Andy. You knew I didn't have a job and you ought to have given me an allowance. And Mrs Quicke ought to have been more understanding and given me a lump sum, so that I could keep up with what Jake expects of his girlfriends.'

Ellie said, 'So it's our fault now, is it? Angelica, you have to grow up sometime. You've made a series of bad decisions and now you have to take responsibility for them. The money business is one thing, but I'm even more concerned about the girl who died. You've avoided that subject. Who was she and how did she die?'

'How should I know?' Eyes wide, an air of total innocence.

Was she lying?

Ellie said, 'Andy, you were shown some pictures of her. What did you say? A redhead with no identification?'

Andy nodded, tight-lipped. He was finding it hard to process what he'd heard. He flushed a deep red and then paled. Jealousy, anger and humiliation fought for predominance. 'A redhead. I didn't know her from Adam.'

Ellie said, 'True redheads are few and far between. Angelica, do you remember a redhead at the party?'

Angelica pulled a face. 'No, of course not.' She met Ellie's unforgiving gaze and her voice trailed away. She tried tears again. It was a marvel how she did it. The tears appeared and hung on her lashes, suspended, but not yet ready to fall.

Ellie said, 'That was a lie. You do remember her. Was she a latecomer?'

'Don't badger me! How can you expect me to remember? There were people coming and going all over the place. I was in the kitchen, trying to get Jake to loosen up, and if someone came in late I wouldn't have seen them, would I?'

Ellie thought the girl was lying. But why?

It was then that Susan landed the killer blow. 'I wonder . . . Jake's previous girlfriend. Is she a redhead by any chance?'

'What?' A pretty trill of laughter. 'Who? How should I know?'

'You'd know. What's her name? If it's the same girl, I think he brought her to the pub once. A redhead. High heels and expensive tastes.'

A pretty shrug. 'Well, I suppose it might have been Kate. Not that I noticed her particularly. I don't know her second name. She is such a drama queen. No wonder Jake got tired of her. She's not a true redhead, anyway.'

Ellie said, 'You saw her arrive at the party. Before or after Jake left? Did she come to fetch him?'

'How should I know?'

'You'd know if you were as much in love with Jake as you say you are. You would have noticed her straight away. Jake was in the kitchen with you. He didn't see her?'

'I suppose . . . if it was her . . . and I'm not saying it was because I didn't see her properly . . . I suppose she might have gone straight into the sitting room, looking for him. He didn't see her. He left, saying he'd ring me . . . and he hasn't!' Tears clouded her eyes again.

'When he walked out of the flat, you went after him?'

She pouted. 'Well, of course. If it was Kate, which I'm not sure that it was, well, I didn't want him going back in and finding her, did I? I thought that if I asked him to take me with him, he would . . . but he wouldn't listen. He said . . . he said I should call the police as the party was getting out of hand and anything might happen. And I thought that Kate might get pawed by some of the rough guys and I was glad! She pretended to be so high and mighty. She was asking for it. She shouldn't have chased after him. It was all her fault!'

'Did you go back in?'

'No, of course not. I was terribly upset. I sat outside on the wall for a while and I had a little weep, because nothing had gone right and I didn't know what to do, and there was nobody to help me. And then Timmy Lee came out and said the party was a bore and we should go on to a club and have some fun, and he had his scooter there, so I . . . I was exhausted, you see.'

'This Timmy. Where does he live?'

'Dunno. The other side of the river, I think. He's Chinese. Or something. Maybe Japanese? His surname is spelled L.I. something. And his first name is unpronounceable, so we all call him Timmy Lee. He doesn't mind.'

'How do you know him?'

'Oh, he's just around. You know. A student. I see him in the coffee shops and in the pub and at parties and that. He didn't realize it was my party. And, well, I thought everyone would go home eventually and I suppose I did have a teensy little hope that Kate might get roughed up a bit, not that I bore her any ill will or anything.'

'Didn't you worry about the damage the partygoers might do?'

'Well, no. Not really. Obviously, Andy's insurance would cover it. And Lesley's such a bitch, turning me out of their flat as she did. It served her right if she had to clear up some beer stains or whatever.'

Andy said, 'If I hadn't given you a key, Angelica, I could have claimed on the insurance. But as I did, I'm afraid the insurance may not cover the damage.'

Another shrug. 'Well, how was I to know that? It's not my fault if you haven't got proper insurance.' She looked at the clock on the mantelpiece. 'I really must go. My friend will be getting worried.'

Ellie said, 'You're not going anywhere, Angelica, until we've put Lesley in the picture. Yes, Andy, it's awful that your flat's been wrecked but everyone seems to be forgetting that a girl has died. Surely that's more important than your problems? So the first thing we have to do is tell Lesley what Angelica knows.' She started to her feet. 'Oh. Where is Lesley?'

FOUR

L esley wasn't in the kitchen, or the downstairs toilet. The door to the sitting room was usually kept open, so they would have heard her if she'd crossed the hall and gone upstairs, wouldn't they? Where was she?

Andy shot up the stairs from the hall and opened bedroom doors, calling Lesley's name. No response.

'I know!' Ellie went down the corridor which led to the kitchen, up the back stairs and along the landing to what had once been their housekeeper's bedsitting room. Lesley had spent the night there once, before her wedding. There was a shower room and a toilet next door.

And, yes, Lesley had managed to get up there before sprawling on the bed, her hand still clutching her mobile phone and tear stains on her cheeks.

Fast asleep.

Ellie told herself she was pleased that Lesley was getting some rest, but that didn't stop her worrying about her friend. Something was very wrong with Lesley. But what could it be?

Ellie tried to take Lesley's pulse by feeling her wrist but wasn't sure how to do it. Did you put your thumb this way or that? She tried both but couldn't decide whether what she felt was her own pulse or Lesley's.

It was probably the best thing for Lesley to have a nap. Ellie took off Lesley's tight-fitting shoes. Lesley didn't stir, so Ellie undid and pulled off Lesley's jeans as well. Still Lesley didn't move. Ellie took a pillow and a duvet out of the cupboard and made her friend comfortable.

Someone was breathing hard behind her. Angelica.

Ellie put her finger to her lips. Angelica bent over Lesley, not to kiss her but . . . what was she up to?

Ellie would have screamed if she hadn't remembered it would

waken Lesley. Instead, Ellie grabbed Angelica, towed her out of the room and down the stairs to the kitchen. And confronted her there. 'Give it here!'

Angelica put her hands behind her. 'What?'

'Lesley's mobile phone.'

'I need it. I know she'd be happy to let me borrow it while she's asleep.'

'No, she wouldn't.' Ellie turned the girl round and retrieved Lesley's phone.

Angelica's ready tears flowed. 'You don't understand. When Jake phones he won't be able to get through because Rafael's got my phone. I need to use Lesley's, now!'

'Tough,' said Ellie, determined not to let her have Lesley's phone.

Andy blundered in, looking harassed. 'I can't find Les anywhere. Where could she have got to?'

Susan followed him. 'Mrs Quicke, I've just thought. Would she be in your old housekeeper's room?'

'Yes, she's there and fast asleep.' Ellie held out the phone to Susan. 'Lesley's phone. I can't cope with these new-fangled things. Can you check to see if she managed to ring her boss at the station about Angelica hosting the party before she went upstairs?'

Susan pressed buttons and frowned. 'I don't think she did.'

'Well, that's good, I suppose,' said Andy. 'It gives us some time to think what to do next.'

Ellie said, 'I'm sure we ought to tell the police about Rafael. Lending money at a high rate of interest is legal; I know that. Having met the man, I'm sure he knows exactly how to keep within the law. But robbing a girl in the street is another thing.'

Susan fidgeted. 'I really don't think he'd go so far as to rob someone in the street. Angelica said that she offered him her bag of her own accord.'

Angelica shrieked, 'You can't tell the police about me borrowing money! If you do, I shall deny everything! I'll say I lost my handbag on the bus . . . yes, on the bus or . . . no, in the taxi. You can't prove otherwise.'

Ellie wondered how the girl had reached the advanced age of twenty-one without meeting an untimely end. The worst of it was that, unless Angelica bore witness against Rafael, the police would be unable to arrest him.

So back to basics.

The corpse in the garden.

Ellie said, 'All right, but we do have to let the police know the name of the girl who died. Think of her parents, who must have missed her by now and be agonizing about what's happened to her. They'll be sitting by the phone, ringing all her friends, ringing the hospitals. Kate something. What was her other name, Angelica?'

Angelica tossed her curls. 'I have absolutely no idea. And if someone gatecrashed my party, someone I might have seen in the distance a couple of times, then it was nothing to do with me.'

Susan muttered, 'You are incredible.'

Ellie said, 'Nevertheless, Angelica, we have to tell them what we know. It would be helpful to let them have Jake's name, too. The police will want to have a word with him.'

Angelica became hysterical. 'No, you can't! You mustn't drag him into this! He'd never forgive me!'

'Tough,' said Ellie, repeating herself and enjoying the experience even more this time round. 'If he's that insecure you wouldn't want him as a boyfriend anyway.'

Angelica tried to grab the phone from Susan, who swept her arm up and round, knocking Angelica off her feet and across the room . . . where she sat on the floor, looking shocked and, for the first time, frightened. A girl who'd fantasized that she was a little princess and found the reality rather different from her dreams. Possibly she'd never been manhandled in her life before.

'Sorry,' said Susan. 'I don't know my own strength sometimes.' Her face contorted. Was she trying not to laugh?

'Susan! How could you!' Andy was not amused. He lifted Angelica off the floor and placed her tenderly on a chair.

Angelica took a deep breath and screamed.

Susan folded her arms at Angelica. 'Oh, shut up, you stupid little girl. How does your fancying a toffee-nosed git weigh against the loss of a girl's life?'

Angelica wept. 'I'm not telling you, I'm not! It's my future that's at stake here and you can't make me! You can put red-hot needles under my nails and I still won't tell you! *Oh! By dose is bleeding!*'

And so it was. With a wail, Angelica fled for the toilet. Andy trailed after her, asking if she were all right, which she obviously wasn't.

Ellie picked up the card which Rafael had left them. 'Susan, there's another way to find their names.' She fetched her own mobile phone from her bag in the hall and sat at the kitchen table. 'Now, let me concentrate.' She dialled Rafael's number and he answered straight away. She said, 'Rafael, this is Mrs Quicke here.'

'Really? I must confess I'm somewhat surprised. I hadn't thought to hear from you so soon.' A mellow tone of voice, pleasant to the ear.

'I dare say. I want to fill you in on what we've discovered Angelica's been up to. It may affect the decisions you make concerning her debt to you. You say that you knew she'd planned to use her cousin's flat for a party. It wasn't your scene and you didn't go. You know someone died during the course of the evening. Angelica thinks the girl might have been an ex-girlfriend or family friend of the boy she's been dating: first name Kate, second name unknown. A redhead. Angelica's current boyfriend's first name appears to be Jake but she refuses to tell us his second name. I am thinking of the agony Kate's parents may be undergoing, not knowing where she may be and what may have happened to her. I think the police should be told what we know. Do you know this Jake or the girl, who might have been a previous girlfriend of his?'

'Yes, I know him, slightly. He comes to the pub now and then. Yes, he used to go around with a redhead. Striking looks. I don't think I've ever heard her second name. He's usually with Angelica nowadays.'

'Do you know where Jake can be found?'

'We're not on visiting terms.'

Ellie thought about that. 'You have Angelica's phone. Jake rings her on that phone and presumably there are contact details there. Would you give me his number?'

'I'm a businessman. Angelica owes me a great deal of money. She gave me that phone of her own free will to offset some of my losses. It has gone to be stripped of its current details and made ready for resale.'

'I don't think you'll have got rid of it until you've done your best to raise a ransom for it from Angelica or her friends. I would hazard a guess that you still have it on you.'

He was amused. 'How shrewd of you. My contacts inform me you are a good businesswoman and I see that they were correct.

Well, Mrs Quicke, you are halfway right. The phone is no longer in my possession as I feared Puss might try to claim that I'd robbed her when all I did was pick up a handbag that she'd dropped in the street . . .'

Ellie almost laughed. What a plausible rogue he was, to be sure!

'But I daresay I could let you have the details on Puss's phone. At a price. As one business person to another, I'm sure you appreciate that I am not a charitable concern, while you, dear lady, have the power to clear Puss's debt with a wave of your hand.'

'I cannot see myself passing you off as a charity.'

'Why not? Am I not the victim of a scam, and therefore deserving of help?'

'The difference is that you have a contract with Angelica, not with me. Also, you charge interest, whereas my charitable trust doesn't expect any return on the money we pay out.'

'I use my capital to help others, much as you do with your trust fund. I get many requests for help, as you do. I vet the ability of my customers to repay me, as you do. It is true that I made a mistake regarding Angelica. I did not check her out thoroughly enough. But I shall not make that mistake again. Another difference between us two is that I refuse to accommodate those whom I consider unable to repay their loan on easy terms.'

'We vet our customers' honesty and the depths of their need, and we do ask for a return on investment, though I agree we don't always expect it in sterling. Like you, we occasionally make investments which turn out badly. But we start from a different point of view. We try to alleviate suffering wherever we find it.'

'So do I. Now, don't tell me you haven't given money occasionally to rogues and scoundrels, or to no-hopers who will never climb out of the pit.'

She had to smile. 'You're right, of course. But we do try to avoid it. I hate to waste money that way.'

'My grandfather used to say that the Deserving Poor Are Never Grateful, no matter how much you give to them.'

'Which is why we mostly give to organizations – schools, clubs and so on.'

'And yet you cannot find it in your heart to help Angelica?'

Rafael had led her up the garden path and dumped her in the sewage.

Rethink, Ellie. She said, 'Susan and I have found some bags of clothing which Angelica bought this morning. We will take them back to the shops and reclaim the money spent on them. Then we'll hand that money over to you in part payment of Angelica's debt, and in return you will let us have Jake's details.'

He groaned. 'My dear Mrs Quicke, how unworldly of you. Some of the shops may give you money but most will only give you a voucher to be used against future purchases. However, I will meet you halfway. Send me a thousand pounds from your charity to set against Angelica's debt and I will let you have Jake's details. Then you can make arrangements directly with Puss for her to repay you.'

Ellie was tempted. 'No. I can't do that. Two wrongs don't make a right, and I can't see any way she can repay me. Let's put it this way: you say you have to turn away many who cannot afford the interest you charge. That must make you feel unloved, unappreciated. Suppose I say that the trust will be happy to receive applications from some individuals who don't fit your criteria but might still be helped by us?'

'Now what on earth would I get out of that?'

Ellie said, 'Something you don't often receive, I suspect. Gratitude. A blessing.'

Would he go for it? Her first impression of him as a villain was not altogether accurate. She felt she could trust him to a certain extent. Perhaps he was not without a moral code?

And, yes, he laughed. 'You offer nothing more tangible, Mrs Quicke? How about a case of good wine?'

'Certainly not. And let's be careful here. You send me no rogues or scoundrels. Also, I think we should place a limit on how many people you send me. Shall we say, five referrals over a period of a year?'

'How about one a month?'

Ellie smiled. 'Six over a year. One every two months, and I retain the option to send them away if they don't appeal to me. You will let me have Jake's number within half an hour?'

'Within five minutes, dear lady. And I will get someone to drop Angelica's handbag into the nearest police station, with a note that I found it on a bench in the Ealing Broadway shopping centre. Her cards are all maxed out, by the way.' He rang off.

Susan had been listening to this one-sided conversation with a grin. 'Did he fall for it?'

'Actually, I rather like him.'

Susan's smile widened. She nodded. 'Yes, he can be very charming when he chooses, but he's going to put you to a whole lot of trouble, dealing with hopeless cases who need money and can't repay.'

'Granted that it's easier to deal with institutions such as schools and clubs, but it is rather soulless. Perhaps he's giving me a push to deal with the Mr Micawbers of this world, who might be able to dig themselves out of a hole if given a helping hand or two.'

'And down-and-outs?'

'Them, too. The other trustees might not approve but I think that we should get down in the muck sometimes. And, yes, some of it won't be very savoury, but . . . well, it feels right.'

Her phone rang and Rafael said, 'There is no information on Angelica's phone for anyone named Kate, but she has the phone number for Jake Hartley Summers. He lives in a flat just off Wimbledon Common. Have you a pen and paper to take down his address and phone number?'

Ellie had, and did. The phone clicked off.

Susan said, 'Good for Rafael. He's a man of his word. Usually. You'll let the police know? Meanwhile, I think I'll look in on Lesley. I'm worried about her.'

'Aren't you supposed to be back at college?'

'I'll make the time up. This is more important.'

Ellie agreed. 'All right. Take her up a cup of tea?'

When Susan had departed, Ellie sat on, thinking about what she ought to do next. She could ring the police now and speak to Lesley's boss. Hand over the information she'd gathered and leave it to him to investigate Jake and Kate and whoever.

But Ellie had a history with the Detective Inspector, whose large ears turned bright red whenever his blood pressure rose. Most unfortunately, Ellie – who hadn't known his name when they first met – had referred to him as 'Ears'. The nickname had shot through the station staff and become common knowledge. Ears had of course eventually heard about it and had been known to speak harshly and at some length about interfering old women who . . . *insert words of choice.*

Ears would not welcome any intelligence she might have to offer, and might even go so far as to dismiss it as unimportant.

Ears was an officer of medium intelligence who had probably been promoted as far as he would go. Ears disliked women in the force, and clever women like Lesley were an especial abomination. Ellie could well imagine that he'd been secretly amused that Lesley's flat had been vandalized in her absence. If Ellie rang and gave him this piece of information, Ears might decide that as Jake had left the party early and Angelica hadn't been sure that the redhead she'd spotted had been his previous girlfriend, then they would be no further forward in their efforts to identify her.

On the other hand, if this Jake really had known the girl, then *he* could tell the police her name, her family could be informed and Ellie could keep out of it.

She was aware that this was, perhaps, the coward's way out, but it would surely be the best in the long run.

Ellie dialled Jake's number. 'Is that Jake? Jake Hartley Summers?'

'When I'm awake, yes. Who are you? Don't tell me. Let me guess. Your company thinks I've been in an accident and will want to sue for damages or . . . No, those people are usually ringing from Bombay. Are you still on about that bank insurance thingy? No, that's an automated call, isn't it? I know, you want me to compare lifestyle choices, which I haven't the slightest intention of doing. Right? So, who are you?'

He sounded amused, as if he enjoyed baiting cold-callers. His voice also told Ellie that he'd been educated privately, gone on to university, didn't have to work hard for a living – if at all – and that he thought he was Prince Charming.

Ellie said, 'My name is Ellie Quicke. Mrs Ellie Quicke. A girl called Angelica is currently staying with me.'

'Oh. Right. Angel's fairy godmother. What's the silly chit done now?' A yawn. 'Apologies. Late night last night. Poker. Groan. Did I lose, or did I lose? Next question: why am I not at work? Answer: I'm on gardening leave.'

'What does that mean?'

'I've been put on the naughty step, sent home to "find myself", rapped over the knuckles. In other words, I deleted some files that I hadn't oughta and they're getting in some nerd or other to try to recover them. Total waste of time, anyway. The stuff wasn't worth keeping.'

'I see,' said Ellie, grasping only the fact that the lad was in some sort of trouble at work. 'Well, it's about Angelica. She hosted a party on Saturday night, which I believe you attended for a short time. Is that right?'

'So . . .?'

'You know a redhead called Kate? I believe she used to be your girlfriend. Yes?'

'Mm. Sort of. We used to go around together.' He was wary, taking time over his answers.

'Did you see her at the party?'

'Kate? No. I wasn't there that long. So what?'

There was no easy way to break the news. Ellie said, 'On Sunday night, the body of a redheaded girl was found in the garden of the house in which the party had been held. She had no identification on her. The police are involved. Someone said it might be your ex-girlfriend, Kate.'

A long silence. Ellie said, 'Are you still there?'

'Yes. I mean . . . No identification, you say? I don't understand. And why have you contacted me?'

'I'm following up something someone said about you having a redheaded girlfriend. It might not be the girl you knew.'

'Who said it was my ex?'

'Angelica.'

A long pause. 'I suppose I could give Kate a ring, check that she's all right.'

'Yes, you do that.'

Another pause for thought.

'Mrs . . . what did you say your name was? If what you say is true . . . I'd better have your number, hadn't I? . . . I suppose, if it is Kate . . . but I don't understand why no one's identified her. What a bore! If it is her, the police will jump to all sorts of wrong conclusions. I mean, we were friends, yes. But nothing more. Or at least, not recently. Months ago, we had a sort of . . . I suppose the police will want to know if we were sleeping together, which we weren't, not now. They'll assume the worst, and there'll be endless questions about this and that and . . . How did I get mixed up in this?'

He was beginning to accept that the girl in the garden had been his ex. Well, that was a step forward.

He said, 'Our families go back a long way, you know. Our mothers went to the same nursery or whatever, way back when Moses was alive. Her brother's just graduated. And her father! He'll go spare. He's devoted to her. Her mother died last year, you know? No, why should you know? It probably isn't her.'

Ellie had had enough of Jake. Self-centred whatsit! He could at least pretend he was upset that his girlfriend had died . . . though, of course, it might not be his Kate at all. 'Have you a paper and pen to write my name and number down? You need to ring Kate's parents, and then the police, to check if it's the girl you know or not. You can ring me back any time. I won't be going out.'

'If it is Kate, I'll be gutted.'

So maybe he did have a heart, after all. She said, 'I'm sorry. I hope for your sake it isn't her.'

'Yes, but . . . wait a minute. How did she die? Was it drugs? Did Angelica have drugs at the party?'

'Drugs? No, I don't think so.' Ellie put the phone down and the front doorbell rang.

She opened it to find two plainclothes policemen on the doorstep, flourishing shields to prove they were the real thing. Not 'Ears', thankfully.

Ellie said, 'Ah, police. Right. You need to speak to . . .?'

They asked for Susan. And Angelica.

Ellie went to the foot of the stairs and called the girls to come down. 'It's the police, wanting a word.'

Susan descended, looking strained. 'Of course, of course. I'm happy to speak to the police but, Mrs Quicke, I'm worried about Lesley. Can you keep an eye on her?' And to the police, 'I'm sorry, I really don't know anything about the party on Saturday. I was out with some friends. We went to the cinema.'

They were not impressed. 'If you'll just come down to the station . . .'

Andy appeared at the head of the stairs. 'Who is it? Oh, police? Officers, I have to tell you I was mistaken when I said that Susan must have arranged the party at our flat. It wasn't her, but—'

'Yes, it was!' Angelica appeared. Incredibly, and in spite of her tears, she looked as distractingly pretty as ever, but she had taken the precaution of picking up a pack of tissues in case she needed to burst into tears again. 'Officers, I would never, ever have done such a thing!'

The police looked puzzled. Susan folded her arms and raised her eyes to heaven.

Andy said, 'Look, officers. There's been some mistake. My cousin didn't mean to . . . She was—'

Angelica said, 'But I have an alibi, officers! I can prove I left the party early!'

'Perhaps,' said the taller of the two policemen, 'it would be a good idea for us to talk this over down at the station?'

'Oh, no!' cried Angelica. 'I can't! I mustn't! You couldn't be so cruel!'

'What a good idea!' said Susan.

Andy fidgeted. 'Look, officers, I . . . This is all a bit embarrassing. I didn't mean to suggest that Angelica would know anything about—'

'That's for us to decide,' said the taller of the policeman. 'I really think it would be best if the two ladies come down to the station and we can sort out their alibis.'

'Oh, no!' wept Angelica, turning her flower face up to Andy.

He responded, 'Would you like me to come with you, Angelica? I mean, I've got you into this mess. Do you want me to get you a solicitor?'

Angelica turned adoring eyes on him. 'Oh, would you? I'm so frightened.'

Susan said, 'Humph!' to the air. She marched outside, calling back to Ellie, 'Don't forget Lesley!'

Andy ushered his cousin outside. The two policemen disposed of the girls in the back of their car. Andy got into his to follow them. And then the house was empty again.

Except for the sleeping beauty upstairs. Ellie went up to have a look at Lesley, who appeared to be drowsy but not as deep in sleep as before. And rather flushed. Ellie put her hand on Lesley's forehead and decided that Susan was right to be concerned.

Lesley half opened her eyes and tried to sit up. She failed. 'Oh, dear, have I wet the bed?'

Ellie pulled back the duvet and saw the stain spreading out from between Lesley's legs.

'Lesley! You're pregnant?'

Lesley tried to laugh. 'Bad timing, right?'

Ellie felt as if the room were going round and round. She pushed herself upright. This was no time for her to faint. But if Lesley were to miscarry . . .?

Ellie tried to work moisture into her mouth. In her mind, she slid back through the years to when she had had miscarriage after miscarriage herself, when her whole life had been focused on producing a living child . . . when she'd failed, time and again, when she'd ended up in tears every month . . . when Diana had been the only baby who had survived.

Ellie told herself that her weakness was not going to help Lesley. She told herself to be strong. *Lord, help me. Lesley shouldn't have to go through what I suffered.*

Ellie knew that sometimes miscarriages can't be stopped. Ellie wanted nothing to do with what was happening. She wanted to run screaming from the room, but no. Her desertion wouldn't help Lesley.

With an effort, Ellie pushed her friend back on to the pillows. 'I think you're in danger of miscarrying. Keep still. Don't move. I'm ringing for an ambulance.'

Lesley wailed, 'Oh, no! Don't say that! I want this child so much.' She breathed deeply, and then drew up her knees as a contraction took hold of her body. 'Oh!'

Ellie stumbled down the stairs. She'd put her own phone down somewhere. She couldn't think where. Had she left it in the kitchen? She made it to the landline in the hall and dialled nine-nine-nine. 'Ambulance, please. Yes, it's an emergency. My friend is miscarrying. Yes, my name is . . .'

The doorbell rang.

Ellie tried to concentrate. If she didn't give the operator the right address the ambulance wouldn't find them. But the doorbell! She couldn't think what to do. There wasn't anybody else at home, was there? If only Thomas hadn't been called to an emergency on the other side of London.

She continued to give the operator their details. 'Yes, that's her name. Lesley with an "ey" at the end. She's bleeding heavily and having contractions . . .'

The doorbell rang again.

Ellie was informed an ambulance would be there directly. She crashed down the receiver and opened the front door.

A young man stood there with his hand raised, ready to press the bell again. A motor scooter was parked behind him. Baseball cap on backwards. Black and tan clothing, expensive and clean. Chinese or Japanese, maybe. A tiny moustache. Dark eyes. Intelligent. The student known as Timmy Lee? What on earth was he doing here?

'Mr Lee?' said Ellie. 'You're looking for Angelica?'

Was that a cry from upstairs? Ellie was torn. Should she tell this lad to get lost and attend to Lesley? She dithered, not knowing what to do.

'My apologies, Mrs Quicke. Angelica did say you were like a second mother to her. I gave her a lift from the party on Saturday night, and I wondered, as she has not been in contact with me, if you might know . . .?'

Well-spoken, educated. The very slightest of lisps? Ellie hesitated, thinking that if Lesley were miscarrying she ought not to be left alone. She ought to get rid of this man, but . . . He should be down at the station, helping the police with their enquiries. He could clear Angelica of all involvement.

He solved her dilemma by stepping towards her so that she gave way. And now he was in the hall and the front door had shut behind him.

She said, 'Look, the police have Angelica down at the station, asking her about Saturday night. They need to know whether or not a girl called Kate was still alive when she left the party . . . although, of course, it might not be Kate. But if you can give Angelica an alibi then you really must tell the police when you left the party.'

He had narrow eyes, very black. 'A girl from the party is really dead?'

'Did you see a redheaded girl arrive at the party?'

'Yes, perhaps. Where is Angelica? I need to see her, urgently. I gave her a lift home from the party when things got a bit tight. That is the right word, is it not?'

'One of them, yes,' said Ellie. And turned her head to listen again. Was that Lesley calling for help? She tried to get rid of the man. 'Angelica is being questioned by the police as we speak. She could do with an alibi. Look, I'm sorry to throw you out but I have a friend upstairs who needs medical attention.'

He sat down on the hall chair. 'I will wait until Angelica returns.'

That wasn't at all what Ellie had had in mind. She glanced up the stairs. That really had been a cry for help, hadn't it? 'I must attend to my friend.'

Timmy waved her away. 'I wait. And I will think about what I did see.'

'No, that's not what . . . Oh, well, you'll have to excuse me for a minute.' Ellie bounded up the stairs, slowing down near the top. She found Lesley on the floor in a foetal position. 'Sorry, Ellie . . . your mattress and duvet! Such a mess . . . Oh!'

Another contraction. Ellie helped Lesley back on to the bed when the contraction eased. The miscarriage was well on its way. No amount of bed rest was going to stop it.

Lesley's head rolled back and forth.

Ellie said, 'How far along are you?'

'Seven weeks, almost. Aagh!' She convulsed again.

Nearly fifty days. Ellie tried to think backwards. Lesley had conceived before Susan had been eased out of Lesley's flat and while the wedding preparations had been going on. Lesley had been pregnant when she and Andy had had a spat over the amount of attention Andy had been showing to Angelica. At that time, Ellie had seriously wondered if Lesley should have gone through with the wedding. Ellie had feared, even then, that the couple were mismatched. But then, seemingly mismatched couples often made a solid partnership in marriage, with each person respecting the other's strengths and weaknesses.

Ellie had kept her misgivings to herself. She'd thought Lesley must be besotted by the man to excuse the selfish way he carried on. But now, in view of what she'd just learned, perhaps Lesley had gone through with the marriage because she knew she was pregnant?

Ellie got a wet cloth and washed the perspiration from Lesley's face.

Timmy Lee's voice floated up the stairs. 'Ambulance arriving. Shall I let them in?'

Ellie sang out, 'Yes, please do.' And to Lesley, 'I'll come with you.'

Lesley panted, clutching at Ellie's arm. 'No. Don't come. I'm better off by myself. I made this mess; I'll get through it by myself. There's something I have to tell Andy, but . . . I can't think straight.

What was it? Tell him to look in the piano.' She panted as another contraction took hold of her. 'I'm losing the baby, aren't I?'

The paramedics burst into the room with a merry, 'What do we have here?' Then got down to business. Ellie, feeling weak, took the stairs to the ground floor. Slowly. And only when she was in the hall did she remember her caller. Timmy Lee. Chinese, perhaps. Only, there was no sign of him.

FIVE

Monday teatime

Ellie clutched her head. Events were moving too fast for her. Murder and miscarriage. Moneylending and mayhem.

Do murder and moneylending go hand in hand? Probably.

Be practical, Ellie. Lesley would need some things if she were being taken off to hospital. She'd need her handbag and a change of clothes in with her for a start. Now where oh where was Lesley's luggage? Had Andy dumped Lesley's stuff in the guest room upstairs or . . .? How long would they keep Lesley in hospital?

Down the stairs shot one of the paramedics and out of the front door. To fetch something from the ambulance?

The phone rang and Ellie dithered. She told herself it was no good dithering. She looked for her own handbag because Lesley would need . . . What would she need? A mobile phone, for a start.

Oh. Where was Lesley's phone? Ellie couldn't think.

The paramedic burst back into the hall and ran up the stairs hauling a piece of equipment with him.

Ellie answered the phone. 'Yes?' For the moment, she couldn't even remember her own phone number.

By great good fortune, it was Thomas, her husband. 'Are you all right, Ellie?'

'Um, yes. I'm fine. Things are happening, though.' How could she explain?

He sounded taut. Stressed. Thomas had officially retired from being in charge of a parish while continuing to work as the editor of a national church magazine. However, he was still at the beck and call of friends and acquaintances in trouble. As now.

He said, 'Things do happen around you, Ellie. You attract happenings. Listen, I've been invited to stay for supper with my old friend. His wife's just been diagnosed with cancer and neither of them is handling the situation well. I'm not sure what I can do, but maybe just being there and being ready to listen to them talking about it might help. But if you need me I'll cut it short and come back early.'

Ellie would have loved to have him back that very minute, but if he was needed elsewhere, then elsewhere was where he must be. She could cope, couldn't she? She braced herself to be brave. 'No, no, I can manage. The only thing is that Lesley seems to be miscarrying.'

Thomas knew what her own miscarriages had meant to her, all those years ago. 'Ellie, I'm coming straight back.'

'No, don't do that. You're needed there.' She stilled her breathing, which had quickened. 'I'm not panicking. Really, I'm not. I can manage. I've phoned for an ambulance and it's just arrived. I suspect they'll take her straight off to hospital, so a spot of prayer would come in useful.'

'Yes, of course. Lesley will take it hard if she miscarries.'

Ellie thought that wasn't the only thing Lesley was going to take hard. The paramedics came into view and descended the stairs, slowly, carrying Lesley in a collapsible chair between them. Lesley's eyes were closed. Tear tracks stained her cheeks. And talk about looking 'as white as a sheet'!

Ellie said goodbye to Thomas and located her handbag. 'Lesley, I've put your mobile phone somewhere for safekeeping. Take mine. Ring me when you know what's happening. I'll bring whatever you need to the hospital later on. I'm praying for you and so is Thomas.' She thrust her own phone into Lesley's hand.

Lesley opened her eyes. 'The baby . . . gone.' Desolation.

'Oh, you poor dear.'

'They'll check that all's well. I may have to have a tiny op to make sure it's all come away, and then they'll send me home. May I come back here afterwards? The flat . . .!' Tears pooled on her cheeks.

'Of course,' said Ellie, wondering if Andy would want to share the big double bed with Lesley or . . . Well, think about that later.

Ellie held the front door open for them to take Lesley through. Lesley's car had gone. Of course, Andy had taken it to go after Angelica and organize a solicitor for her, hadn't he? Would Lesley's handbag still be in their car?

Lesley held up her hand as she passed by. 'Ellie; I've just

remembered. Tell Andy to look in the piano.' Her voice was hardly more than a whisper.

The girl was hallucinating. Ellie was alarmed by how weak Lesley sounded. 'Yes, of course I'll tell him.'

Then they were gone and the drive was empty.

As was the house. Ellie went back in and shut the front door, wondering what she ought to do next. Something struck her. She felt hollow. She'd missed lunch and ought to do something about it.

A figure loomed up out of the shadows and Ellie nearly jumped out of her skin.

He said, 'I have made tea and I have found the biscuits. Is tea right? Do you wish for coffee instead?'

Timmy Lee. She'd forgotten about him. His English was almost perfect. 'Tea would be lovely.' He was carrying a tray with the rarely used best china cups and saucers on it. He'd even found the tea cosy to put over the teapot, put milk in a jug and laid some biscuits out on a plate. Clever boy.

Unusual, too. Perhaps it was the custom in China to housetrain the boys as well as the girls.

She ushered him into the sitting room and sat down. 'You can be mother.'

'What?' He hadn't removed his baseball cap, which annoyed her slightly. She told herself she was getting old and was not keeping up with the fashions of today's youth, but in her day men did not keep their headgear on when they entered someone else's house.

She laughed at herself. In her mother's day there were silver tongs to handle sugar cubes and a strainer. Also, they'd used loose tea leaves instead of the now-universal teabags.

She said, 'Oh, sorry. People say, "You can be mother" if they want someone else to pour the tea. As in, "You pretend you're the hostess and pour the tea for me". You are a student at the university?'

'Indeed. I come to improve my languages, to take my degree, to learn to be English.'

Ellie wanted to correct him to say it should be 'British' and not 'English'. But didn't. It seemed he wanted to talk, so she must let him do so. Besides which – she took a sip of tea – he made a mean cuppa, and it was going down a treat. 'Where do you come from?'

'Hong Kong. And you? I have learned that many people in London come from other places.'

'You are right, but I was born in West London, so I'm a native. How do you know Angelica?'

'She is always at the student parties and in the clubs at night. So pretty. So short of money.'

Ellie did a double-take. Was he hinting that Angelica had been selling herself for money? No, surely not. She must have misunderstood him. It was so easy to get the wrong idea when communicating across language barriers. Did Timmy know about Angelica's boyfriend, Jake? Surely he would know if he saw her about at parties and in the clubs. Time to clear up one problem at a time. 'So you know Angelica well? And her boyfriend?'

'I see them together, yes.'

'Why did you say she was short of money?'

'We are friends. She tells me this.'

'Did she tell you how she meant to solve her problem?'

A stare. 'No. It is not my intention to be involved. She is pretty girl.' And he gave a tiny shrug.

There it was again, a hint that Angelica had been selling herself for sex. Ellie frowned. She didn't think Angelica had been doing that. Did Timmy know about Angelica's deal with Rafael? And if not, then he couldn't be as close a friend to the girl as he had implied.

He said, 'I, myself, do not pay for sex. When I go home, it is to join my uncle's company and marry my cousin. It is all arranged. I Skype my family and my fiancée twice a week.'

It did indeed seem that Timmy knew nothing about Rafael. Ellie decided that it would be better not to mention him. She said, 'As a friend, you were invited to Angelica's party at the weekend?'

'I go to all the parties. I do not drink much but if there is food, I eat. It saves me much money. Angelica says there is a party at this address and I make a note of it. I arrive, but what I see I do not like. Is a bad scene. Men pushing, shouting. Girls screaming. Some of them meaning it.'

'This is important. Did you see a redheaded girl at the party? She might have arrived about the same time as you.'

He concentrated, taking his time to answer. 'I try to remember. So many people. Shouting. Spilling drinks on the floor, all over the place. The noise! The telly and a radio and a ghetto blaster, too! Did I see redheaded girl? I think, maybe. I am not sure. I do not stay as there is no food. I leave. I find pretty Angelica in tears outside. I say, "Shall we go to a club?" She says, "Yes". But on the way, she says she is tired and wants early night. So I bring her here and I see she goes into the house with her key all right, no problem.'

He narrowed his eyes at her in speculation. 'Angelica says you are lovely lady, you are like a mother to her. It is a big house, indeed. Do you have many lodgers?'

She was amused. 'No, no. I inherited this house and there are a lot of bedrooms so I can have people to stay if I want to. I do have another girl staying with me at the moment, but she helps in the house and is part of the family. You may have met her – Susan is her name – and she is studying at uni to be a chef.'

'Susan?' He thought about it. His face cleared. 'Ah, the girl with the big . . .' He made a gesture with both hands which Ellie interpreted correctly as referring to a girl with a big bosom.

'Yes,' she said. 'A delightful girl.'

He twitched a smile. 'She is one fine English girl. I understand that I can look but I must not touch.'

Ellie laughed. It was a good description of Susan. 'Well, Angelica came to stay recently. She asked if I could let her have a room for a few nights, and I did. She will be moving on soon.'

Very soon, thought Ellie. Tonight, if possible.

Timmy frowned. 'She says you are a relation to her. She says that is why you invite her to stay.'

'No, she is no relation of mine. She is related to a friend of mine but they don't have enough room to put her up. I have the space but I'm getting old and perhaps I don't understand how you young-sters like to live. We – my husband and I – go to bed early and get up early, but Angelica . . . Well, it's a small thing, but irritating.'

'She is not fitting into the household?'

'No, she isn't.' Ellie stopped there. She didn't need to tell this man how Angelica flouted the house rules and how she had lost no opportunity to be rude to Susan. If Timmy was a friend of Angelica's he didn't need to know what a difficult house guest she had been. Angelica needed all the friends she could get.

Ellie reached for another biscuit and found it was the last one on the plate. How many had she eaten already? It would do her waistline no good. She said, 'When Angelica came, she said she had nowhere else to go. I couldn't turn her away then, but I think now that I ought to have made sure she had somewhere to move on to pretty soon.'

'But you have taken her in, so you are responsible for her.'

Timmy judged her to be a fool? Perhaps he was right. If Ellie had known more about Angelica when she first came to the door, would she still have taken her in? Mm. That was a difficult question to answer. The girl had said she was in trouble and Ellie had responded automatically to an SOS call. She had thrown the door wide and allowed Angelica to move in. And now . . .?

She said, 'Angelica has to take responsibility for her actions sometime, and while she's got a room here for the moment it is not going to be for ever.'

'She thinks . . .' An assessing look. 'She says you are a lady with a big heart. She says you help her out of some difficulties she has, with a grant from a trust fund.'

'She is mistaken. The trust is not for foolish girls who don't work and expect others to subsidize them.'

'It is my understanding that you give money to those who need it?'

'Not exactly. The trust exists to give people something so that they can then help themselves. It might be to replace old camping equipment for a Scout group or to enable a school to buy better equipment. We will not be paying Angelica's debts, if that is what you mean. We wouldn't throw good money after bad.'

'She tells me that you will help her, because she is so much in need.'

This conversation was going nowhere. Ellie changed the subject. 'If you are her friend, you have a chance to help her now. The police have taken her in for an interview. They will want to know what responsibility she had for the party, who she invited, who came, what she saw and when she left. She admits that she did see a redheaded girl at the party and that she recognized her as her boyfriend's ex. She says you can be a witness to this, that you can confirm that Kate was alive when Angelica left. You agree that you picked Angelica up and brought her back here. You say you saw her safely inside. In other words, you can give her an alibi for the time of the girl's death, which will clear her in the eyes of the law.'

Ellie stood up, giving him the cue that the interview was now over. She waited for him to move but he didn't. She put the pressure on. 'So from here I suppose you will be going down to the police station to make a statement?'

He stayed where he was, eyes down.

She tried and failed to understand him. What was he thinking about?

He said at last, 'Angelica is OK, no need for help from me. She will cry and they will feel sorry for her. That is the way she works. I do not have to say anything or do anything.'

Ellie took a deep breath and sat down again. 'Do I understand you have no intention of going to the police to clear her name? Why not? Isn't it your duty as a citizen? Oh, well. I don't suppose you feel you are a British citizen, because of course you aren't. But is there any other reason why you don't wish to go to the police?'

'You are calling me a liar?' A flat stare. Intimidating. It was like a blow in the face. Totally unexpected. For the first time, she wondered if she had been wise to let this man into her house. She was all alone. Everyone else was out. Thomas wouldn't be back for hours – if at all.

She made her tone conciliatory. 'Surely you can see that the police will want to speak to you, to check Angelica's alibi? I don't understand why you are not anxious to help her. She will give the police your name to clear herself. You can't deny you were at the party.'

'Also, many other people. They will speak to the police. There is no need for me to speak, none at all.'

Ellie persisted. 'If you don't tell them what you know and Angelica says that you took her home early, the police might begin to think that you didn't come forward because you had something to hide. They might wonder, for instance, if you killed the girl yourself and—'

'No, not I!' A note of . . . what? Amusement? No, no. Surely not amusement. He said, stolidly, 'It is true I saw her there. A redheaded girl. But then I left.'

'Then why not tell them so?'

No reply. Ellie wondered if there might be another reason for him to avoid going to the police. 'Perhaps you don't wish bringing yourself to the attention of the police because your papers are not in order? Has your student visa expired?'

'Of course not. It is ridiculous to say that.' Yet he shot her a calculating look.

Ellie didn't normally have a suspicious mind but she began to wonder if what he said were true. There was something about the way this young man had turned up on her doorstep . . . She shook her head at herself. She was seeing shadows were none existed. Yet there had been a certain something in Timmy's story which left questions in her mind.

She said, 'Really? Your papers are in perfect order?'

A bland look. 'I admit there was a mix-up, a real mess, a while ago. Someone else with my family name attempted to enter here, but that matter has all been ironed out and I have nothing to fear. One more year and I will have my degree.'

'A mix-up in your papers? We hear lots of excuses at the trust. Perhaps you have five children who are all sick and your father is an alcoholic?' She almost laughed at his look of incomprehension and hurt pride.

He said, 'My father is a revered academic and my mother is a teacher at a top school. I do not understand your reference to alcoholism.' There was a note of annoyance in his voice.

'Sorry. I was thinking of the standard set of excuses used by those who fail in life. You are right. I apologize for my levity. But I still do not understand why you do not wish to go to the police when you could so easily clear Angelica of murder.'

'It is not good to be running to the police every five minutes. Angelica is in no danger and I am innocent of everything but giving her a lift home.'

Ellie considered what he had said and not said. 'If the police find that your papers are not in order—'

'Which they are.'

'But if there was some doubt, I believe that you have a right of appeal to stay for some months. In which case, you would be able to stay here till after your exam.'

'You keep saying that my papers are not in order, but I assure you that they are.'

By now, she was pretty sure that they were not. There was something about this young man which she did not care for. He sat there, solid as a jade figurine. Almost threatening.

No, why did she think he was threatening? That was ridiculous!

Nevertheless, she would be glad to have one of her lodgers return. Even Andy's presence would be welcome. She said, 'Oh, look at the time. I must really get on with—'

He interrupted. 'It is not true, what you said. I do not think they would let me sit the exam if it is known there is a problem with my papers. Therefore, you will not talk about this to anyone!'

So there really was a problem with his papers? She hadn't imagined it?

For the first time, he showed signs of agitation. 'This is all Angelica's fault. If I had not given her a lift, nothing would have happened. If you tell the police on me, if they take me down to the station and start looking into my papers, I will refuse to give your girl an alibi. Why should I help her when she has got me into this mess?'

Ellie's brain plunged this way and that. He was right. If his papers were not in order he couldn't risk anyone looking at them, and surely Angelica could talk herself out of trouble without any help from him.

No, he was wrong! He was conveniently ignoring the fact that a girl had been murdered.

But if Angelica did manage to convince the police she had had nothing to do with the murder, then it wouldn't be necessary to call on this lad to say what he knew, would it?

No, that was sophistry. She didn't know exactly what the word 'sophistry' meant, but she was pretty sure it was the right one in this context. Thomas would know. If only he were here! Well, she could ring him on his mobile and tell him all about it. He could help her decide what to do.

Correction: she knew what Thomas would tell her to do, which was *not* to ignore the fact that Timmy was flouting the law of the land.

That is, if he were correct in saying there was nothing wrong with his papers.

Oh, dear. It would be so much easier to say nothing. What would be the harm in letting Timmy complete his course, take his exam and get his degree?

But if he'd misled the university about his papers then what else had he lied about? Was he shading the truth about other things?

She said, 'Sorry, Timmy. Now you've told me what happened,

I can't pretend I don't know. You'd better tell the university that there's been a problem with your papers and see what arrangements you can make to get your visa extended so that you can still get your degree.'

He was shocked. 'I have been open with you, and this is how you repay me? What harm have I ever done to you that you should want to ruin me . . . and not only me, but bring shame on my parents and my fiancée who is waiting for my return, and my uncle who has arranged a job for me in his factory?'

'Don't exaggerate.'

Cheeks flushed, he was almost shouting. 'You don't understand. I'm telling you nothing but the truth! You can't mean to throw me into prison—' He bounced up on to his feet and stood over her.

She quailed, thinking that there was no one else within earshot, that he was bigger than her and could attack her . . . Her heart beat faster, thudding away . . . He lifted his hand to hit her! She wanted to pray for help, couldn't think of the words.

The phone rang. Or was it the doorbell?

It broke his concentration. He lowered his arm and looked around the room . . . for the phone?

She said, 'I'd better take it.' She got out of her chair, moving stiffly, and made her way around him and out into the hall.

It wasn't the phone. It was the doorbell.

Someone in a uniform was at the door, holding out an identification badge. It was the gasman, to read the meter. A thin stalk of a man with a long nose, looking not at her but past her, down the hall, to identify where the meter might be.

Trying to think what to do about Timmy, she opened the cupboard under the stairs to allow the gasman to read the meter.

Timmy had followed her into the hall and now stationed himself rather too close to her for comfort. Waiting for the gasman to leave.

And then what did Timmy intend to do?

Ellie tried to think. She didn't believe – she hoped – that Timmy really meant to harm her. Yes, he wanted to frighten her, to deter her from giving him away to the police, but that was a different matter, wasn't it? She wanted him to leave . . . Oh, yes! How she wanted him to leave! He was sticking to her elbow, waiting till she was alone again.

What to do? Well, she could tell the gasman that Timmy had

been threatening her and ask him to call the police. But, if Timmy denied it, then how could she prove he'd threatened her?

She could understand the lad's point of view. It was hard to think that one little slip, some slight defect in his papers might ruin his life.

If only he would do the right thing, confess his problem to the authorities and deal with the fallout! She didn't think he'd be thrown into prison for an infringement of his visa, although she supposed he might be detained somewhere for a while. But with a good solicitor, he'd get a slap on the wrist and be free to get on with his life. If necessary, she would put him in touch with her own solicitor and help him that way. Would that be condoning his transgression? Well, possibly. But only a very little.

She decided she would give him one more chance. How? Well, perhaps she could use the gasman's presence in some way.

The gasman got out his torch and dived head first into the cupboard.

She said, 'Timmy, I've given you some good advice and I hope you take it. I shall check, you know. Meanwhile, I expect you're anxious to get down to the police station to give Angelica an alibi. Perhaps you'll let yourself out.'

He didn't move. 'We haven't finished our discussion yet.'

The gasman re-emerged, mouthing figures to himself. He entered the numbers on his computerized gadget, his eyes on the job. He hadn't even looked properly at Ellie. He hadn't been listening to what she'd said. If he left Timmy in possession of the field, as it were . . .? The prospect did not please her.

The gasman was so focused on getting in and out of houses quickly that he wouldn't remember anything that had happened during his visit. He'd be gone in seconds if she didn't do something to imprint the situation on his mind.

The gasman said, 'That's it, missus.' He shut the cupboard door and turned back to the front door.

She put herself in his path. 'Do you fancy a cuppa?'

'Huh?' He focused on her for the first time. Then looked at Timmy, who glared at him, probably wishing him to Hades.

The gasman looked back at Ellie. 'You have a problem with your gas, missus? I'm only here to read the meter, but if you want me to make a report, I can do that.'

Ellie gushed, 'How good of you. You've got my name down, have you? Not just the number of the house? Mrs Quicke, that's right. My visitor here, Mr Lee, doesn't know anything about gas and he's just leaving, aren't you, Timmy?'

Timmy chewed his lip, his eyes darting here and there, seeking some way out of the situation. 'I'm staying for a while,' he said.

SIX

Ellie wondered how on earth she could she use the gasman's presence to get rid of Timmy?

Inspiration struck. Ellie said to the gasman, 'What it is, I've been thinking about signing up for a service agreement for the boiler. I was wondering if you have time to talk it through with me?'

The gasman shook his head. 'Sorry, missus. On a tight schedule here. But I'll make a note that you want someone to ring you about the service agreement, right?' He tried to step around her.

Ellie sidestepped, too. 'You don't have any literature about it in your car, do you?'

'No, sorry.' He sidestepped again.

Ellie said, 'Timmy, where are your manners? Open the front door for the gasman and don't forget to shut it behind you as you go.' Burbling away, Ellie took Timmy by the arm and tried to lead him to the front door. He resisted her, his arm hard under her hand.

'Come along, now, Timmy,' said Ellie. 'We don't want a scene in front of the nice gasman, do we?'

The gasman's eyes focused on them. Sharp and shrewd. 'You want him to leave, missus?'

Ellie nodded. 'He's leaving, yes.'

Timmy muttered, close to Ellie's ear, 'I can give you names, lots of names, of people who were at the party.'

The gasman said, 'You want I should give him a helping hand out of the door, missus?'

'That would be most kind,' said Ellie, relieved to find the gasman had finally cottoned on to what was happening. 'Mr Lee came for a cuppa, but we don't want him to outstay his welcome, do we?'

Timmy narrowed his eyes at her. 'You are . . .!'

She gave him a little push. 'Out you go.' And out he went, stiff as a wooden soldier, out of the front door and over to his scooter.

He didn't look back but she thought he was trying to contain his fury as he bestrode his machine, not bothering with a helmet, and drove off, watched by Ellie and the gasman.

'That one's trouble, I can smell it,' said the gasman, looking at his watch. 'I've lost a few minutes' time, but . . . You alone in the house, missus?'

'Not for long,' said Ellie. 'And thank you.'

'You really want a service agreement?'

'Actually, yes, I do. You'll arrange for someone to call?'

'Tell you a thing, missus. You keep your mobile phone on you, ready to call the police if he comes back, right?'

'I'll do that,' said Ellie. And then wondered where her own phone was . . . she'd given it to Lesley, right? So where was Lesley's?

She watched the gasman leave.

A gust of wind blew some seeds into the drive from the sycamore trees in the road outside. A dark car drew up and parked across her driveway. Two men sat in the car. She didn't know either of them, but they looked at her and kept looking.

The car didn't move.

The men didn't get out.

They were there to see that no other car entered her drive? Or left it?

Or they were waiting for someone else to arrive, to talk to her? About what?

She closed the door and double-locked it. Then shot the bolts.

Her mouth was dry. She tried to swallow.

She was all alone in the house. Thomas wouldn't be back till late. Susan and Angelica were in the hands of the police. Andy was there, too. Lesley was in hospital.

She had no mobile but the landline was still working. She checked, wondering who to call. Thomas was on an errand of mercy. Yes, he would return if she called him, but it would take him a good hour and a half to get back, if not more. Her closest friends were all away, on holiday.

She could ring the police and complain that a car was blocking her driveway. They'd laugh. Complaints about illegal parking went to the town hall, which closed before five o'clock – and it was nearly half past four by now. The town hall wouldn't do anything about it that night.

She would think who to ring in a minute. The priority must be to make sure all the doors and windows on the ground floor were safely shut.

It was a big house with a number of doors and windows on to the outside world. She couldn't remember how many windows might be open on this fine summer's day. She went down the corridor to the kitchen, locked and bolted that door. She locked the door from the conservatory into the garden, and the French windows from the sitting-room ditto. The library windows were open. She shut them.

She hesitated when she got to Thomas's Quiet Room, which he used for devotional purposes and which she sometimes sat in when she needed to get away from the phone and think.

She needed to think, now. She went to the window to see if the car was still there. It was.

Dear Lord, I really don't know if I ought to be panicking, but that's exactly what I'm doing. The people in that car out there may be on a perfectly innocent errand, waiting for a friend or looking at a map because they've taken a wrong turning.

Wrong. They're bad news, whoever they are.

Finally, an idea borne out of desperation.

She returned to the hall and picked up the phone. Where had she put that card? Ah, she found it in her pocket. That was lucky . . .

She dialled and waited for the man to pick up at the other end.

She said, 'Rafael, you probably didn't think I'd get back to you so quickly, but . . .' She tried to still her breathing, but her heart was beating so strongly that she knew she sounded odd.

He was quick on the uptake. 'Something's wrong, Mrs Quicke?'

'I don't know. You'll laugh when I tell you, but I'm alone in the house and there's a car with two men in it, parked across the driveway so that no one else can get in or out. The two men are just sitting there. Watching the house.'

'Can you describe them?'

'Not really. Bulky. One has a shaved head, I think.'

'Suits or shirts?'

'Sweatshirts, dark.'

'White British or—'

'One is. The other, I'm not sure. I think they're waiting.'

'Yes, I expect they are.'

'You didn't send them?'

'Not my style.'

'Do you know them?'

'I might know *of* them. They're after Angelica, of course.'

'She's not here. The police took her down to the station to make a statement and she hasn't returned yet.'

'Ah. You won't let them in, will you?'

'No, I've locked all the doors and windows, but . . . it's stupid to be frightened, when the sun is shining.' And that sounds stupid, too.

'You're not stupid, Mrs Quicke. You've decided not to call the police?'

'What would I say? Someone is parked illegally across my driveway?'

'Yes, yes. I'll be round in ten. I would suggest you don't answer the door, or the phone, and if someone comes tapping on the window—'

'I'll lock myself in the loo.'

'When I arrive, I'll press the doorbell with the Mayday signal. You know it?'

'Three short, then three long . . . or is the other way round?'

He laughed and disconnected.

She put the receiver down with a hand that shook. Stupid woman! She was going to pieces. When Rafael arrived he'd discover a raving lunatic, mopping and mowing and . . .

Pull yourself together, woman!

She went into the sitting room, collected the tea things and took them out to the kitchen. The doorbell rang. She ignored it. She began to hum a little ditty. 'Polly put the kettle on, Polly put the kettle on.'

The phone rang. She ignored that too, crossing her fingers that it wasn't Thomas or Lesley trying to get through.

Ten minutes, he'd said. She looked at her watch, which was running slow. She'd been meaning to take it in to have it serviced, or cleaned or adjusted, or whatever it is that you did to watches that ran slowly.

She was not going to answer the door. Or the phone. Or even look out of the window

She put the tea things into the dishwasher.

Someone tapped on the kitchen window and she dropped a cup.

But didn't look at the window. She picked the cup up. Thankfully, it wasn't broken. It was a fine china cup, one of her mother's prized possessions. She only had three cups left now, out of . . . how many?

She turned the radio on. Turned the volume up. Someone was talking about the weather. It was going to turn hot tomorrow. In Scotland it was going to rain.

She opened the fridge door. Someone rapped hard on the window a second time.

It was no good – she'd have to go to the loo and lock herself in. The window there was so small that no one could climb through it, whereas if they broke the kitchen window it was large enough for them to get through.

Except . . . she rinsed her hands under the cold tap . . . if she locked herself into the loo, she couldn't open the front door when Rafael arrived.

Dear Lord, I'm shaking!

Someone yelped. She risked a glance at the window and saw two arms flailing wildly . . . and then they disappeared with a thump! But the phone was still ringing. It was doing her head in.

She closed the fridge door. She couldn't think what they were going to have for supper. Susan might not be back in time. They could go out somewhere, perhaps? If Rafael managed to get rid of the intruders.

What makes you think you can trust him? He's a moneylender, and you know they have a shocking reputation. Some of them charge one hundred per cent a month.

Well, Ellie Quicke, you're a moneylender, too. Of sorts. And I think Rafael has a code of honour.

The phone stopped.

The relief!

Three long and three short rings followed by three long. Mayday.

Of course, the baddies might have tortured Rafael into revealing the code.

Well, probably not. Let's hope not.

She rushed to the front door, pulled back the bolts and managed to open the door.

Rafael stood there in black leather biker gear with a shining helmet under his arm. A powerful motor bike was parked behind him. The car that had been blocking the driveway had gone.

Thank the Lord! Praise be! A dozen times.

She said, 'Thank you,' and tried to smile. 'Do you want a cuppa?'

He said, 'Have you any green tea? My mother and my grandmother swear by it.' He stepped inside, 'Earl Grey will do, if you don't have green tea.'

Her voice wobbled. 'I'll have to look. I'm not sure what I've got. How did you get them to leave?'

'They know me. Or rather, they know of me. I promised to do what I can to return their property to them.'

She reached for the back of the hall chair and managed to sit on it before her legs gave way.

He put his helmet down. He looked amused. 'They frightened you? Suppose I make you a cuppa, right?'

'I don't expect to be menaced by thugs in broad daylight, in my own home.'

'Exactly. Can you make it to the kitchen? Shall I give you my arm? It's this way, isn't it?'

She was not going to let him support her trembling footsteps! Certainly not. She got to her feet and with only the lightest of contacts with the wall, made it to the kitchen. He put the kettle on. She sank into a chair and said, 'Those men were drug dealers, right?'

'Support staff, yes.'

'Angelica isn't actually on drugs herself, is she? No, I don't think so. But . . . let me see if I've got this right. We know she needed money. Could she really have been so stupid as to invite a dealer to push drugs at her party?'

'For a consideration. To provide her guests with entertainment. Or so Milos says.'

'I can't believe it! I suppose the drug dealer – you say his name is Milos? – thought he was on to a good thing, because Angelica seems to have been letting people think that the flat belonged to her. I understand she's most inventive, and has been telling people I'm her favourite auntie or words to that effect. What went wrong?'

'He says he'd been invited by Angelica to send someone to the party to sell drugs, on the understanding that she'd get a cut of the takings. He says his salesman hasn't reported back and is not to be found at his usual place of residence. The man has dropped out of sight, together with the money he took and the rest of the drugs. Milos believes Angelica knows what has happened to him and the goods. He wants his property returned and reparation made.'

'I understand that he might consider her responsible because she arranged the party, but she left early so how can she know what happened to his salesman?'

'Milos can be inventive, too. He says she must have seduced the man into splitting the proceeds with her before helping him to disappear. That's why he's gunning for her.'

Ellie made a gesture of frustration. 'She couldn't have been so stupid as to think she could double-cross a drug dealer, could she? No, surely not!'

'He thinks so.'

'Every time I think I've plumbed that girl's depths, I discover another layer of stupidity. She can't have been thinking straight.'

'Question of the week, definitely: is Angelica capable of joined-up thinking?'

'You're right. She disconnects her brain every ten seconds. Impulse rules, OK. And if her half-baked schemes go wrong, she believes someone else will always get her out of trouble. Why did those men come here now, today?'

'I'm afraid that was my fault. I took Angelica's phone, remember? And answered it when it rang. I recognized Milos's voice because he has difficulty with his r's. He demanded to know where Angelica was. I must admit, I was feeling somewhat annoyed with the girl, so I told him she no longer owned that phone and why. He knows of me. I don't do drugs, and he knows that, too, but he thinks of us as being on the same side. Suppliers to people in need. He asked if I'd taken her phone because she owed me money, and I said yes. He asked if I'd tried her family yet. I said I'd tried but didn't think it would work.'

'Because you'd met us.'

He nodded. 'Because I'd met you. I told him my chances of recovering what I've lent her through you were not great. He didn't believe me.'

'Ouch. So he's going to approach me himself?'

He gave her a sideways look. 'You've not dealt with anyone like him before?'

'No, and I don't know how to handle him.'

'There is one way. You could help Angelica out.'

'No, I won't do that. He'll have to work things out with her another way.'

He looked around him. 'You're not hiding the drug pusher somewhere, are you?'

She spurted into laughter. 'No!'

'Milos thinks you are.'

Ellie clutched her head and gave a little scream.

He twitched her a smile. 'All right, all right. You aren't. But it's not impossible, is it, that Angelica knows where the man has gone? And that she knows what happened to the money and the remaining drugs?'

'Come on! We know the girl left the party early, courtesy of Timmy Lee. How would she possibly know what happened to him?'

'Milos thinks she's in it up to her neck. He thinks she brought the money from the sales and the remainder of the drugs back here when she left the party. I promised him that I would search for them for him.'

'What?'

'That's the price of removing his goons from your driveway.' He looked around. 'I agree it's unlikely, but it's better I search than that his men do it. So, if you were Angelica and you'd brought back a package from the party, what would you do with the stuff?'

'I can't believe it!'

'Try. Or Milos tries for you.'

Ellie tried to concentrate. 'Well, it's not in her bedroom. Susan and I have just turned it out.'

'You weren't looking for money and drugs, were you?' He poured them both a mug of tea, brought them to the table and sat down beside her. 'Let's think. A package of drugs and money wouldn't take up much room. Did you look under the mattress?'

'Yes. Susan helped me to clear her things out of the big guest room, and as there were two of us, we turned the mattress. There wasn't anything under it. Do you think we'll have to search every room in the house? No, come to think of it, we needn't bother with the top floor because that's Susan's domain, and Angelica wouldn't go up there as they don't get along.'

She tapped her forehead. 'Let me think. It would be after midnight when she got back. I sleep lightly and usually half wake and look at the clock if either of the girls come in very late. Which Susan doesn't, much.

'Angelica has been getting back sometimes between two and three, but I honestly can't remember hearing her on Saturday night. One thing: I don't think she'd have risked going into one of the other bedrooms on the first floor in case I heard her moving around where she had no right to be and got up to find out what was going on. So, if it's not in any of the bedrooms on the first floor, she must have hidden the stuff down here.'

She got to her feet, looking around her. 'The kitchen would be my bet, except that Midge – our cat – often sleeps in here when he's not on our bed. Angelica is not fond of cats and avoids any room that he's in. Midge was up with us last night but I can't remember where he was on Saturday night. Oh dear, we're going to have to look everywhere, aren't we?'

'I'll help you. Milos thinks the drugs were in a Marks and Spencer's bag, which is distinctive. Look for a dark green plastic bag.' He began on the cupboards to the right of the door. 'Let's be systematic about it.'

'Right. Freezer and fridge.' She started on those. 'Nothing untoward. She's not very tall. Would she have put anything in the top cupboards?'

'She might have stood on a chair. Don't worry. We'll find the stuff and I'll get rid of it for you.'

She opened the oven door, and then told herself that was the last place Angelica would hide something. The family used the oven almost every day but Angelica had never been known to cook for herself or anyone else. She said, 'If the police find out . . . Thomas and I could be arrested for possession! I can't believe this is happening. That girl is amoral.'

'Agreed.'

Ellie moved on to the larder. Susan loved the larder and had filled the shelves with shining, gloriously colourful jars of jams and pickles and marmalades.

Ellie groaned. Every single one would have to be moved to make sure nothing was hidden behind it. 'I could murder the girl.'

'Pretty face. Pity about the lack of common sense. Nothing here. What's down the passage?'

'Toilet. Utility room. Door to the backyard. I can't think what is to become of her.'

He raised his voice as he dived into the back quarters. 'Realistically, the best thing would be for her to work for a pimp who runs a stable of high-class girls. She wouldn't deal with money and she'd be looked after, medically. Alternatively, she could marry some brainless idiot who has money and ruin him.'

Ellie blinked. She would never have thought of Angelica working as a call girl. What a horrible thought! She had to admit it was practical, although not a solution a Christian would care to consider. Oh, but it would never come to that.

She said, 'Her cousin Andy fancies her, but if he shed his wife and married Angelica she would certainly bankrupt him within months. She couldn't live on a deputy head teacher's salary.' She backed out of the larder. 'There's nothing here.'

'Nor out back. Besides which, she's madly in love with Jake. Or so she says. Where next?'

'The dining room, which we only use for meetings of the trust fund. I don't think Jake reciprocates her feelings.' She led the way and he followed.

'You've spoken to him? What did he say?' He looked around him. 'Nice room. Good proportions.'

She nodded. He appreciated quality, didn't he? The chairs stood to attention around the long mahogany table. Victorian rectitude. Long velvet curtains. 'I'll look in the sideboard. You check the curtains?'

'Jake?' he probed.

'Oh. He didn't impress me. La-di-dah, as my mother would have said. But he did admit he knew a girl called Kate. And he did say he'd check on her and inform the police if it really was her who'd turned up dead.'

They checked the dining room and came up empty.

He said, 'Nothing here. Where next?'

She led him down the corridor and opened a door on to what had once been a morning room and which Ellie now used as her study. Desks and chairs, old-fashioned filing cabinets, bookshelves, a computer, files of paper . . . and a large ginger cat who woke up from his nap on top of a cabinet and stretched fore and aft.

Before Ellie could warn Rafael that Midge didn't usually take to strangers, her visitor had reached out to rub behind the cat's ears. Midge was supposed to be a good judge of character. Ellie held her breath. Midge might well lash out . . . or . . . Midge raised his head for another rub and then sat up, curling his tail around himself.

'I like cats,' said Rafael, smiling. 'What did you say his name was?'

'Midge. Don't laugh. He can open any door or cupboard which has a handle instead of a knob. Knobs still defeat him.'

Rafael addressed Midge. 'Now, if only you were a dog, trained to sniff out drugs, you'd save us a lot of time, wouldn't you?'

Midge sneezed, jumped down to the ground and wound himself round Rafael's legs, his tail waving. Ellie relaxed. Midge was not going to attack Rafael.

She cast a quick look around. 'I can't see that anything's been disturbed and I don't think Angelica would have left anything in here because she knows that I have a part-time secretary who might well squawk if she found anything untoward. And, come to think of it, the same applies to Thomas's study. Come, I'll show you.'

She led the way down to the end of the corridor and opened the door on to a large room looking both on to the garden at the back and the drive at the front. 'This is the library, which Thomas uses for work. He edits a quarterly Christian magazine. The summer issue went out some time ago and the autumn issue is at the printers as we speak, so his secretary has taken time out for a holiday. I don't think Angelica would have hidden anything in here in case someone turned it up by accident.'

He looked around him. Shelves of books. Piles of books. Two desks piled with paper. Chairs ditto. Computers, currently quiescent.

He said, 'I see what you mean. And, if she had hidden something here, how would we ever find it?'

'We wouldn't.' She shut the door and led the way back down the corridor. 'Thomas's Quiet Room is the only place left on this corridor. There's not much furniture in there but there is a cupboard which she might have used for a hiding place.'

She let him into the room and lowered her voice. 'This room is special to Thomas. He prays here a lot. Perhaps you can feel it?'

He looked around. Assorted chairs, a small table, a woollen picture of the Good Shepherd. An air of quiet. It was slightly tidier than usual. Thomas had a habit of referring to different editions of various bibles and commentaries if he wished to check on something. He would dig the relevant tome out of the cupboard and leave it open on the table or the floor. Once a week these books would be picked up by the cleaners, dusted and stacked away again in the cupboard, which is where they were now. Ellie opened the cupboard and prodded at the books, but saw nothing that shouldn't be there.

He looked around. 'A quiet room, yes.'

She bent to pick up a toy car which had strayed under Thomas's chair. 'I look after my grandson a couple of mornings a week. He likes this room and, if he's going to lie down and take a nap, he'll do it in here.'

Rafael said, 'I can understand why he likes it.' He held the door open for her. 'What next?'

'I'm beginning to lose hope.'

'Don't do that.'

She looked at her watch, comparing it with the clock in the hall which was about to strike the hour. Putting the toy car on the ledge by the door, she said, 'I must ring the hospital and find out how Lesley's getting on. And Susan! Surely they can't keep her much longer at the police station?'

He said, 'Tell me about the police coming to fetch the girls.'

'Two policemen arrived and asked for them. Angelica protested but Susan went with them willingly. Andy trailed along behind.' She turned into the sitting room and gestured widely. 'Here we are. This is the last of the rooms downstairs. You take that side and I'll take this.'

'You said Susan was happy to go off with the police?'

'She was, which was more than I can say for Angelica. Anyway, they both had alibis. I'd better fill you in on . . . Oh, look! There's that magazine that Thomas was looking for. I thought I'd thrown it away. He'll be pleased.' She placed it where he'd see it when he came in, on the table in the window.

'Susan,' prompted Rafael, moving the settee to see if there was anything under it.

'Right. Well, I'll have to go back a bit.' She did so, starting with her phone call to Jake and his reaction to the news of Kate's death, followed by the police calling for the two girls and Timmy Lee's visit. She ended up by describing how she'd got rid of the student with the help of the man who came to read the meter.

This amused him. 'Mrs Quicke, I am full of admiration,' said Rafael. 'If only you were ten years younger and I were ten years older . . . what a ball we would have had.' He stood upright. 'I can't see anything untoward.'

Ellie felt herself blush. She thought how silly she was being. Almost coquettish. A pang in her right hip reminded her of her age and caused her to ease her back. She sat down in her favourite chair. 'There's no drugs or stash of money here. Your friend Milos must be mistaken. I expect his salesman went off with the goods.'

'It's possible, but Milos doesn't think he'd be that stupid and neither do I. The consequences would be . . . life-changing.' Rafael didn't elaborate. He said, 'What about the conservatory? And is there a shed in the garden?'

'Go and look, if you like. I don't think Angelica's ever set foot in the garden.' She looked at her watch, which was running slow, as usual. She really must get it looked at. 'I'm so worried about Lesley.' She looked at the clock on the mantelpiece.

When were visiting hours? How long was it since the police took Susan and Angelica away? Timmy Lee could give Angelica an alibi, but I don't think he's any intention of doing so, which means the police may hold her . . . Oh, I hope they beat the truth out of her! No, I don't mean that, exactly. But she's got Andy dancing attendance on her when he ought to be in the hospital, looking after Lesley. What a mess.

He said, 'I'll check the conservatory. You ring the hospital.'

He was being a bit high-handed, wasn't he? But it was sensible to divide the tasks they needed to perform. She phoned the hospital. The nurse said that Lesley was being kept in overnight, and visiting hours were from six thirty p.m.

Now, could she manage to get to the hospital with some clothes and toiletries for Lesley before she had to produce supper? She expected Susan and Angelica to return at any minute, also Andy. Don't let's forget Andy. They'd all need food. Ellie couldn't think what she had to give them.

Rafael reappeared, holding a corpse. 'Any ideas for disposal?'

SEVEN

Monday, early evening

E llie recoiled, moving her chair back a pace. 'A mouse? But we don't have mice. Midge doesn't allow it.'

'Perhaps he's brought it in from outside. Where is he, anyway?'

Nowhere to be seen.

Ellie felt the situation was getting way out of hand. Murder, she could cope with. Mice? No. 'What do you suggest?'

'A mouse trap. If you've got a nest, there's going to be more than one mouse around. Cats like to play with mice before they kill them. This particular dead body must be some of his work. I repeat, what would you like me to do with it?'

Ellie tried to think. 'Plastic bags, drawer nearest the freezer. Then dump it in the rubbish bin. Sanitizing hand cream on the ledge above the basin.'

'Shouldn't the corpse go into the compost? My parents had a big garden and everything which decomposes went into the compost.'

'I daresay. But in London we get flies and pigeons and crows and magpies, not to mention foxes, who swoop on anything that they think is food. You didn't find the nest?'

'No.' He disappeared across the hall, his voice floating back. 'Your boiler could do with a service. I don't think it's set right.'

No, it probably wasn't. The boiler was due to be serviced next month. Thomas had been chuntering on about the settings for some time but . . . what business was it of Rafael's?

Ellie was annoyed. Who was this man, anyway? Some kind of businessman who flourished on the edges of the law? What right did he have to walk into her house and order her around and . . .?

Here, Ellie clenched her fists.

Susan had reacted in a most peculiar way when she'd brought Rafael into the kitchen. Susan had said things afterwards which indicated she knew him fairly well. Susan occasionally mentioned a boy who was on the same course as herself. His name was . . . what? Ellie couldn't remember. But he seemed to be more of a friend than a lover. A reliable companion.

Susan had said that Rafael could be charming.

Rafael had asked about Susan. Not once, but twice.

Rafael was interested in Susan?

No! Not possible.

Susan wouldn't be interested in him. Never! Perish the thought! But . . .

Ellie remembered Rafael's first entrance. Susan had answered the door and brought him into the kitchen. Susan had stood by the door and let him pass in front of her. He had walked past her, smiling slightly. Not looking at her.

Susan's eyes had been lowered. Why hadn't she looked at him?

Rafael returned, rubbing gel into his hands.

Ellie said, 'You've met Susan before?'

He half laughed, then turned to look out at the garden. A light drizzle was falling outside. Clouds obscured the sun.

He said, 'Susan? Angelica used to talk about Susan. Said she was a lump of lard. I don't think they got along, did they? Something to do with Susan throwing her weight about.'

She persisted. 'You know her well.'

'Why, I've seen her around. In the pub. And once at a club.' He was not being open about this, was he? Why?

Oh. Dear. Susan had only ever gone out clubbing once. It was true that in the past Angelica had made fun of Susan until the girl had begun to think of herself as unattractive. Then one day Susan had realized that showing off her wonderful bosom had a considerable effect on men. That very evening, one of her friends had persuaded her to go out clubbing. Susan had returned home in the early hours, discarding a pair of pink fairy wings and a headdress in the hall on her way up to bed. She'd been escorted home by . . .?

Ellie pointed her finger at Rafael. 'It was you who took her clubbing and brought her home afterwards?'

He didn't blush, exactly, but he didn't meet her eyes. 'I . . .'

'*You?*' she said. 'You tried to get—'

'A little too close, and got a knee jerk that I can still feel today. Yes.'

Ellie grappled with the scenario of this smooth man-about-town propositioning Susan, and how his advances had been received. Susan had kneed him in the groin, hadn't she? And now he'd come back for more?

Why?

She said, 'So you are taking an interest in this case not just because Angelica owes you money but because you can see an opportunity to get close to Susan? Are you planning to pay her out for rejecting you? Do you intend to play with her as the cat did with the mouse? You want to make her fall in love with you, and then you plan to dump her?'

He put his hands in his pockets and jingled coins. 'Actually, no. I might have thought that, at first . . . but,' he shot a glance at her. 'I'd like to help *you*, Mrs Quicke. Sincerely.'

Ellie snorted. She didn't think he knew what 'sincerely' meant.

He took his hands out of his pockets, and then put them back in again. 'Look, you've got me all wrong.'

'I don't think so.'

'I swear to you that—'

'Don't swear. Anyway, I wouldn't believe you. Listen to me, young man. If you harm one hair of Susan's head you'll have to reckon with me. Understood?'

'Yes, Granny.' Meekly. 'Honest, I'm not—'

'Oh, yes, you are. You're the closest thing to a scumbag I've met in ages, and you're not fit to—'

'Wipe the floor that she walks on? Yes, I know that. But, you can't blame me for trying, can you?'

Ellie found her handkerchief and blew her nose. 'I'm very fond of Susan.' Indistinctly.

He grimaced. 'She's a girl, like any other. She can be romanced like any other. It's up to her whether she goes along with it or not.'

'You only want her because she had the impudence to reject your advances.'

'Now you're becoming quite Edwardian. "Oh, Sir Jasper!" and all that.'

'I want you to leave this house.'

'No, you don't. Because if I go, you won't have anyone to fight your corner, and when Angelica talks – which she will – and tells the police that she stashed the drugs and the money here, they will arrest you for possession of drugs and stolen money. You need me to keep you out of jail.'

'Are you threatening me? Do you really think I'd sell you Susan to keep the police off my back? You are mistaken. You may live in a world of compromise and half-truths, and yes, I can see the logic in going along with your suggestion. But I try, however difficult it may be, to do the right thing and not to compromise. And I bet I sleep more soundly than you do.'

He sat down, producing a smile charming enough to lure any woman under eighty into his arms. 'Shall we let Susan judge for herself? I promise to be good. We know that Susan can defend herself when she considers it necessary to do so. I concede that I did misjudge her and she did punish me accordingly. We both know she can do the same thing again if she considers I am getting out of hand. How about that?'

'I don't trust you.'

'I don't trust me, either. Mrs Quicke, this is a new situation for me. I am trying to do the right thing. I am, I must say, quite astonished at myself for trying, but there it is. I promise to behave myself if she turns me down again. All right?'

'I still don't trust you.'

'No, but you are wondering if the love of a good woman can rescue a bad man. Right?'

She had to laugh. 'I don't think you are that bad a man.'

'Don't fool yourself.' Grimly. 'I've been with dozens of girls and told dozens of lies about my intentions. Matrimony is not on my agenda. Why should the leopard change his spots?'

'Hmm.' She sat back in her chair, considering the man before her. 'I don't think you've ever left a girl pregnant?'

'No. That would be messy. I don't like mess. I promise not to leave Susan pregnant.'

Ellie blew her nose again. 'I can't stop you romancing her. I have to trust her common sense not to be taken in by you. Or, if she decides to go along with your flimflam, then I'll be there to pick up the pieces. I'll give it some thought in prayer.'

His lips twisted. 'You think your prayers will save her from me?'

'I think prayer works.'

'Let's shake on it.' He held out his hand and, somewhat reluctantly, she took it. He shot her one of his glancing smiles. 'And now I'd better ring Milos and give him the bad news that we haven't been able to find the money and the drugs. He will not be amused.'

He took out his phone and frowned at some messages that had come in. 'He's getting impatient. Can't blame him. You really don't want him coming over here to look for the stuff himself. I'll see what I can do to head him off.'

He pressed buttons and got through. He said, 'Cool it, Milos. Mrs Quicke and I have searched the place and haven't found anything of yours yet . . . No, Angelica's not here. She's been taken down to the police station to answer questions about the party. When she comes back, I'll have another go at her, get her to tell me where she's put the stuff . . . Yes, she'll tell me where, I assure you. She should be back any minute now. I'll ring you when I've spoken to her.' He killed the call.

The front doorbell rang. Ellie started to her feet. 'I expect that's her now.' She hurried to the hall. 'I may have shot the bolts after I let you in. Yes, I did. Can you reach the top one for me? It's a little high for me. I can't think how I managed to reach it earlier.'

'Fear,' he said, drawing back the bolt for her. 'Let me have a look, see who it is before . . .'

The front door opened, almost sweeping him off his feet. And there was Susan, looking as if she'd very much like to chop something into teeny weeny pieces and throw it into boiling water. 'Who double-locked the door?'

Behind her came Andy's car, with Angelica in the passenger seat.

'You!' Susan pointed her finger at Rafael and advanced on him. No shrinking violet here. 'I might have known you'd move in on Mrs Quicke when my back was turned!'

He held up his hands, backing away, laughing. 'No, honest! I'm the cavalry, riding to the rescue!'

'As if! You . . . you slug!'

'Have a heart! I really am trying to help.'

Ellie noted with interest that his smile had disappeared altogether.

Angelica flew into the house and cast herself upon Ellie. 'Oh, I can't bear it! If it wasn't that I knew you'd help me, I don't know what I'd have done!' Tears sparkled, lips quivered, curls bounced. 'Oh, it's so wonderful to be home!'

Wonderful for her, maybe, but not for Ellie, who tried to make the girl stand upright only for her to cling all the closer.

Andy came in, shutting the door behind him. 'I told her not to say anything at all, and she didn't. What a girl!' Full of admiration for Angelica.

Susan turned away from Raphael, dismissing him from her mind, to speak to Ellie. 'I'm sorry to have been so long. The police had to check that I really did go to the pictures on Saturday evening—'

'Me, too!' said Angelica, curls bobbing. 'They couldn't find Timmy, horrid boy, the one who gave me a lift home after the party, but I told them about Jess and Gina and their friends arriving at the party just as I was leaving with Timmy, they contacted them and they confirmed it, naturally. And, oh, I'm so sorry about the party, Andy. I thought it would be just a few friends round but some horrid people came and it got out of hand, and I was so frightened, I didn't know what to do, and it's true – I ran away!'

Great tears glistened in her eyes, and she removed herself from Ellie to hang on Andy's arm.

Andy smiled down at her. 'There, there! You couldn't have known what would happen. I'm sure the insurance will pay up, and if not, well, it's not the end of the world.'

Susan made one of her sick-making noises, with which Ellie fully agreed.

Angelica was all smiles. 'Oh, you are all so good to me! I am such a lucky little girl!'

Rafael said, 'So now you're back, little lady, have you worked out how to solve your money problems?'

'Oh, yes!' She was all smiles. 'You'll never guess what happened. I had no idea someone was going to bring a drug dealer to the party but there he was, and I was thinking this was not a good idea when a fight broke out and someone was going to take him off to the hospital to be looked at, so before he disappeared he pushed this bag into my arms. I didn't even look to see what was inside it because I was so upset, he was all over blood, and I realized this was getting to be a really bad scene, and then Jake said he was going, and that upset me all over again, and then Timmy offered me a lift home, and I got on the back of his scooter without thinking, and only when I got home did I look in the bag and realize he'd given me some pills and all the money he'd collected! Wasn't that wonderful? So now I can pay you off, Rafael, and we can all be friends again!'

Ellie blinked. Pinched herself. Had the girl really thought . . .?

Susan said something softly to herself. A prayer, possibly.

Andy gaped. And swallowed. 'But Angel, it's not your money.'

Angelica was ecstatic. 'Don't you see, the drug man can't come after me for the money because what he was doing was illegal, and obviously it was *meant* that it finished up in my hands. Aren't I the luckiest?'

Rafael rubbed his forehead. 'Give me strength! All right, girl. Where did you hide it?'

'Oh, that was so clever of me, too.' She started off down the corridor. 'Thomas didn't like it when I went into his Quiet Room to light a joss stick, which everybody does when they want to meditate, don't they, although personally I don't go in for that sort of thing much, but I thought he'd like it, and he really didn't need to be quite so rude to me about it, did he? I told him, I said, I was taught at school to say the Lord's Prayer, although obviously I've long since forgotten how it goes . . .' She opened the door to Thomas's Quiet Room and dived into the cupboard in the corner. 'So I put the bag in . . .'

She gave a little scream.

Rafael said, frowning, 'It's not there. We searched this room earlier.'

Ellie slumped into the nearest chair. A particular sequence of events trickled through her mind and she knew, or rather, guessed what might have happened to the package . . . and then she thought, no, she must be mistaken.

'Oh my God!' Angelica whimpered. 'Someone's stolen it! Get the police!'

Andy made a strangled sound and stated the obvious. 'Angel, we can't go to the police asking them to track down illegal drugs which you brought here.' Then, rather bravely, he eased Angelica to her feet and patted her shoulder. 'Perhaps you came back and moved it to another hiding place, later?'

Ellie felt for her mobile phone, which would have certain numbers on it. Her hand fell away from her pocket. She'd given her mobile phone to Lesley, hadn't she?

'No, no, I didn't move it!' cried Angelica. 'I thought it was safe there, and if anyone found it and blamed Thomas for having the drugs then it would serve him right, wouldn't it? Because he really was so unkind to me. You do believe me, don't you?' She slitted her eyes. 'Someone watched me hide it, and then they came down and stole it.'

Ellie thought, I know what's coming. No, surely, she wouldn't dare!

And it came.

'Susan!' Angelica whirled round. 'You stole it, didn't you?'

Susan gaped. 'What? But . . .! Come off it! I didn't know anything about drugs until this very minute.'

'You were listening for me, spying on me when I came in on Saturday night, and then you crept downstairs and found the package and took it for yourself.'

'No, I didn't. I don't hear you when you come in late at night. My bedroom is not over yours. I've never heard you come in, except once when you banged the front door by accident and woke me up.'

Angelica cast herself on Rafael. 'She did it! I know she did it! She's always been jealous of me! You'll have to get it out of her. And you can make it right with the drug person, can't you? I know you can. You can do anything!'

Rafael took hold of her wrists and held her away from him. 'I can't come between you and Milos. Now you've admitted having possession of his property he's going to come after you, my dear, and I certainly won't try to stop him.'

'But Rafael, I thought you were my friend!'

Ellie thought hard. She must have those phone numbers some-where else . . . perhaps not in her usual address book, but . . . in her study somewhere? Of course, she might be mistaken, and someone else had found and taken the drugs and the drug money, but . . .

What was that noise? Her landline was ringing.

She hastened back to the hall and picked up the phone. Thankfully, it was Lesley, who sounded faint and weary. 'Ellie, is that you? I was ringing so long. I thought you must have gone out.'

'I wish I had. But I've got a house full at the moment. How are you?'

Susan had followed her, and after Susan came Rafael. Susan said, 'Is it Lesley? What's the news?'

Lesley's voice was a mere whisper. Sedated? 'They've got me on a drip, would you believe? And then tomorrow they'll make sure everything's come away properly and tidy me up. I'll probably be allowed home in the evening.'

'Tell me what you need and I'll get it to you. Nightdress and toilet things, a jumper and jeans? What else?'

As Lesley talked of shoes and a jacket, Andy emerged from the Quiet Room with his arm around Angelica, who was leaning on him.

Susan gestured to Ellie that she'd like to talk to her aunt.

'Yes, yes,' said Ellie, trying to make notes. 'Now, Andy and Susan are here. Shall I hand you over?'

'Does Andy want to speak to me?' Lesley sounded distant.

Ellie said, 'Andy? It's Lesley on the phone. They're keeping her in overnight.'

He hesitated, detaching himself from Angelica, but not exactly hastening to take the phone which Ellie held out to him.

Lesley sighed. 'Don't bother him, Ellie.' And cut the call.

Ellie put the phone down.

Susan said, 'Why are they keeping her in?'

Ellie looked not at Susan but at Andy. 'She lost the baby.'

Andy registered concern, and then what looked very much like relief. 'Did she? Well, I . . . but I suppose she'll take it hard. That's bad. To be honest, I didn't want to have a baby so soon, but she—'

Angelica said, 'It was extremely selfish of Lesley to saddle you with a baby before you wanted it.'

I would very much like to strangle Angelica. Slowly.

Susan flushed and burst into tears. 'Oh, no! Oh, how awful!' Susan didn't weep prettily, as Angelica did, but her tears were real. 'Oh, poor Lesley! Is she all right? Can I visit her? She must be shattered.'

Lesley had said she was destroyed.

Rafael put his arm around Susan. 'She'll need some things. I'll take you to the hospital and wait for you.'

Susan elbowed him away. 'Don't be ridiculous! This is nothing to do with you.'

Actually, if he were to make it his business, we might all get through this adventure with as little trouble as possible. But not, of course, at the expense of Susan's peace of mind.

Dilemma. Is it a good idea to have an ally with a spotty past? Answer yes or no.

Er. Yes. Sometimes. Probably.

Andy dithered. He didn't know whether to show grief for a lost baby or concern for his wife. Perhaps Angelica was right and Lesley had wanted a child, but he hadn't. Or he hadn't wanted one yet. Yet his upbringing taught him that he ought to display distress in such circumstances.

He lifted his arm to put it around Angelica's shoulder again, and then let it drop. Even he could see that cuddling Angelica was inappropriate at that moment. He said, 'What ward is she on? I'd better get down there.' He spoke without enthusiasm but he did say it.

Ellie wondered if Lesley wanted to see her husband or not. Perhaps, when he saw her lying there on a drip, having lost their child, it might rekindle his love for her? 'What a good idea,' she said.

Angelica had another role in mind for him. She gave a little scream. 'Oh, Andy, no! You can't leave me here without protection. Those horrid drug men will be round any minute, wanting their things which I don't have, and none of this is my fault, and I know they're going to be so cross with me and they'll threaten to beat me up and mark my face so that I'll never be able to go out of the house again! Oh, I'm so frightened!' And she cast herself on him again.

'Oh, come now,' said Andy, showing a mixture of embarrassment and tenderness. 'It can't be as bad as all that.' He tried to make her stand on her own two feet, but she was having none of that and clung all the closer.

'She's right, you know,' said Rafael, who showed neither embarrassment nor tenderness for the girl. 'She's got herself into a right mess, owing money left, right and centre.'

Angelica screamed. She had a nice, tight scream. It went up to the roof and assaulted their ears. 'What am I to do? Mrs Quicke, you've got to help me out. Lend me enough to get them off my back and I swear I'll pay you back.'

'With what?' said Ellie. 'Promises?'

Angelica sprayed tears, clasping Andy's arm. 'Andy, you'll help me out, won't you? If they kill me, or maim me, you'd never be able to forgive yourself! It's only a couple of thousand, when all's said and done. And the drugs, of course. But I'm sure they'll understand that I don't have them any more.'

Sweat broke out on Andy's forehead. 'But Angel, the flat's in such a mess, it's going to cost an arm and a leg to put right, and I really don't have that sort of money.'

Ellie had had enough. Time was passing and she needed to be on the track of the lost drugs. And for that, she needed her mobile phone. She drew Susan to one side. 'Listen, this is important. I gave Lesley my phone and it has some numbers on it which I desperately need. Can you get it back? You have Lesley's phone, don't you? If we can find her a change of clothing and her night things, you could be at the hospital in half an hour. I'll give you money for a minicab each way.'

Susan blew her nose and gulped. She was still weeping but trying to concentrate on what Ellie said. 'You want me to go as well as Andy?'

'Yes.'

'But he's her husband.' Susan looked at Angelica. The girl was pressing herself up against Andy, who was trying to fend her off but not being firm enough about it.

Susan said, 'I get you. He's not much of a husband, is he? I'm only her niece, of course, but I am very fond of her. You think that her getting pregnant was a mistake?' She let the question hang in the air. Then she shook her head. 'Well, even if it was a mistake, Lesley would have wanted to keep the baby. She wanted children. Yes, you're right. I'll go, too.'

'Andy won't think of taking the things she'll need, so that's your excuse for going with him. And whatever happens, get me my mobile phone, right?'

'It's that important?'

'Yes. And it's that important that she has someone to comfort her. I'd go myself, but . . .' She gestured to include Andy, Angelica and Rafael. 'A house full. And remember to tell Lesley she's welcome to come back here when she's discharged from hospital. Let's get some things together for her.'

As they started for the stairs, they heard Andy sweeping across the hall, followed by the light clip-clop of Angelica's shoes. Angelica was breathless. 'Don't leave me, Andy. Let me come with you!'

The front door banged behind him. Opened and banged again. Exit the pair of them.

Susan halted. 'Shall I call him back? He's forgotten to take Lesley's things.'

Ellie added, 'And he's taken the thing that Lesley will not want to see. Let him go.'

Susan said, 'You're right. I think I know which are Lesley's cases. I bought her one of those suitcases on wheels for her last birthday.' She started up the stairs.

Ellie would have followed Susan but Rafael laid a hand on her arm. 'A word.'

He knew? Or guessed that she knew where the drugs had gone?

Ellie sang out, 'Susan, can you cope? I'm going to see if Lesley left anything in the bedroom over the kitchen.' Nodding to Rafael to follow her, she led the way up the stairs, round the landing and into the old housekeeper's room. She threw open the window. The ruined mattress and duvet lay where Lesley had left them. And nothing else. Not even her handbag. Where was her handbag? Still in the car with Andy? Was it going to be safe there? Would Angelica plunder it?

Rafael said, 'What is it, Mrs Quicke? I saw some thought strike you as soon as Angelica opened the cupboard door. You think you know where the drugs may be? Yet we searched there earlier and you didn't react then.'

'No, Rafael, I don't *know* what's happened to the drugs and the money. I suspect that . . . but I may be quite wrong. As soon as I've got a minute, I'll make some phone calls.'

'You've thought of someone who might have had access to the cupboard since Sunday night . . .'

EIGHT

Ellie said, 'I can't think that someone I trusted would have stolen from me, but what do I know?'

He gave her a sharp look but changed the subject. 'How shall we dispose of the old mattress? Do we throw it out of the window or drag it downstairs?'

She said, 'Drag it downstairs.'

He grabbed the mattress and lifted it on to one edge. Seemingly without effort. He might look slender, even willowy, but there was strength in them there willows.

She held the door open for him, deciding to share her suspicions. 'I use the services of an agency to clean the house. I've had the same two people for years, but one is off work having her bunion seen to, so someone else comes with Annie for the time being. It's not always the same person. They came early this morning. Annie has been with me for years. I could have sworn that . . . but anyone can be tempted, can't they? A moment of madness?'

'You suspect your cleaner found the stash and lifted it?' He began to ease the mattress out of the door and along the corridor.

She bundled the duvet up and followed him. 'It's possible, yes. They did clean the Quiet Room this morning. I know that because all of Thomas's books had been picked up and put back in their rightful place in the cupboard. Annie's daughter wants a boob job. Annie and her husband were going to help their daughter out with the cost but they neither of them earn a lot and, when they'd done their sums, they realized they couldn't afford it. In her coffee break this morning, Annie asked me for a loan and I refused.'

He laughed without sound. 'Welcome to the club. I'm always turning people down for a loan. They can get quite vocal about it.'

'I don't usually have individuals approaching me. In the trust, everything is done through a committee by letter or email. I feel awful, because if I hadn't refused Annie she wouldn't have been tempted to take the money. And now, unless I can get it back straight away, the police are going to be involved and . . . Oh, this is all horrid. I pay the bills to the agency so I've never needed Annie's home address. I know she lives in Greenford – she takes the bus to get here – but I don't know precisely where. Her telephone number, for use in emergencies, is on my mobile phone, and I gave that to Lesley when she was taken into hospital.'

He'd pulled the mattress as far as the head of the stairs. 'Shall I slide it down or throw it down, or what?'

'What do you mean?'

He said, 'One . . . two . . . three . . . and . . . Whoosh!' He launched the mattress into the air. It bumped and slid and stuck, hovering halfway down, and then, gathering momentum, flumped and bumped all the way down to the bottom of the stairs where it lay, puffing out dust. He put his hands on his hips and laughed.

Ellie caught the infection. She giggled. She folded the duvet over and over, tossed it up into the air and let it tumble over and over and come to rest sitting on top of the mattress.

'Success!' he said. And then, 'What fun!'

'What . . .?' said Susan, frowning as she reappeared with a small tote bag.

'It's the child in me,' said Rafael, running smoothly down the stairs to pick up the mattress and stow it upright at the side of the stairs.

'And in me,' said Ellie, 'although heaven knows, there's not much to laugh about at the moment.'

Susan looked as if she didn't know whether to join them in a smile or continue to frown. The smile won. 'You're both crazy.'

Rafael took the bag off Susan. 'Let's go. That is, if you don't mind riding on the back of a motorbike. It would take too long to fetch the car. Now, Mrs Quicke, don't you try to lift things while I'm away. Double-lock the doors behind us and don't let any suspicious characters in. I'll be back in an hour or so to help you tidy up any loose ends, so to speak.'

Ellie was alone at last.

She felt limp.

The house seemed to sitting down on its haunches. Listening. Waiting.

Were there any watchers outside? She looked out of the window.

No watchers. No motorbike. No bodies. She checked the locks on all the windows and doors and shot the bolts on the front door.

Suddenly, like a swarm of bees, problems screamed out for attention in her head.

What if the drug people came back now, while she was alone?

Well, they couldn't get in, could they?

Er, yes, they could, if they broke a couple of windows and climbed in that way.

She shuddered.

And then she took a deep breath.

Dear Lord, give me courage. It's probably ridiculous to imagine I'm going to be tracked down in my own house . . . except that bad things are happening. Look at that poor girl, Kate. Killed at a party.

Oh, dear. I'm in such a mess. So many people in trouble and I don't know which way to turn or what to do next.

Please, Lord, look after Lesley. She's going to need everything her friends can do for her to get through this.

What to say about Andy? Well, I certainly don't know what to hope for there. But if you could keep an eye on him? Perhaps he's just the product of an overindulgent mother who has told him that he deserves a life of wine and roses . . . which is certainly not what ordinary life is about.

And Susan, dear Susan. Keep her safe. And yes, look after that rogue Rafael who is possibly not as black as he's been painted, but if he does have designs on Susan, then . . .? But you'll know best how to help her through the heartache when he's had his wicked way with her and dumped her. Because, if the truth were but known, I don't think many women could withstand Rafael's charm.

I don't know what to hope for re Angelica. Yes, she's one of your lambs but, oh, dear! Give me some advice?

I must admit I'm afraid of what the drug man will do now he knows that the drugs definitely came here only to disappear. He'll hold me responsible, won't he? And perhaps, in a way, I am. Because if I hadn't refused Annie that loan for her daughter's boob job she wouldn't have been tempted to steal. It's out of character for her to take something that isn't hers but I couldn't let her have the money for a boob job. It was a ridiculous thing to ask for, very expensive and totally unnecessary, and the family has no means of paying me back for it, so in effect they're almost as bad as Angelica, except that . . .

No, Angelica isn't in the same class as Annie. Annie is the salt of the earth: a hard-working, opinionated gossip who has been part of my life for years. We've exchanged news about our families and our ups and downs over tea and biscuits so many times.

How could she have stolen from me? I feel betrayed. I wish . . . if wishes were . . . what? Fishes? No, not fishes. Can't remember what they're supposed to be like. Something down to earth, no doubt.

I keep forgetting that a girl died at that party. Kate, her name was. I don't know anything else about her except that she had red hair. But you know all about her. You watched her grow up and go to the party looking for Jake. You watched her die. You know who is grieving for her. If you want me to do something about finding her killer, then you'll have to point me in the right direction because I don't have a clue.

Meanwhile . . .

She lifted the phone and dialled. She didn't think she'd be able to get the information she needed over the phone because the agency would be closed at this time of day, but she must try.

A girl called Maria ran the cleaning agency which Ellie had used for years. Maria was not only a friend of hers but was also married to the general manager of Ellie's charitable trust, so there were many ties binding them together. Maria wouldn't mind being interrupted after hours, would she?

'Maria? Sorry to trouble you after work . . .' Ellie could hear Maria's two little girls playing in the background. Little screams of delight. Water splashing. Were they in the bath? Or the paddling pool? Was it their bedtime already? Ellie looked at her watch . . . running slow . . . and looked at the clock. Yes, time flew when you were having fun, didn't it?

Maria sounded stressed. 'Ellie? Can I ring you back? The doorbell's just rung and—'

'It won't take a minute. Do you have Annie's phone number on you?'

'Well, no. It will be in the office. I can get it for you in the morning if you like. Is there a problem?' Maria took the phone away from her head and shouted to her husband, 'Can you get the door?'

To which he replied, faintly, 'I'm on it, I'm on it!' Rather sharply.

Maria returned to Ellie. 'Sorry, chaos here. We're trying to get the girls to bed before the babysitter comes. We're going to my parents for supper. Look, I'll ring you tomorrow first thing when I get into the office, right?' Down went the phone.

Ellie replaced the receiver at her end, too. She had hoped that Maria might be able to access the office computer from home somehow. Not that Ellie knew how it might be done, but Maria was young and bright and knew all about such things, and perhaps she might have been able to come up with Annie's phone number. Well, she hadn't done so.

Ellie wondered about ringing Maria back, but no . . . they'd be on their way out any minute now and explanations would take too long.

Ellie considered the alternatives. She was *not* going to ring the police and say she'd been robbed of money and drugs.

In the first place, she would have to admit she'd a house guest who had stashed drugs in her house. She could just imagine how Ears would react to that! And how Thomas would react . . . horrors! And then, if it got into the papers that drugs had been found in his house – which it would do – how all his colleagues would react! He would be accused of bringing shame on the church and, oh, untold problems!

In the second place, she didn't want to get Annie into trouble, because they'd known one another for ever. All right, she'd never be able to trust Annie again, but give her away to the police? No, it was out of the question. Ellie realized that somehow or other she'd decided to get the stuff back off Annie and delivered to the drug dealer without recourse to the police, even it meant she would be saving Angelica from the results of her behaviour.

Frustrated, Ellie stamped on the hall floor. And then said, 'Ouch!' because that had hurt.

When Susan returned with her phone, then she could ring Annie. Why hadn't she written the number down somewhere in her study? Because Annie had told Ellie that she didn't need to. Annie had one of the latest phones, had put her own number on Ellie's phone for her and shown her how to access it. Annie had pictures on her phone and could show videos of her grandchildren. Altogether, she was far more advanced in such things than Ellie.

Ellie rubbed her forehead. Questions without answers. Problems without solutions. Time wasn't on her side. It was no good letting problems squirrel round and round in her head because she was only going to get a headache.

She needed to work out what to do for supper. Only she didn't know how many people there were going to be. She started to count on her fingers, and the doorbell rang.

It wasn't Rafael. It was someone with a more uncertain touch pressing the bell. One long, one short.

She froze.

The silhouette of a man?

Not tall enough for Rafael. And too chunky.

She tiptoed to the door . . . how ridiculous to tiptoe! She looked through one of the clear panes of glass in the stained-glass window. No one she knew.

A chunky hunk with dark hair. Young. A rugby player? Conservatively dressed.

Rafael would have told her not to open the door but a name had popped into her head and, well, curiosity had always been her middle name. So she opened the door a crack.

'Mrs Quicke?'

Yes, she knew the voice. She opened the door wide to let him in. He looked around, assessing her and her position in society. He was perhaps in his late twenties, casually but expensively dressed and nicely barbered. A young professional but . . . in what field? He didn't look super intelligent. Rugby playing? Definitely. Perhaps his family had found him a sinecure?

'Jake. We spoke on the phone. You told me about Kate.' He was jingling keys in his pocket. His shoulders were held stiffly. Gold rugby balls for cufflinks. Ill at ease? Yes.

'I've just come back from the police station. I told them it might be Kate. They showed me pictures and then took me to the mortuary to check. And it was.' His voice cracked. 'What a shock. I mean, we've known one another since nursery school. Our mothers are cousins and . . .' He ran one hand back through immaculately cut, dark hair. His eyes were dark brown and slightly liquid . . . Contact lenses?

He gestured widely. 'It's knocked me for six. I mean, you don't expect, do you . . .? They, the police, asked how did I hear, and I

said you'd rung me and they said how did you know, and I said it
must be because of Angelica. Is she here?' He looked up the stairs
as if expecting to see her run down to greet him.

'No, she's gone out with her cousin.' No need to tell him where.

He took a couple of steps forward to look into the sitting room.
'I must talk to her. The police wanted to know why I left the party
early and I had to tell them that it looked as if it was going to
degenerate into chaos and I wanted no part of it. Then they wanted
to know what time I left, and I had to say I had no idea. I didn't
look at my watch. I didn't think about needing an alibi. I mean, it
was such a crazy evening. I went outside and Angelica followed
me and we had words but then I left. I assumed she went back
inside the house. What do you think?'

Ellie thought he wanted to put the idea in her mind that Angelica
went back into the house and in a minute was going to suggest that
Angelica killed Kate because, whatever he felt about Kate, she was
of his world and Angelica wasn't, and he'd quite like to shed the
pretty poppet now . . . What better way to get rid of Angelica than
by suggesting that she might have been responsible for killing Kate?

Ellie said, 'I really don't know.'

Again, his eyes went up the stairs. 'She's really not here? I
thought, if I could have a word with her, she might come clean and
tell the police a bit more about what happened that night. Confirm
that I left when I said I did. That sort of thing.'

'No, she's not here.'

'You're sure?' Brown eyes had turned hard.

*I was a fool to let him into the house. He's sitting on a lot of
. . . what? Anxiety? Tension? Pressure of some kind.*

'She went out with her cousin some time ago.'

Something shifted at the back of his eyes. 'Ah, the soft-touch
cousin?'

'Is he?' Ellie wasn't sure how much this man knew. Or thought
he knew. Uneasiness grew. By her own stupidity, for the second
time that day she'd let a large young man whom she didn't know
into her house when she was all alone. She hoped she wouldn't
regret it but was rather afraid she might.

The doorbell rang. SOS style. Rafael? Thank the Lord.

She almost ran to open the door and, yes, there he was.

He stepped inside. 'Susan said I should come back, that I

shouldn't have left you alone. She'll let me know when she's ready to leave.'

'Thank you, Rafael.' Ellie gestured towards her other guest. 'I think you know Jake Hartley Summers? A friend of Angelica's. Jake says he knew Kate, the girl who died, but he says he left the party even before Angelica did.'

Rafael's face was a mask. He inclined his head towards Jake. They knew one another.

Jake's eyes narrowed. 'It's Ralph, the Ready Reckoner, isn't it?'

An insult? Rafael smiled faintly. 'And . . . Jackie Jam Pots?'

Insult returned. Ellie looked from one to the other. Jake looked wary. Rafael looked watchful. Two alpha males.

Jake postured, throwing his powerful shoulders back. *Look at me! How strong I am!*

Rafael was as still as a cat can be when watching a mouse hole. Concentrating.

Rafael, thought Ellie, was a fully mature person. He could play the child and throw a mattress down the stairs for fun. He could also walk into a dragon's den and emerge unscathed. Perhaps because he was a dragon himself?

Ellie came to the conclusion that she rather liked Rafael and almost trusted him.

Jake jingled coins. 'So did you drop in on Angelica's party on Saturday night? What a crazy chick she is. I can't think what possessed me to say I'd go, even for five minutes. I left as soon as I caught a whiff of trouble. How about you?'

'The opera. With Melinda.'

An open-mouthed guffaw. 'I gather her parents don't approve.'

'No?' Giving nothing away.

A tinge of pink in the smoothly-barbered cheeks. 'Kate, of course . . . Well, we've known one another for ever. I suppose it's not surprising that Angelica was jealous.'

'Was she?' Again, giving nothing away.

A slighter deeper pink in the cheeks. 'Well, of course she was. Made scenes, you know? I mean, Kate had everything: the private education, the good job, the family tree, the indulgent parents who have always expected us to pair off.'

'I heard she was a bit of a drama queen.'

A light laugh. 'Yes, I suppose . . . the two girls were well matched

in that way. Poor little Angelica. Out of her depth there. It's no
wonder she felt at a disadvantage. I gather she went back into the
party after I left . . .'

Did she? Now that's news to me. No, surely not.

He continued smoothly, 'It would be amusing to find out what
happened next between her and Kate.'

'Amusing?' Rafael tried out the word. He didn't seem to think
it was appropriate.

'Oh, I suppose you'll stand up for her but let's face it. She is a
bit of rough, what? A nasty temper when the tears don't work. What
do you think happened? I imagine they set to, hair-pulling, scratching,
throwing things . . .'

No reaction from Rafael.

Jake shifted his feet. 'Right. Bad taste, that. Forget I said it. Tell
you something: this has knocked me for six. You can say it won't
do my street cred any harm, two bitches fighting over me but, when
all's said and done, I have known Kate for years and I'm shocked
to the core by what's happened.'

Rafael said, 'I didn't know Kate. I heard she was a nice girl.
Decent. Got a good job. Her parents must be devastated.'

'Yes. I must call round. Perhaps later this evening. You don't
know them, do you?' Another pointed remark, trying to put Rafael
down.

'My parents know them, I think. I wouldn't wish to intrude. Do
you know how Kate died?'

A shrug. 'The police wouldn't say. I suppose it was drugs. What
else? Once Angelica had invited a drug dealer in, the odds were
that someone was going to get topped.'

'So it was true? Drugs were involved?'

He reddened. 'I have no idea. Have you?'

'Did Kate do drugs? Did any of your crowd? I hadn't heard that.'

'Would you know?' A sharp laugh. 'Forgive me, but I didn't
think you were on close terms with Kate, or anyone else in our
crowd.'

A slight inclination of the head. 'One hears things.' A penetrating
look from under his eyebrows.

Jake shifted from foot to foot again. He looked at the clock and
checked the time by his gold wristwatch. 'Well, busy, busy. Mustn't
keep you up beyond your bedtime, eh? Mrs Quicke, you'll tell

Angelica I called, right? Say I want to speak to her. Not tonight.
Things to do, places to go. You understand? I'm sure she's nothing
to worry about regarding the police. She only has to tell the truth,
even if it does mean she . . . well, we all know she's a trifle what
. . . impulsive, shall we say? A woman scorned and so on and so
forth.'

He swung past Ellie and made an exit, carefully shutting the front
door behind him.

Ellie took a deep breath. 'Rafael, do you think he's told the police
that Angelica killed Kate with a drug? That's what he's been trying
to tell us, isn't it?'

'It is.'

Ellie said, 'But Angelica couldn't possibly have done that. Or
could she? She told me she left the party soon after Kate arrived
and immediately after having words with Jake out in the street,
and that Timmy Lee gave her a lift home. He confirmed that.
The only thing is he probably won't back her up because he
doesn't want to draw the attention of the police to the state of
his visa.'

'I have come across Timmy Lee now and then. I don't think I'd
rely on him for anything.'

'So you do know him?'

'Slightly. He's not tried to borrow from me, if that's what you
mean.'

She said, mimicking his tone, 'You called that man "Jackie Jam
Pots". What was that about?'

'The family business is making expensive jam, marmalade and
pickles. He's their senior sales rep.'

She put her head on one side. 'He called you Ralph, the Ready
Reckoner? You two know one another more than "slightly".'

'We were in the same year at university but were never close.
My uncle died and left me some money in my final year. I made
use of it to help out a couple of friends who'd got into difficulty
with their bills. They repaid me with a reasonable rate of interest
and that's how I got started. I'm into all sorts now.'

'Is it "Ralph"? Or "Rafael"?'

He smiled – his sudden, warm smile. 'It really is Rafael. My
mother was Italian. Jake and I have issues.'

Ellie was amused. 'You took a girl away from him?'

He laughed. 'Oh, that. Yes. But more importantly, I turned him down for a loan and he's never forgiven me.'

'What did he want the loan for?'

He shook his head. 'My lips are sealed.'

'Something his family wouldn't have liked, if they'd been approached? Ah . . .' She thought she knew. 'He got a girl into trouble and—'

'Hush. Perhaps we all do things we regret later. And you're off the mark, anyway.'

She didn't think she was. She looked at her watch and then at the clock. When Susan came back, she would grab her own phone and ring Annie. In the meantime . . .

He said, 'When did you eat last, Mrs Quicke?'

She blinked. 'Er, I can't remember. I seem to have missed lunch but I had some biscuits at teatime, I think. Are you trying to look after me or are you hinting that you'd like some food yourself?' She looked at her watch and then at the clock, which showed a time fifteen minutes apart. 'Oh dear, how long is Susan likely to be? And, I must ring Thomas . . . No, I can't, can I? He's on an errand of mercy. I honestly don't know what to do about supper.'

Rafael took her by the elbow and guided her down the passage to the kitchen. 'Let's investigate the fridge, shall we? And you can tell me how you came to take Angelica in and under what terms.' A phone appeared in his hand and he looked down at it.

He said, 'Forgive me, I must take this call. Business.' He turned away, spoke softly into the phone and then listened.

Midge appeared from nowhere, with the intention of annoying Ellie until he was fed. She obeyed and he settled down to ingest his food. Noisily.

She opened the fridge door and took items out, more or less at random. She listened in to Rafael's conversation, of course.

'. . . But no, I haven't found it. Yes, I'm back at the house. The girl's gone; she's been out of it for some time. I'm going to try to persuade Mrs Quicke to let me search the whole house . . . Yes, we searched the ground floor, but the client is at odds with someone who occupies a flat at the top of the house and I'm wondering if she might have hidden the stash up there, trying to make trouble for her . . . Yes, I'll keep you updated.' The phone disappeared.

Ellie gaped at him. 'You think Angelica might have hidden the stuff in Susan's quarters because she didn't like her? I grant you Angelica might have thought about it, but she told us she'd decided to put it in Thomas's Quiet Room instead, and you saw how she reacted when she found the cupboard empty. She really did think it would be there.'

'I lied. It's gained us a few hours.'

Midge jumped up on to the table, eyed Rafael closely, decided he was an acceptable table companion and started to groom himself.

Rafael rubbed Midge behind his ears. Midge gave him a level look and washed behind his ears all over again.

Ellie said, 'Midge is not supposed to be on the table. Put him on the floor, right?'

Rafael obeyed. Then, 'Tell me how you know Susan.'

NINE

So now Rafael wanted to know about Susan, not Angelica?

Ellie said, 'Lesley, who is a very good friend of mine, asked Susan to be one of her bridesmaids. Susan is her niece, and when she came up to London to study to be a chef, she moved in with Lesley and Andy for a short time until she found somewhere else to stay. There really wasn't enough room in Lesley's flat for her. Lesley knew that my dear housekeeper, who'd been with us for years, was failing and that I needed someone to help look after her. Lesley asked if I'd like to have Susan for a while to help me out with Rose, and I did. It worked beautifully. After Rose died, I asked Susan if she'd stay on for a while and she did. She's part of the family now.'

'She pays rent?'

'She volunteered to do so, and I accepted because this house is expensive to run. Susan also cooks for us sometimes, which we really appreciate. She keeps her rooms immaculate and she's a very easy person to have around.'

'Angelica isn't?'

Ellie sighed. 'Angelica is Andy's cousin. She's always been treated with indulgence by her family. Andy asked her to be the second bridesmaid at his wedding, which gave her an opportunity to tease Susan unmercifully. Fortunately Susan rose above it. Angelica had also been staying with Lesley and Andy, until she assumed too much and got on Lesley's wick. Lesley threw her out. And that's when, shortly before the wedding, Angelica turned up here in tears, saying she had nowhere to sleep that night. It didn't seem right to turn her away when I have all these spare rooms and I'd already taken Susan in. Angelica said it would only be for a few days, but—'

'She lied. She took you for a sucker.'

Ellie fished some frozen tubs of homemade soup out of the freezer. 'She lies beautifully. So do you.'

A gleam of white teeth. 'What, me? Never. Well, I admit I lied to Milos, but that was to help you out of a hole, right?'

'Asparagus soup, ham, cheese and salad. That do you?' Without waiting for his reply, she emptied the two tubs of soup into a pan and put it on the stove. 'Is it right to lie? Ever?'

He said, 'Sometimes. Socially and for business. But not without having weighed the consequences. And don't tell me you've never lied to get yourself out of trouble.'

Of course she had. She poked at the frozen mass of soup. 'Next you'll be telling me you have an active conscience and that your business decisions are all ethical.'

No smile this time. 'I try, yes.'

Perhaps he did. She began to assemble a salad while he took out his phone, turned away from her and listened to a message. And replied to it. This time she couldn't hear what he said.

When he'd finished, he put away the phone and said, 'Susan told me she has an understanding with someone on her course, that they plan to work in other people's kitchens for a couple of years and then set up together in their own restaurant. She said they intend to get married then. What do you think?'

Ellie couldn't think how to reply to that. She pressed her thumb on the wrapped cheeses, one by one. Were they ripe enough to eat today? Yes. She stirred and poked at the defrosting soup. She'd thought at one time that it would be quicker to defrost soups in the microwave but had come to the conclusion that the old-fashioned method worked better.

The salad was ready. There was a bottle of homemade dressing in the fridge. The soup would be another few minutes. She found a fresh loaf and cut some slices, located the butter and the marg. Thinking about what he'd said.

Rafael waited for her to reply to his question. He could be patient; she had to grant him that.

Finally she thought she knew what to say. 'When I first knew her, Susan was self-conscious about her figure. She'd been teased about it for ever. Angelica was the worst of her tormentors. On the plus side, Susan had discovered that not only could she cook but she could also make friends. She'd made friends in college, both boys and girls, in a jolly hockey sticks way. Some time ago she told us that she hoped to team up with someone on her course in order that they might open a restaurant together.'

'So it's true?'

'It *was* true, then. I'm not sure that she still thinks the same way now. Lately Susan has discovered that displaying her figure properly leads to people treating her differently. A short while ago my level-headed Susan went out clubbing for the first time and experienced what it was like to be admired, until—'

'I brought her home and made a pass at her.'

'And she reverted to type. She hasn't been clubbing since.'

'But she hasn't been covering up her beautiful bosom, either.'

'No, she hasn't. So if you ask me whether her arrangement with her fellow student is still on or not, then all I can say is that I don't know.'

'She's halfway between what she was and what she might become?'

'Rafael, we've only just met and I don't know you very well, but I think you're getting fond of Susan and I must warn you that she's a straight up and down sort of person, who tries to live life as a Christian should.'

He grinned. 'She's never been tempted by someone like me before.'

'You might well sweep her off her feet for a short romance but then what? Think how devastated she will be when you dump her. Because you're not in the market for a faithful companion in life, are you?'

'You make her sound like a Labrador. No, I'm not. Mind you, my parents would probably fall over themselves with delight if I took Susan home with me. He's a retired solicitor and she does good works. I'm the black sheep of the family, who toils not and neither does he spin. All I do is shift money around. Rather success-fully, I might add. I may have started out as a moneylender to my friends but I have invested in the property market, too. Buy to let, that sort of thing.'

Ellie nodded. Yes, he had the air of a successful businessman.

He said, 'Girls have always thrown themselves at me. And yes, I admit that I was intrigued and annoyed when Susan rebuffed me. She's not my usual type. I tell myself that she's no good for me but I can't seem to get her out of my mind.'

He was serious. Ellie said, 'Leave her alone. I don't want either of you to get hurt.'

'Thanks for the advice.' Eyes down. He had no intention of leaving Susan alone.

Midge finished his grooming and leaped on to the top of the fridge, from which vantage point he could observe everything that was happening. Rafael's phone appeared in his hand and he turned away from Ellie to talk into it.

The phone rang in the hall. Ellie went to answer it.

A hard voice, male. 'Well, have you found my property yet?'

A slight lack of the r's. The drug dealer? 'Are you Milos?'

'Who else?'

'No,' said Ellie. 'It's not here. Someone has stolen it. I'm trying to find out who.'

'I'll help you find it. I'll be round in ten.' He disconnected.

I should have lied. Now what have I done?

Ellie walked back to the kitchen, slowly. Rafael gave her a sharp look.

She said, 'That was Milos. I suppose it's about time I met him. He's coming round straight away. When I explain what has happened—'

'You think he'll see reason?' Rafael threw up his hands. 'You think he'll wait patiently while you try to find out who has stolen the goods? You're out of your mind!'

'What can he do about it? I don't have Annie's telephone number till Susan gets back from the hospital—'

He paced up and down, thinking. 'Tell you what, I'll ring Susan and . . . No, that won't work. If we could track down this Annie person before Milos gets here . . . No, that's hardly likely. He'll be here in ten minutes or less. You'd better get out your chequebook because he's going to hold you responsible.'

'I'll tell him it was Angelica who took his property. He knows what she's like and he'll understand.'

He pressed buttons and put his phone to his ear. 'No, Mrs Quicke, he won't understand. Why should he? She stole his property. Let's face it: if she'd stolen some of your things you'd want them back, wouldn't you?' And to the phone, 'Come on, Susan! Pick up!'

'If she's on the ward, they won't like her using her phone—'

'Then I'd better go and fetch her. No, I can't, can I? I can't leave you here by yourself.'

Ellie started back for the landline phone in the hall. 'I'm going to ask the police to come round—'

He followed her. 'That's not a good idea.' He continued to hold his mobile to his ear. 'Even if they do come, what are you going to tell them? That you've been robbed of some illicit substances and a pile of cash?'

'No, no. I shall tell them that Timmy Lee confessed to taking Angelica away from the party and can give her an alibi. That ought to keep them happy for a while.' She found the number of the local nick in the phone book and dialled.

Rafael gave up on his phone to address the air. 'How did I ever get involved in this mess? I *never* get involved in my clients' troubles. Ever. I don't particularly want to be here when the police come but . . . Tell you what, I'll wait outside in the street and warn Milos when he arrives – which will be any minute now – that you've called the police. He won't want to mix with them, so with any luck that will give him cause for thought. Of course, you realize that it won't stop him coming after you in the long run. All he has to do is wait till the police leave and then he'll come down on you like a ton of bricks! And then what? Susan will never forgive me if anything happens to you on my watch.'

She waited for someone at the station to answer her. 'Stop worrying, Rafael. There's more than one way to skin a cat. What's the time now? About seven? The man I want should have gone home by now or taken a break to eat. Hopefully.'

Someone picked up the phone at the station. A human being, not a robot. Hurray. The woman said, 'What is your name, please?'

Ellie put on her 'slightly potty little old lady' act. 'Oh, am I through to the police? Yes? Do you think you could put me through to "Ears", please. Oops! Naughty me. My dreadful memory. It's DI Bottrill, isn't it? Have I got that right?'

Rafael stared at her. 'You're barking mad, you know that? You can't ask for a DI by his nickname!'

'I'm so sorry!' Ellie apologized to the girl at the other end of the phone while smiling sweetly at Rafael. 'Please, forget I said that. I do know his name really, but sometimes I . . . Yes, I really would like to speak to him. But first, can you confirm that he is in charge of the case of the redheaded girl who died at the weekend? He is? Oh, good. Well, I might have some information for . . . Oh, sorry, again. My name is Mrs Quicke. Ellie Quicke. I'm a friend of Lesley Milburn's, who as you know is . . . Yes, you're quite right and she was on honeymoon but she's back now . . . Oh, you know about that? Yes, of course you would do, what with it being her place where the body was found. Did you see her when she was called in to the station today? Yes? Well, you may not know what happened afterwards, but she's been whipped off to hospital. Yes, it was all very sudden . . . No, it's not that serious. Well, I suppose it is in a way. She had a miscarriage. Yes, awful, isn't it? She's so distressed. Her niece is with her at the moment but she'll probably be staying with me here for a couple of days after she leaves hospital because her flat is . . . Yes, you know what's happened to her flat, don't you?'

Rafael narrowed his eyes, trying to work out what Ellie was up to.

Ellie sent him another smile and sat down on the hall chair, to continue her conversation with the WPC – or maybe the phone was being manned, or womanned, by a civilian nowadays?

'Yes, of course I'll tell Lesley that you'd like to be remembered to her. I suppose the station will want to send her some flowers, or something. I hope she won't be kept in hospital long. Anyway, what I was really ringing about was that I wanted to speak to "Ears", I mean, to DI Bottrill, but you do know who I mean, don't you? I'm afraid we've never really got on – he thinks I'm a dreadful old fool – but I do have some information which might . . . Oh, yes of course. I hadn't realized it was so late, and naturally he will have finished for the day. You'll leave a message for him? Tell him he can come round at any time tonight or tomorrow to suit him. Thank you so much.'

She put the phone down and drew in a deep breath.

Rafael repeated her words. '"He can come round at any time".' He nodded, once. 'Yes, of course. If Milos knows the police can come round at any time, then he'll steer clear. I'll tell him.'

He shot out of the door and Ellie sighed with relief. She could trust Rafael to put the drug dealer off. And if Ears did bother to send someone round, she could deal with that when it happened.

Meanwhile, the soup was probably boiling over in the kitchen, and she must attend to that before doing anything else.

Except . . . the phone rang again.

Only, there was no one at the other end when she picked it up. It might just be a nuisance sales call. Or it might not. It might be Milos, checking that she was still in the house. Or it might be an automated sales call which hadn't connected her to the outside world. Hopefully it was only that.

Her breathing was just a trifle too fast for comfort. She was *not* going to panic. Definitely not. And if she didn't unstick her feet from the floor and get out to the kitchen, the top of the stove was going to be swimming in soup and would take ages to clean. She made it to the kitchen just as the soup was beginning to bubble over the sides of the pan.

And here came Rafael, looking thoughtful. 'I told Milos you've asked the police to call on another matter, and he's agreed to give you twenty-four hours to produce his stuff. After that . . . you are crazy, you know? What makes you think you can stop Milos in his tracks? I mean, he's really on the warpath.'

'Mention of the police did it, though. Didn't it?'

'For twenty-four hours. Don't you have any sense of danger? Do you know what he routinely does to those who don't pay up? I've heard that . . . well, I don't want to frighten you, but it's not nice.'

He frowned, clicking his fingers. Almost to himself, he added, 'Why is he so angry? I suppose he has every reason to be annoyed if his man got beaten up and robbed, but . . . well, I wonder if Angelica got someone to do that? Nah. Not her style. But . . . who was it who had a fight with the drug salesman at the party? Would it have been someone Angelica knew? Or some stranger who'd gatecrashed the party?'

'I'm too hungry to speculate. Are you ready for some soup?'

There was a stir in the hall, and Susan's voice called out, 'I'm back! Where are you, Mrs Quicke?'

Ellie raised her own voice. 'We're in the kitchen.' And to Rafael, 'I thought you were going to fetch her.'

'I arranged to send a car for her and texted her it would be waiting. I didn't want to leave you alone.'

Susan appeared, her red-gold hair curling loose around her head instead of being drawn back into a ponytail. 'Oh, Mrs Quicke! Poor Lesley . . .' And, on seeing Rafael, she stopped to say, formally, 'I must thank you for the car. The driver refused to take any money. You must tell me what I owe you. I'll pay you back, of course.'

Rafael held out a chair for Susan. 'My pleasure.'

'I insist,' said Susan, taking the seat. Not meeting his eye.

Ellie poured soup into bowls and set them on the table. 'Sit down, Rafael. Eat up, Susan, and tell me how you got on.'

Rafael said, 'Yes, how is Lesley, and where's the villain of the piece?'

Susan tore some bread into pieces and dunked them in the soup. 'Boy, am I starved!' She slurped a mouthful and closed her eyes in pleasure. Took two more mouthfuls, and was prepared to talk. 'Well, when I got there, I found they'd put Lesley in a side ward. She was as white as a sheet, with a drip in her arm and her eyes closed. Andy and Angelica were arguing over her bed and they wouldn't shut up. It was upsetting Lesley, so I called a nurse, who told them to calm down.'

'What were they arguing about?' asked Ellie.

'Angelica wanted Andy to take her to a hotel to get away from her drug dealer, and he was trying to attend to Lesley but, as he kept saying, he's not good with people who are sick. Angelica didn't pay any attention to Lesley but wanted Andy to concentrate on her, when it was all her fault that this has happened. Then the nurse said Andy could stay but Angelica must go, and she had hysterics! Yes, really! There and then, in front of everybody. So they called another nurse and Angelica was hustled out, and Andy didn't know whether to go after her or stay with Lesley. He really isn't much good with sick people, you know. And Lesley said . . .'

She screwed up her face, fought for control, put her soup spoon down and took a deep breath, at which her magnificent bosom heaved. Rafael's eyes widened and his spoon hovered in the air.

Susan said, 'Lesley told him to go. And he went.' Susan gulped.

Ellie said, 'But you stayed, being the brave girl that you are.'

'I held her hand and stroked it, and said a lot of stuff about how everything was going to be all right, and I put in a spot of praying, too, though I don't know that she believes, but it made me feel better. At any rate, Lesley stopped crying, and I think she drifted off for a while. They brought round some food round but she didn't want anything. The nurse kept checking on her. Lesley has to go down to surgery in the morning to make sure everything came away properly. Then Rafael texted he was sending a car for me and I left.'

She took another deep breath. Rafael made an odd sound in his throat and almost spilled his soup.

Susan said, 'Thank you for the soup, Mrs Quicke. I'm perfectly all right, honest. I just need some food. I missed lunch.' She went back to work on her soup.

Rafael said, 'So where are the missing couple?'

Susan shrugged. 'Don't ask me. Angelica wanted them to elope to the Orkneys or something. Gretna Green, perhaps? He didn't want to go but he didn't want to stay with Lesley, either. He's conflicted.'

Ellie nodded. That was her reading of the situation, too. 'I don't think Angelica will go anywhere without her make-up and a change of clothes, so she'll come back here for her things before she goes anywhere.'

Rafael said, 'Angelica has no sense of danger, has she?'

Susan scraped up the last spoonful of soup. 'Experience has taught her that no matter what sort of mess she gets into, someone will always get her out of it. She's elected Andy as her saviour for the moment but,' a tiny smile, 'I don't think he's as anxious to ride to her rescue as he used to be. He's beginning to suspect that she's out of his price range.'

Ellie collected empty soup bowls and dished out plates for ham, cheese and salad stuffs. 'Did you retrieve my mobile?'

'I knew there was something else I had to tell you. I took Lesley's phone with me, to swap them over. I gave Lesley hers, or rather I showed it to her and then put it in her locker, although I don't think she was really taking in what I said. I don't know where her handbag is, by the way. She didn't seem to have it with her. When I asked her for your phone, she nodded and then she drifted off. They came to take her blood pressure and check on the drip so I looked in her locker, top and bottom, but I couldn't see it. Then Rafael rang to say a car was coming for me. Lesley didn't answer when I spoke to her and I didn't know what to do. So I said I'd see her again in the morning or as soon as it was allowed, and I left. I'm sorry. I know you said it was important.'

Ellie felt a cold spot forming in her stomach. This was really bad news. She'd hoped to contact Annie and reclaim the goods that night. Oh, dear.

Milos had given her twenty-four hours to return his things, so she did have some leeway. If she could get hold of Annie through the agency first thing in the morning, all might yet be well.

Ellie worked her way through the ham and salads. They all concentrated on eating. Without much enjoyment. They really ought to have had something hot and filling, but Ellie hadn't had time enough to prepare anything else.

Susan got to her feet, squaring her shoulders, causing Rafael's eyes to widen. 'I think we all need carbohydrates. Let's see if I can find something in the freezer to line our stomachs with. I made some individual sticky toffee puddings some time ago . . .'

Rafael fanned himself. 'Do you make bread as well?'

'Of course.'

Rafael said, 'I'm hyperventilating. Will you let me watch next time you make bread?'

A perfunctory ring on the doorbell and in marched Angelica, trailing Andy behind her. 'Oh, Mrs Quicke! It's so wonderful to be home again! I can't tell you what a dreadful day I've had!'

Andy said, through gritted teeth, 'Not as bad as Lesley.' Andy looked harassed. There were lines around his eyes that hadn't been there before. Perhaps he really was distressed about Lesley? Or had the hours in Angelica's company worn him down?

Angelica was her usual sunny self. 'Oh, poor Lesley. But she's in the right place. She's being looked after properly and I'm so hungry! Can I manage a drop of that soup? I think perhaps I might.' She seated herself next to Rafael, pulling Andy down on the other side of her. She looked as fresh as a daisy and quite as bewitching.

Andy looked ten years older than he had that morning.

Susan transferred individual puddings into the microwave and whipped up a sauce, saying, 'The last I saw of you, Angelica, you were being escorted from the ward. Where did you go?'

'Oh, it was so awful! Poor, poor Lesley. I did feel so sorry for her. I went down and waited for Andy at his car, and when he came I just burst into tears, I was so upset, and he had to take me for a drink, only the best place was closed, and you wouldn't think they'd close at this time of the evening when everyone needs something to help them face the world, would you? And he wouldn't take me into a pub on the way back, even though they are open all day.'

Andy put his head in his hands.

Ellie said, 'Angelica, pay attention. I'll feed you now and you can stay the night in the spare room, but tomorrow you're out of here and no argument.'

A pout. Angelica was not taking the threat seriously. 'Oh, I know you don't mean that! I've nowhere else to go.'

'Try your mother. She lives somewhere in London, doesn't she?'

'Yes, but she's got this horrid boyfriend, and he said . . .' She gulped most beautifully, while tears hovered on her eyelashes. 'He said I mustn't go back there any more. Anyway, I'm a lodger here, bona fide, and if you want me to go, you'll have to give me thirty days' notice, and then the magistrate will probably say I have another thirty days to find somewhere else, so you can't turn me out, just like that, so there!'

Ellie said, 'That's not true, Angelica. You have not signed any contract with me to rent the room and have never paid me any rent. You're a house guest, only, so I can ask you to leave whenever I like.'

'But I know you won't!'

Did the girl really think that? Ellie had another card to play. 'Angelica, I've got your drug dealer coming here tomorrow, looking for you, so you really do have to find somewhere else to go.'

Angelica wailed, 'But you'll protect me, won't you? I haven't got his stuff. I swear it!' A calculated look. 'If you don't help me, I'll have to tell him that Susan stole it from me!'

'As if!' said Susan. 'Try facing up to your responsibilities, Angelica. You caused the problems. You deal with them.'

'You!' Angelica hissed. 'What do you know about the problems a pretty girl like me has? Stupid Susan! I suppose you know Rafael bet on getting into your pants by the end of term?'

Rafael half started up out of his chair. 'Susan, believe me! That was before I—'

Susan laughed. 'Silly girl. Of course I heard about it. I asked the man who'd taken the bet how much my virginity was worth and he said fifty pounds. I said that wasn't enough. Make it fifty thousand, I said, and we'll split the proceeds.'

Rafael subsided into his chair, laughing. 'That's my girl!'

Susan aimed a wooden spoon at him. 'I am not your girl. I am myself. Now, anyone want a pudding?'

Andy shook his head but everyone else took one.

Ellie said, 'Now you're all here, I wonder if we can get any more information about Kate, the girl who died at Angelica's party.'

'*Not* my party!' said Angelica, but even Andy shot her a look which said, *Shut up!*

Ellie said, 'How come you all know one another, anyway? Not you, Andy, but Susan and Angelica and Rafael? And, come to think of it, also Jake and Timmy Lee.'

Susan said, 'The catering section is only one of the courses which the university runs. There are lots of other ones. There's a student bar, but it's crowded and can get noisy, so some of us prefer going to the Queen's Head up the road. That's usually where we meet up to make plans for the weekend, go clubbing or go to festivals. Some of us socialize only with the people on our own courses, but some of us mix and mingle with others. I've seen Timmy Lee there, and Angelica with Jake . . . though I don't think he's a student. He was slumming it, probably.'

Rafael said, 'That he was. The Queen's Head is noted for its talent, which is why I used to drop in occasionally. Pretty girls aplenty, all looking for a good time. I don't do that now, of course,' he added. 'I'm a reformed character now.'

Susan dished out puddings and sauce. 'Hah! When hell freezes over.'

Angelica said, tears sparkling, 'How can you say that Jake was slumming it? He was really serious about me until that horrid girl Kate told on him to his parents and everything went wrong.'

Ellie said, 'How did you come to be at this pub, Angelica? You don't usually expect to pay for yourself, do you? And you're not a student of anything.'

A wriggle. 'If boys like to treat me to a drink, why shouldn't I enjoy myself, too?'

Ellie persisted. 'You organized a party to impress Jake at your cousin's flat because you knew it would be empty. Who else did you invite?'

'Well, Timmy, I suppose. But it doesn't really work like that. You tell the people you want to be there, and they tell others, and they all come and bring some drink and we have fun.'

Ellie said, 'But you went out of your way to invite Milos the drug dealer to send someone as well. How did you know him?'

TEN

Monday suppertime

Ashrug. Angelica said, 'I didn't know him. You've got it all wrong. I didn't invite him. Clay – you know him? He's always in the pub, offering pills for this and that . . . Well, he heard I was having a party and he said everyone would enjoy themselves more if he came along, and I agreed without realizing what he meant.'

Ellie's eyebrows rose and so did Rafael's. Did the girl really think they'd swallow that?

Susan said, 'Ha!' and dealt out dessert spoons to everyone. 'Eat up.'

'It's true,' said Angelica earnestly. Perhaps she even believed it herself? 'Clay knew lots of the people who came to the party. He was a student at the uni himself, once. Photography, I think. Till he dropped out.' A wrinkle on the perfect brow. 'I think the pub banned him recently but he still hangs around, like, and people can always get his phone number if they want it.'

'And you didn't know he worked for Milos?'

'No, of course not.'

'Pull the other one,' said Rafael. 'But I'm interested to know what sort of cut Clay was going to give you?'

Another wriggle. 'You make it sound so horrid! It wasn't like that at all. He just said that he'd love to come to the party and he'd make sure I wasn't out of pocket. I had all these horrid bills to pay, and it's no fun not being able to afford pretty things, so of course I said he could come, and I didn't know there was going to be trouble, did I?'

'What sort of "trouble" are we talking about?'

Lowered eyes. 'How should I know? People getting high. Pushing and shoving. You know. I don't like to think of such things.'

'Come on, now,' said Rafael. 'You nicked the proceeds after the fight, or whatever it was. Probably just a scuffle? So you must have been there when fists were thrown around. You told us that it was only because this man Clay got knocked about in a fight that he gave you his stash to take care of.'

Angelica threw off a tinkling laugh. 'Oh, no! I didn't see what happened, honest! He came reeling out of the sitting room with blood on his face and thrust this package at me, but then Jake came and I was trying to talk to him and hardly took in what Clay was saying. It was a real shock to me when I found out what he'd given me, and that's why I hid it. And now someone's stolen it from me, and you're all looking at me as if I had done something dreadful, when all I was doing was trying to give my friends a good time.'

Ellie started to say, 'But—' and got cut off.

Angelica said, 'Look, everyone at the party was grown up, like. They didn't have to buy anything from Clay if they didn't want to, did they? I don't know how he got hurt and I don't want to know. I was upset when Jake said he didn't like my party when I'd been to all that trouble to set it up. Then I spotted Kate arriving and I didn't want them to meet, of course I didn't. So when Jake left I followed him, and then . . .' Tears spilled over. 'He went off down the road, and I . . .' Gulp, gulp. 'I was so miserable that when Timmy came along I agreed to go clubbing, only then I thought that Jake might call me and I remembered I had all that money on me, so I said he should drop me here and I know nothing at all about anything else, so there!'

Andy hadn't been listening. He got up with a sudden movement. 'I'm going to ring Lesley, see how she is. If she can't answer I'll get hold of the ward sister or someone. I shouldn't have left her.' Off he went, getting out his mobile phone.

'Better late than never,' said Rafael, looking after Andy as he left.

Angelica half rose from her seat. Was she really going to try to follow Andy? Um, no. He'd been too quick for her this time. The girl sat down again, looking flushed. Pouting.

Ellie was not at all sure that Andy going after Lesley was a good thing. If he wanted to stick to Lesley, was that the best thing that could happen to her? Wouldn't it be better for her if she had a clean break and took another dip into the marriage market later? But she had chosen to marry Andy, and in Ellie's book marriage was for life, so . . . Ellie shook her head. It wasn't her business. Her job was to find out what had happened to that poor girl Kate. She said, 'Angelica, who else did you invite to the party?'

A twist of the shoulders. 'No one. Everyone.'

Rafael tipped his chair back. 'Let me think who she'd have invited. There's a couple of girls who frequent the Queen's Head. Gina and her friend, what's her name . . . Jess? They hunt as a pair. They're waitresses at one of the coffee shops in the Broadway, aren't they? Always up for a spot of fun. Or so I've heard. No personal experience.'

Ellie said, 'Angelica, didn't you say earlier that you'd told the police about two girls who arrived when you were about to leave the party? Are those the ones you meant? Gina and Jess?'

'I suppose.' Her colour had risen. Why?

'Where can we find them?'

'Dunno. At the pub, I suppose. That's where they go in the evenings. But, honest, it's no use thinking you'd get any sense out of them. They're both slags.'

Susan looked thoughtful. 'I know them both by sight. They are not slags. And you wouldn't have invited them if they had been. They're all right. They're hard-working girls who like to party, yes, but I've heard they always turn up on time for their shifts the following day. They're older than most of the students. They're streetwise and not into drugs. If they were at the party, they could at least tell us who else was there. They're probably at the pub by now. Rafael, they may not have heard about Kate's death and have no idea that the police might be interested in what they saw on Saturday night. Perhaps you could ask them what they know?'

Rafael said, 'You want me to fetch them for you to interrogate?'

Susan dimpled. 'You might as well make yourself useful.'

He got up and bowed. 'Your wish is my command.'

'I wish,' said Susan. She glowed with the knowledge that she was desirable. Her hair twisted in golden-red curls around her head. Her skin was nectarine-soft. Her bosom swelled. Her bosom was remarkable, and Rafael was very aware of it.

He looked at his watch. 'Mrs Quicke, is this all right by you? It won't take me long to see if one or both of the girls are in the pub.'

'Ridiculous!' said Angelica. 'As if anything those two tarts said could be of interest. Trust me: they'd make up any sort of lies to get their pictures in the papers.'

Ellie wondered why Angelica was getting so aerated. She also wondered what sort of stories the two girls would tell which might upset Angelica.

Susan clashed mugs on to the table. 'Rafael, you may have your coffee on your return, right?'

'Never fear, my dear! Neither of them will ever stir my pulse as you do. Think of me as the cat sent to bring back the mouse. Will either one of them do, Susan? I can only fit one at a time on the back of the bike.' And off he went.

Andy put his head round the door. 'They're not happy about Lesley. I'm going back to the hospital to see if they'll let me sit beside her.' He vanished, too.

Susan said, 'I'm beginning to wonder what else Little Miss Angel Face has been up to. What time did you say you left the party, Angelica?'

The girl tossed her curls. 'I'm not staying here to be accused of all sorts when I've done absolutely nothing wrong. I shall go up to my room for some peace and quiet.'

Susan piled plates into the dishwasher, saying, 'I only asked what time you left. Why does that upset you? Oh, and don't forget you're in the small guest room tonight.'

Angelica flounced out. She had a pretty rear end and knew how to make the most of it.

Ellie covered the leftovers from supper with cling film and stowed them in the fridge. Susan was hovering, frowning to herself. Ellie said, 'Yes, Susan? What is it?'

Susan shut the door to the corridor. That door was usually kept open, so she must require secrecy for what she had to say. She also put her finger to her lips, enjoining silence.

Then she set the dishwasher going. More noise, to cover her softly spoken words. 'Will you come upstairs with me, Mrs Quicke? I may be completely wrong, but I have a horrid feeling that we might find something in my flat which doesn't belong to me.'

Ellie also lowered her voice. 'Really? We cleared out the bedroom Angelica had been using and there was nothing untoward there. She hid the drugs and drug money in Thomas's Quiet Room because he'd annoyed her. You've annoyed her even more, but I can't think of anything that she could have planted in your rooms that might worry you.'

Susan's expression showed that she didn't like her suspicions. 'I know. I'm probably way off the mark, but you and I and Thomas all went to church yesterday morning, while madam said she was too tired to come. She was alone in the house all morning. I just have a nasty idea that it might be as well to check.'

Ellie nodded. 'Straight away.' She opened the door to the corridor and blenched at the noise. Angelica didn't care who else she inconvenienced when she wanted to play pop music, did she?

The two women trod quietly up the stairs to the first floor, and then took the second, smaller staircase to the attic.

Ellie said, 'I'll take the sitting room and you the kitchen.'

Susan said, 'Mrs Quicke, would you mind if we stuck together and didn't search separately? If there is anything wrong here, I want us to witness that we found it together.'

Ellie nodded. 'You're right. That's only sensible. Sitting room first.' She threw open the door. Everything looked fresh and neat. There were no obvious places where you could conceal something. And, in any case, what would that 'something' be? They moved chairs and tables, looked through magazines and CDs. Nothing.

'Where would you hide something, Susan? It can't be anywhere obvious that you'd find when you did routine cleaning. Let's try to think like Angelica. She's sneaking upstairs with a bundle of something she wants to hide. Where would she go? I think . . . the kitchen?'

They went into the kitchen. Susan had washed up her breakfast things before she went out that day. Susan pulled out drawers in the fridge/freezer. And shook her head.

Ellie started on the cupboards. 'We don't know what we're looking for.'

Susan said, 'Something quite small, I think.'

It wasn't that small.

Ellie found it in what might once have been called a 'broom cupboard' which had been created out of the space under the eaves. The cupboard now contained the vacuum cleaner, a rudimentary toolkit, boxes of candles for emergency use and a bag of batteries for the smoke alarm, the remote control and so on.

'What on earth?' Ellie fished a plastic bag out from behind the toolbox and opened it up.

It was a woman's clutch purse with a diamante letter on the front.

It wasn't large as such things go. It wasn't one you would take out for a dinner party, but something you might tote around for a visit to a pub or an informal get-together.

Susan gasped. 'Is that . . .? That's not Angelica's, is it?'

Ellie took the plastic bag to the kitchen, shook out the purse and opened it up. Her fingers trembled and she had some difficulty with the catch.

Susan's voice wobbled. 'That's a "K" for Kate, isn't it?'

Ellie nodded. She upended the purse and out fell a diary, a lipstick, some used tissues, a comb, pressed face powder and an empty wallet. Well, the wallet was empty but for a travel card with a picture of a redheaded girl on it. A clean tissue tucked into a side pocket held something that glittered: a fragile necklace in gold filigree. Also a pair of diamond-chip earrings.

Ellie backed away. 'I shouldn't have touched the purse. Fingerprints.'

'These are Kate's things?' said Susan, unable to believe the evidence of her eyes. 'Angelica killed her? And then she robbed the body to hide her identity? I can't believe it! How could she?'

Ellie shook her head. She didn't know how anyone could do that, either.

Susan held out the wallet. 'No money. I suppose Angelica's spent it already. But the jewellery? It's pretty recognizable. Do you think she kept it with the intention of selling it later?'

Ellie couldn't believe her eyes. 'I can't make sense of this. Angelica couldn't have killed Kate, could she? No, I don't believe it!'

Susan gestured to Kate's belongings. 'I wouldn't have thought she'd be up to stealing from a corpse, either, but here's the proof. What do we do now?'

'So you found the stuff?' Angelica had arrived, unheard. 'I thought to myself, who would want to steal from a corpse and the answer, of course, was Susan. I'm glad you've found it, Mrs Quicke. Now Susan can pay for what she's done.'

'What!' A red tide rose up in Susan's face. 'Angelica, does this mean what I think it means? Did you kill Kate?'

'No, of course not.' Outraged.

'Then you found her lying in the garden, dead. And robbed her? Surely not even you would do that!'

Angelica bounced on her toes. 'Nothing of the sort. You know perfectly well that I left the party early. No, this is proof that you did it. I suppose you thought we wouldn't look in your rooms for the missing things.'

Susan gasped. 'But Angelica, I didn't! I wouldn't!'

'You were back very late on Saturday night. Long after I'd gone to bed. I suppose you went to the party after I'd left, had words with Kate and killed her. Possibly by accident? Or maybe you found the body lying in the garden and thought you'd help yourself to the girl's money and jewellery.'

'No!' cried Susan. 'I never went near the place—'

'Of course you did. You said yourself that you had a key and were going in to water the pot plants.'

'Yes, but—'

'I don't know how you think you could get away with it!'

Ellie said, 'Angelica, stop that!'

Angelica stopped.

Susan was a fiery red. Was she going to cry?

Ellie knew that some people, even when completely innocent, reddened with embarrassment when accused of a crime. Susan was one of them. It was just possible that Susan might kill someone if she were attacked, or perhaps by accident, but Susan was not, definitely not, a grave robber. Therefore, she did not hide these things in her flat.

Ellie said, 'Angelica, did you kill Kate?'

'Certainly not!' Maybe she was speaking the truth for once.

Ellie didn't know what to think. 'We won't touch anything but let the police check for fingerprints. Let them decide who robbed the body and take it from there.'

'Let me see!' Quick as a flash, Angelica reached out to pick up the purse.

Ellie realized what the girl was up to. She was going to put her own fingerprints over any others which were already on the purse. Why? To disguise the fact that they were already there, which would prove that she'd handled it earlier? If she were quick enough, she'd then go on to touch the wallet, which someone had already handled because there was no money left in it. And if Angelica succeeded in touching everything on the table now, in front of witnesses, there would be no proof that she had ever seen them before.

Fortunately Angelica was on the far side of the table and had to reach right over to touch the purse. So Ellie grabbed Angelica's arm and bore down on it with all her weight, pushing it down on to the table top and holding it there . . . inches before she could reach Kate's things.

'Ow! Let go!' cried Angelica.

Ellie continued to hold Angelica's hand down. 'Susan, get a plastic bag and, without touching anything yourself, use a spoon or tongs or something to shovel everything from the purse into a clean bag. Particularly the wallet.'

Angelica screamed and tried to tug her hand loose. 'Let me go! You're hurting me!'

Susan scrambled to obey Ellie, putting the contents, including the original plastic wrapping, into a large freezer bag.

Only then did Ellie release her hold on Angelica, who whimpered and held her wrist. 'You've sprained my wrist! Ow! Ow! It hurts! I'm going to sue you for defamation of character and assault! Look, there's a bruise coming up already.'

'Serves you jolly well right,' said Susan, carefully easing the purse into a second clean plastic bag. 'We'll give these to the police and let them sort out who touched which items first.'

Angelica made a wild lunge, trying to wrest the bags from Susan's hand. Susan was taller and held them up high above her head. Angelica tried to jump up to get them and failed.

Ellie said, 'Calm down, Angelica. If you're innocent then the police will clear you—'

'I am! I am. It's Susan who murdered Kate and stole her things!'

'If the police find that Susan touched them, then they'll know what to do about it. But I think they're going to find your fingerprints, aren't they, Angelica? How did you come by Kate's things?'

Was Angelica going to resort to tears, as usual? But no, she wasn't giving in so quickly. 'It was Susan, not me!'

Ellie felt very tired. 'You know something, Angelica? I have been trying to make excuses for you. No more. You've got to pay for what you've done.'

Angelica almost spat. 'The police will believe me! When they look at Susan, and they look at me, who do you think they'll believe?'

Ellie lost it. 'Get down those stairs before I box your ears, Miss Angelica!'

Angelica wept. 'Threats and an assault! You'll pay for this!' She stormed off down the stairs.

Susan was also struggling with tears. 'Oh! Oh! I can't believe this is happening. I was speaking the truth, Mrs Quicke.'

'Yes, of course you were. I can't think that Angelica had the strength or the nerve to kill Kate, but I suspect she knows who did. She insists there was a fight at the party and that it was because of the fight that the drug dealer gave her his stash and money. What if the fight was really over Kate instead and she got killed, perhaps by accident? In that case, would a drug dealer who'd been involved in the fight be so frightened of being found with the proceeds of his crime that he would pass the evidence on to Angelica before he fled? Or, wait a minute, didn't Angelica say he was taken off to hospital? Or did I dream that?' Ellie rubbed her forehead. 'I'm getting so confused.'

'When was the fight, anyway? It must have been before Angelica left the scene.'

'When lots of other people would have seen it. We need to talk to more of the partygoers. It hadn't happened when Jake was there or he'd have said something about it. Or Timmy Lee. And immediately after Jake left, so did Timmy and Angelica. So, if the fight hadn't happened before that time, how could Angelica have the money and the drugs when she left? She says it all happened in a whirl, that the drugs were given to her just before she left, but that doesn't make sense, does it? And what happened to the drug dealer? Who was the fight with?'

Susan shook her head. 'None of it makes sense to me.'

Ellie thought about it. 'We're missing something. I wonder, I may be wrong, but suppose the fight happened much later on when only a few people were around, long after Angelica and Timmy Lee had left? And somehow, during that fight, Kate ended up dead. The drug dealer panicked. To delay identification, he took Kate's purse and jewellery. And then what? How did they get to Angelica?

'I suppose he might have phoned Angelica and asked her to help him. He was leaving in a hurry, didn't want the evidence found on him. He knew she was short of money, so he asked her to hide the stuff for him. He must have phoned her to meet him to hand the stuff over.'

'Or he might just have come to the front door here and handed the stuff over. Then he went on his way. Angelica took the money for her own use and hid the rest of the stuff where she thought she could shove the blame on you and Thomas.'

'That makes sense. But what a mess!'

Someone played a rhythm on the doorbell down below. Ellie started for the stairs. 'Bring those bags, Susan. I'll put them in the safe. That's Rafael at the door, if I'm not mistaken. Let's hope he's got one of the party girls with him. I'm dying to find out what really happened on Saturday night.'

Ellie puffed a bit as she reached the hall and opened the door. It was Rafael, ushering a tall, brown-skinned beauty into the hall. The girl was possibly part Indian, part British, with long, wavy black hair and the minimum of clothing. Ellie blinked. The amount of body beautiful on view was quite something. There was a well-filled bikini-style top and tiny white shorts. Really tiny. Diamond studs flashed in the girl's ears and nose and tummy button. Glass bangles tinkled on her arm. She stood as tall as Rafael because she was wearing five-inch heels. Wow!

'This is Gina,' said Rafael with the air of a cat presenting a mouse to its carer. 'She went to the party and would love to tell you all about it. Her mate Jess wasn't in the pub tonight and Gina's worried about her.'

Angelica shouted from the landing. 'Whatever she says, she's a liar. I was leaving the party when she arrived, so there!'

Gina ignored Angelica to hold out a hand with long, false nails on it to Ellie. 'I'm so pleased to meet you. Raff says you might be able to find out what's happened to my mate, Jess. It's not like her, not answering her phone.' There was a nasal twang to her voice which told Ellie she was born and brought up in West London and had attended local comprehensives. She looked around her. 'Raff was right. You got a lovely house.'

Gina was no teenager but probably in her late twenties. Model looks and a sharp mind. Nobody's fool.

'Er, yes,' said Ellie, sending Rafael a *what now?* look. 'Susan, will you take our guests into the kitchen and make some coffee or tea while I put the evidence in the safe?'

'Susan did it!' yelled Angelica from above. 'I'm going to ring the cops and tell them so.' She retreated down the corridor and slammed her bedroom door.

But you don't have a mobile phone now, do you, ducky? You handed yours over to Rafael. More flimflam. Ignore her threats!

Ellie took the two precious bags of evidence to Thomas's study and had a few moments of panic when she couldn't remember the combination. Eventually she got it right. She knew she wasn't supposed to write these things down but couldn't possibly keep all the numbers she was given in her head, what with mobile phone numbers, and credit card numbers, and national insurance numbers, and . . . well, she gave up after that. Thomas was better at numbers than she was, but even he had a secret list of numbers disguised as something else.

Susan had the kettle on and was making proper coffee when Ellie joined the others in the kitchen. Ellie wondered if it were a good idea for her to drink good coffee at that time of the evening but decided that she needed the stimulation. Her brain was feeling tired and coffee might get her through the next few hours.

And here came Angelica, sidling in to take a seat at the table. 'It's boring upstairs. I might as well hear what lies Gina is going to tell.'

Gina sat sideways on her chair, disposing her long legs in seemingly careless fashion while actually calling attention to their shapeliness. Ellie noticed that although Rafael appreciated the view, he wasn't going overboard about it.

Ellie also noticed that Susan looked down her nose at Gina's tactics, but that they didn't irritate her like they were irritating Angelica.

Gina's flashing dark eyes and long, wavy hair – not to mention her long, shapely limbs and her air of amused well-being – made Angelica look pallid.

Yes, Gina liked to be admired. She knew she was annoying Angelica and she didn't care.

Angelica's lips thinned. 'Gina's well known as a gossip, aren't you, G? I mean, no one ever takes anything you say seriously.'

Gina smiled, showing very white teeth. 'Listen to the little bird. Cheep, cheep, cheep. Angelica, my dear, the cracks in your make-up are showing.'

'What?' Angelica's hands flew to her face, as if to reassure herself it was still there.

Rafael's smile widened. 'Concentrate, girls. Gina, how did you find out about the party?'

'Hold on a mo. You said you'd help me look for Jess.'

'And so I will. First things first. Tell us about the party.'

'Well, we met in the pub, the usual. Talked about what we'd like to do that weekend. Jess saw the party advertised on Facebook.'

Ellie said, 'Do you know who put it on Facebook?'

Gina pointed at Angelica, who huffed and puffed. 'Nonsense! Would I do that?'

'Yeah. 'Course you would,' said Gina, standing no nonsense. 'It's a shame Jess isn't here. She saw it.'

Rafael said, 'I expect she's working. You said she helps out at the Indian restaurant some nights.'

'Not on Mondays. They close on Mondays. That's why—'

'Well, tell us how it was that you got to the party, Gina. Start from the beginning.'

'Jess said she'd seen there was a party on at Angelica's. We was sitting with Timmy and Wilf. Wilf was grousing. He'd just had a row with his partner, so he was weeping into his beer and we was trying to cheer him up, like. Big Scotty came over to join us. He's one of the photography nuts. He's always after Jess and me to pose for him. Not porn. For calendars, like. He said it would be good to go to someplace new, try out some poses in a different background. For our portfolios, right?'

Angelica snapped, 'Porn! I tell you, you can't trust a word she says.'

Gina was amused. She smiled. 'You mean Big Scotty never asked you to sit for him?' And to Ellie, 'He's very artistic, like. Dead set on getting the mood right, and the backgrounds. Does he go on about using the right background! We know, Jess and I, that you can put any background you want on any photo, right? But we was at a loose end, so we said "Why not?" But a 'course, Big Scotty does have creeping hands, so we said Wilf must come, too. Wilf has a car, see, so it would cheer him up and it was like it was meant that he could get us there and back safely. Nice old house, it was. I'd prefer something a bit more modern but beggars can't and so on. Pity it got trashed.' A shrug of delightfully bare shoulders. 'Since it was Angelica's, like, we didn't care, did we?'

'You thought it was Angelica's flat?'

'Sure. She'd been boasting about how her parents had set her up in it when they had a spot of cash to spare. More fool them is what I think.'

'How did it get trashed?'

ELEVEN

Monday evening

'How did it get trashed?' Gina shrugged. 'Dunno, really. It was a party, got out of hand. We didn't see much of that, just the start, like, 'cos we was in the big bedroom at the front. Beee-you-ti-ful bed. Big Scotty was in seventh heaven. And the lighting wasn't bad, either. So we tanked up with a bottle of wine we'd brought and had ourselves a ball. Mind you, Big Scotty's hands were everywhere, the scumbag; I shoulda told him to put the brake on then and there, and no mistake. I mean, he isn't called "Big" for nothing, if you get my drift . . .?'

Most of them got the drift before Ellie, but she did catch up.

Gina went on, 'Wilf kept wandering in and out, stupid git! One time he brung in some vodka which was lying around in the other room – little bottles, like. He said as someone as works for an airline brung them. That vodka packs a punch, doesn't it just! Then he come in saying he'd been offered some pills to cheer him up. We screeched at him not to be so stupid and he said, "All right!" and that he'd stick to the vodka.'

Angelica tossed her curls. 'You are nothing but a slut, having it off in my cousin's bed!'

Gina merely smiled. 'Haven't you been getting enough lately, darling?'

Angelica snarled, which was, thought Ellie, rather like a toy kitten snarling at a lion.

Angelica said, 'If you tell lies about me to the police, I'll tell them you were taking drugs at the party. I personally have never seen the need for drugs, being able to get my kicks in the normal way, but I hear that—'

Ellie interrupted what was likely to descend into an argument about drugs. 'Gina, did you actually see someone selling drugs at the party?'

'Good old Clay, yes. He used to be a friend of ours, well, of Jess's really, but then he got nicked for possession and dropped out of uni and now he hangs around, peddling the stuff. Working for some Mr Big or other. There's no great harm in him. I mean, he comes up and offers whatever he's got at the moment, we tell him to go away and that's about it. He's using, himself. I don't reckon he'll make thirty, the way he's going. Pathetic, really.'

'What about the fight?'

'What fight? I didn't see no fight.'

Ellie repeated, 'No fight? But . . .' And looked at Angelica, who was examining her nails and didn't meet her eye.

Gina went on, 'What it was, we was turned out of the bedroom, others wanting their turn, like, and that would be way after midnight, maybe? Nearer one? So we shifted ourselves. It was pretty crowded in the big room at the back, and noisy! Tellies and radios all blaring away, you could hardly hear yourself think. The lights had gone and someone had crashed some glasses on to the floor, so it would have been a bit dicey to join the dancers. I didn't fancy getting my feet cut, wearing my strappy sandals as I was.'

'Did you recognize anyone else who was there?'

A shrug. 'Seen some faces before, maybe, in the pub or in the caff, but not to know their names, like. Plus there was a crowd of low-lifes – no one we knew – swigging back the beer and whatever else they could get hold of, shouting insults, pushing one another around . . . not our scene. No respect! So we left them to it and went looking for Wilf, who was throwing up in the second bedroom. Stupid git! He never could handle vodka. Jess said we ought to clear it up, but as it was Angelica's place, like, we didn't bother. We took Wilf out into the garden to sober up and thought about calling it a day. Clay was hanging around, wanting us to buy something, and we kept telling him to shove off, pardon my language.'

'What was he selling exactly, do you know?'

'Not interested. He said he had something to put the sparkle back in our lives but you can't believe a word he says, and we had a problem, like. Wilf had drunk too much and couldn't drive us home, see? Big Scotty lost his licence some time back, and though I have had some driving lessons you can't keep a car in London; too expensive and not needed for work, which I can walk to. Jess is the same. We talked about if I could drive Wilf's car but it's not an automatic, like, and I said it wouldn't be safe. Big Scotty said he'd risk it, and we said we wouldn't, not on yours. I said we should take a cab back, but Big Scotty lives in Acton, we live in North Ealing and we hadn't enough money on us to get everyone home to our own places.'

'Did you see Angelica's friend Jake at the party?'

'Raff asked me that. Yes, we did. Just for a sec, when we were on our way out to the garden. He was nose-to-nose with Angel here. I couldn't hear what they said, but they wasn't happy bunnies.'

Ellie said, 'You're sure it was Jake? Did you see him leave? What about the fight?'

'Fight? You keep going on about a fight but I didn't see no fight.'

'You said a crowd of low-lifes were pushing one another around.'

'Yeah, but it weren't no fight. Push, push. Fall down. Swear. Get up and find another drink. You couldn't call that a fight. Unless you think what Big Scotty did to Clay was a fight, but nah! Too one-sided, like.'

'Tell us about Big Scotty and Clay.'

'Well, we was in the garden with Wilf and Big Scotty. Now, Big Scotty, he's really moral, like, his parents used to go to church and all. He got really uptight about Clay keeping on at us, wanting us to buy. In the end, Big Scotty picked him up – oh, Lord, how we laughed! – and he dumped Clay in the pond, and there he stuck with his chin on his knees and his feet dancing in the air, screeching fit to bust. Honest, we was killing ourselves.'

Ellie enjoyed the picture Gina had painted for them. Rafael laughed out loud. Susan smiled.

Ellie said, 'That was all that happened?'

'We-ll, Jess, she's that stupid she used to go around with Clay when he first come up to uni, so she's still got a soft spot for him and thinks he'll straighten out as he gets older, which I don't think, personally, is going to happen, but that's what she thinks. Anyway, she got all sorry for him and made Big Scotty help him out of the pond. It's only a titchy little pond, nothing in it much except some scummy water and leaves. No fish or anything. So he was stood standing there, with that wet patch which looked like he'd, you know . . .?' She put her hand over her mouth to stifle laughter and everyone else smiled, too.

Ellie said, 'And that was the so-called fight?'

'Well, that's the only fight we saw.'

'Angelica says that Clay gave her something to keep for him.' Ellie looked around. 'Where's she gone?' For Angelica had disappeared.

Gina shook her head. 'No, no. Angelica had left the party long before that.'

'How do you know? You didn't see her go, did you?'

'Kate said so. She came screeching out of the house into the garden, looking for Jake while we was pulling Clay out of the pond. Kate was yelling that she was going to kill Jake for standing her up. She said someone told her that he'd gone off with Angelica—'

Ellie said, 'Angelica told us she'd gone off with Timmy Lee on his bike and he confirmed it. I didn't dream that, did I?'

If Angelica had gone off with Timmy Lee when Gina and Co. were out in the garden talking to Kate, then how had Angelica managed to get possession of the drugs and the money? Not to mention Kate's purse? This really is the key question.

Rafael was frowning. 'Gina, you must be mistaken. Angelica couldn't have left then.'

Gina shrugged. 'That's what Kate said. And we didn't see Angelica on our way out. Kate was in a right state. Hysterical, you know? A bit embarrassing, really. And nothing to do with us. We'd got enough on our hands with Wilf, who was away with the fairies. Jess thought he might have taken one of Clay's pills, though he swore he hadn't. So we had a confab there and then, in the garden, and Big Scotty and I decided we'd better get Wilf home. We rang Wilf's partner to see if he was still up and was able to look after Wilf in spite of the row they'd been having. And he said that if we took Wilf home he'd look after him, but that he wasn't turning out to act as a minicab at that time of night. So we asked Jess if she was coming but she was fussing over Clay, wanting to know if he'd like to take his trousers off to dry and she'd find him some others, but he wasn't making much sense by that time. Silly girl; she oughta have left him to it. But no, she said she'd stay with him a while. So we left.'

'Kate was all right when you left?'

'Kate? Oh, her. Dunno about "all right". Half left and then some, if you ask me. Talking a blue streak, like. High as a kite. Hysterical. She wanted an audience, it didn't matter who. We couldn't get away fast enough. She was in our faces, wanting us to stay and listen to her troubles. Big Scotty and I had had enough. We wasn't worried about Madam Kate with her soft job and designer clothes. No, we was worried about Jess, but we couldn't get her to come along of us. Big Scotty, he's a bit of a softie, didn't want to leave her there, but me, I said it was all right because Jess hadn't drunk as much as us and knows how to take care of herself, like, only now I'm thinking we made a mistake and we oughta have got her to come away with us.'

'But when you left, Kate was alive and kicking?'

'And vocal with it. Embarrassing, really. Lord alone know what she was on though she said she hadn't taken anything. Maybe she hadn't, but she was half off her rocker, if you ask me, screeching about how she was going to get Jake to come back and fetch her which, from what I'd seen, was about as likely as me winning the lottery. Frankly, I wanted out. It was getting late and chilly. The party was over. People were drifting away, making arrangements to go in one another's cars, that sort of thing. So we left.'

'Who did? You and Wilf, Big Scotty and Jess?'

'Nah. I said. Jess stayed. She said she was going to borrow some jeans from the bedroom for Wilf so he didn't get pneumonia, and she'd see him home and then find her own way back. She's done it before. So we left her there.' She shifted in her seat. 'I wish we hadn't, now.'

'But the party was still going on?'

'Maybe four or five people. Six, max. We could hear them, see them through the windows. The music was still blaring out, though Clay told us earlier that the police had been round asking for it to be turned down. When we left we didn't go back into the house but walked round the side to the road at the front. We couldn't use Wilf's car. We left it there. He fetched it the following afternoon when he'd recovered somewhat. We hadn't enough money to get everyone home to their own places but we phoned for a cab, which took us to Wilf's digs, where he passed out on the floor, but we checked his partner was up and willing to look after him. Then I took the night bus out to Perivale and Big Scotty walked back to Acton 'cos we was out of cash by that time. And, well, that was it.'

'So you left Jess there? With Kate.'

A nod. 'Jess was fussing over Clay. We've told her before, she's got too much maternal instinct, and she laughs, but there it is: she's a sucker for a lad with spaniel eyes, know what I mean?'

They knew what she meant.

Ellie said, 'I'm confused. Angelica says there was a fight, which is why Clay gave her his stash. But you didn't see anything like that?'

Gina shook her head.

'Can we ask Jess what happened after you left?'

Gina put a sparkly mobile phone on the table. 'Now there's a thing. Jess and I, we'd half planned to meet up at my place, yesterday, Sunday, and have a takeaway. She didn't come and there was no reply when I rang her. I thought she'd be at work today and we'd have a laugh over what happened at the party, with Clay in the pond and all, but she never turned up. The boss was mad. I did text her, asked her what was up, 'cos it's difficult being short-handed and she's a mean barista, she really is.'

Gina turned her phone on, looked at messages and shook her head. 'Still nothing. I mean, she used to have these migraines but not so much lately, and if she's ill she always tells me so I can cover for her. We've been friends for ever. Real friends. Not pretend. I was thinking maybe I'd go over to her place later this evening, and then Raff said he'd like me to meet you, Mrs Quicke, so here I am, and he's promised to drop me over to Jess's later.'

Ellie heard a noise in the hall and went to see what was happening. There was Madam Angelica, with two suitcases and a shoulder bag, trying to open the front door.

'Are you leaving us, Angelica?'

Angelica jumped, not having heard Ellie approach. 'I'm not staying where I'm not wanted. I'll send for the rest of my things.' As Angelica opened the door, Ellie caught sight of a taxi in the driveway. And then the door closed.

Rafael came up behind Ellie. 'Did you lend her any money, Mrs Quicke?'

'No. How is she going to pay for the taxi and, come to think of it, how did she call one if you've got her mobile? And where is she intending to go?'

'Where's your handbag?'

Ellie looked around. She'd left it on the shelf, hadn't she? Yes, there it was. Gaping open. Her purse was open, too. Emptied of notes and coins.

Ellie felt very much like crying. 'She's cleaned me out!'

Rafael put an arm around her. She relished the warmth and the support he was offering. It was almost as good as having Thomas there to rely on. Especially since she didn't think Rafael was accustomed to showing affection that way.

Rafael said, 'Did she take your credit cards as well?'

Ellie investigated. 'Yes, she has. But she won't be able to use them without the pin number.'

Rafael had long ago taken Ellie's measure. 'You wrote the numbers down somewhere, in case you forgot?'

'Well, actually, yes. But only as telephone numbers in the address section of my diary. My diary's still here, thank goodness.'

'You'd better report the cards stolen. Even if she can't use them herself, she can sell them on to someone who can clone them or break your code.'

Ellie scrabbled in her bag again. To her great relief, she found that Angelica hadn't taken her bunch of keys. 'My husband uses a security firm who offer to cancel everything after one phone call to them. They gave us these tags to put on our key rings so that if we lose them somewhere the finder can put them into the nearest post box and they come winging back to us. It's brilliant. Once, when we were on holiday, Thomas lost his keys and didn't even know it, and when we got back home his keys were sitting in the mail box here, waiting for him.'

'But,' said Rafael, 'Angelica still has a key to this house?'

'Yes,' said Ellie, dialling the security firm, 'but I can shoot the bolts top and bottom to stop her getting back in. I don't really want to have to change the locks.'

'Nevertheless, Mrs Quicke,' said Susan, who had followed them into the hall, 'it would be safer to do so.'

Long-legged Gina also appeared, to tap Rafael on his arm. 'If you're ready, I really ought to be going. I'm dead worried about Jess.'

Rafael looked at his watch. 'Try her again. Give me a minute to sort something.'

Gina went back to her phone, texting away at a rate of knots.

Ellie reported her loss to the security firm, who assured her they were on it. She put the phone down and hesitated.

Rafael interrupted another of his soft-voiced phone calls to prompt her. 'You are going to report this to the police?'

'I suppose. I can't think why I'm so reluctant to do so. Is it because I feel such a fool for taking her in? I mean, I left my handbag here in the hall where anyone could pick it up. Well, I suppose I can stand a spot of ribbing. I was foolish to trust her. You're right. I must report it. I think you dial one-oh-one for non-urgent calls to the police.'

As she did so, she noticed Susan climb the stairs and disappear down the corridor. By the time Ellie had finished her call, Susan had returned.

'Angelica's taken her make-up and a lot of her clothes. Shall I check she didn't find the stuff she bought this morning? You asked me to put it in Thomas's room at the end of the corridor. And she heard us arrange that, didn't she?'

Susan almost ran down the corridor, opened the door into the library and gave a little scream.

Ellie closed her eyes. 'She took all the stuff she bought this morning?'

Susan returned, looking hot and bothered. 'I'll kill her. She's pulled most of her new clothes out of the bags and left such a mess.'

Gina had been trying to get her friend on her phone, without success. 'Look, I'm sorry to bother you but I'm really worried about Jess. Can we go now?'

Rafael took his phone from his ear. 'In a minute, Gina. Mrs Quicke, can you think where Angelica has gone?'

'I can't think straight. Perhaps to Timmy Lee, or to anyone else who can be fooled by a pretty face?'

'She's left a lot of unanswered questions. Susan, will you stay with Mrs Quicke while I take Gina on to Jess's place?'

Gina, her phone to her ear, gave a little cry. 'She's picked up! At last! Jess, are you all right? I've been so worried about you . . . What? What was that?' She listened, biting her lip. 'But, Jess . . .! No, I do understand why you're upset. But surely, if you explain to the police . . .? Oh. No, I see that . . . but what are you going to do? And where are you now?' Gina listened, her eyes on Ellie and now on Rafael. She said to Jess, 'Hold on a mo.'

Gina took her phone from her ear to say, 'That stupid git Clay has really dumped her in it. He's disappeared and his boss is going mental, trying to find him. He went round to Jess's place and wrecked it, telling her to produce him and she can't. She's sitting in the ladies' loo at Ealing Broadway station, scared to leave.'

Ellie said, 'Tell her to go to the police.'

Gina shook her head. 'He knows where her parents and little sister live. She says he'll do them a damage if she doesn't produce Clay, and she doesn't know, she really doesn't!'

Rafael said, 'I don't like the sound of that. You remember what he did to that family in Southall, in the corner shop? The son was pushing drugs but didn't hand over the proceeds one day, and then . . . ugh! Blood everywhere. The last I heard, the mother's still in hospital and no one will give evidence against Milos.'

Ellie said, 'We have to do something. Tell Jess to get into a taxi outside the station and come here.'

Silence while three pairs of eyes checked that Ellie knew what she was doing.

Rafael said, 'If he finds out that you are harbouring Jess . . .?'

Ellie shook her head. 'He knows the police are coming round to interview me some time today or tomorrow. He won't risk it.'

'Brave words, Mrs Quicke,' said Rafael, 'but he only has to wait till they've been and gone and then he can move in on you. Remember, he's no respecter of women.'

Ellie felt a pang of fear but stiffened her backbone. 'All the more reason to stand up to him. He can't be allowed to go around hurting other people. That's wrong.'

'Yes,' said Gina, 'but who's going to stand up to him? I can't.'

'I can,' said Ellie. 'Tell your friend Jess to come here and we'll see what we can do. After all, Milos won't touch us until after the police leave, so we've got twenty-four hours. Right?'

'Hold on,' said Rafael, back on his own phone.

Gina was also back on her phone. 'Take a taxi from outside the station. If you haven't enough money, I'll pay when you get here. The address?' And she looked to Ellie with a question in her eyes.

'Hold on!' said Rafael.

Ellie gave the address.

Susan had been quiet all this while, but now said, 'Mrs Quicke, I think you're right about standing up to bullies, but Rafael's also right and this lot are trouble. When is Thomas due back? He ought to be told what's happening.'

'I'll tell him right away.' Ellie sat down and dialled Thomas's mobile number . . . which went to voicemail. Which meant he'd switched off. Which meant there was trouble at his end. Which meant he couldn't be summoned back to help them.

Rafael pocketed his phone. He leaned back against the wall, folded his arms and closed his eyes. 'I've survived to be twenty-eight years of age because I don't take risks. I distance myself from the really bad boys. I respect their territory and they leave me alone. What have I done to deserve this?'

Susan laughed, a soft sound of pure amusement.

He opened his eyes and glared at her. 'You can laugh!'

She said, 'Your bad-boy image is slipping, Rafael. You've finally come down off the fence and joined the great majority. Welcome to the real world.'

Rafael said, 'How about if I make a run for it? Disown the lot of you. Pretend I was never here. Because I am not, repeat not, the type to help old ladies over the road.'

'No,' said Susan, 'you're a pussy cat pretending to be a tiger.'

Rafael blushed to his hairline. 'You're thinking of someone else.'

Susan patted him on the arm. 'You may have studied me but I've also studied you. You put on this cynical air to hide a soft heart, and you have been known to charge minimum interest in cases of real hardship. Mind you, your reputation with women is probably well deserved but we won't talk about that, will we?'

Ellie said, 'I think I can hear Jess's taxi. Can anyone lend me some money to pay for it?'

Rafael said, 'You stay indoors, Mrs Quicke. I'll pay and bring the girl in.'

Which he did.

Jess was almost as stunning as Gina, but very white-skinned, with long black hair, green eyes and nasty bruises on her jaw and her wrists. She was wearing a black T-shirt and jeans and boots, all rather the worse for wear. She hobbled into the house, in evident pain.

Gina flew to her friend's side. 'He beat you up?'

'Arnica?' said Ellie. 'And hot, sweet tea.'

'Hospital?' queried Susan.

'No hospital,' said Jess, subsiding with a wince on to the hall chair. 'Nothing's broken. He's too clever for that. And no police. He said not, and I'm not risking it. Painkillers and tea sounds wonderful. He took every penny I had. While he was going through my purse I ran out of the flat without thinking about keys and such. Now I daren't go back.'

Ellie said, 'If you can manage to walk down to the kitchen, we'll get you comfortable and then you can tell us all about it.'

Gina helped her friend to stand. With an arm thrown across her shoulder, Gina got Jess into the kitchen and sat her down on the big old chair at the end of the long table. Susan made and distributed tea and aspirins.

Ellie found the arnica and applied it. She also folded some ice cubes into a clean tea towel and gave it to Jess to hold against her bruised face.

Rafael walked about, talking into his phone in a low voice.

'Now, Jess,' said Ellie, 'can you tell us how you came to be in this state? Gina told us you and Big Scotty and Wilf went to the party at Angelica's. Gina and Big Scotty left with Wilf, who was unwell, leaving you to look after Clay, who'd been dumped in the pond, right?'

Jess's eyes showed that she'd been bruised more than superficially. 'That's right. I can't believe it. I can't believe that I got mixed up with . . . I mean, when I woke up yesterday morning . . . and now I can't go back to my room, or my job. I don't know what to do.'

Ellie was comforting. 'We'll think of something. You can stay here tonight . . .' Fingers crossed . . . had she got a spare bed, because the mattress in the room Lesley had slept in couldn't be used again, could it? 'So what happened?'

Jess pushed her long hair back. Tears glimmered in her eyes but she refused to let them fall. A brave girl. 'I rent a room in a flat. There are four of us but two are away on holiday and the third goes out really early for a run before she goes off to work. Someone rang the bell and I thought it was my mate who'd been out jogging forgetting her key again, so I opened it. There were two of them. Milos I recognized because Clay pointed him out to me once. And another man I'd not seen before. Big man. East Ender? Shaved head and muscles. Sticky-out ears.'

'What did Milos do?'

TWELVE

Monday, after supper

'What did he do? He pushed me right back, hit me here and here . . .' She indicated her jaw and her ribs. 'He picked me up, I was screaming but he didn't care. He threw me right across the room, and I fell on to the little table by the telly . . . and then he kicked the telly . . . Oh, Gawd! The crash as it fell over!'

'Didn't anyone hear the noise?'

'We're over the butcher's shop in the Avenue. It's a big flat, well built. Who would hear? I can't think what my flatmates are going to say when they see the mess. I ran out, without my keys or anything. And now I can't go back.'

'What did Milos want?'

'He wanted Clay. I told him I didn't know. I told him, but he wouldn't listen. He said that no scumbag cheats him and gets away with it, that there was nowhere for him to hide in the whole world. He said that I should give him up or he'd mark me! I was terrified. He trod on my hand, and he said I wouldn't be able to work, ever again if . . . Look!' The back of her hand was badly bruised. 'What am I going to do?'

'So where is Clay?'

'I don't know! Honest to God, I don't!'

'You stayed behind with him at the party when the others left.'

'I thought I could help Clay, for old time's sake. You know? Stupid me. I mean, he really has gone downhill, pushing drugs! I've never, ever! And he knows how I feel. But I was sorry for him, having been dumped in the pond. Big Scotty ought not to have done that. It was dissing him. It was understandable that Clay was upset. I mean, in a way . . . yes, I did giggle a bit, and then he was upset about that, too. Said I was taking their side, which I wasn't, not really.'

'You said you'd fetch him some jeans from the house? The party was still in full swing?'

'Yes, I did go inside. Things were calming down. Someone shouted out that the cops said they'd be around again if we didn't cool it, so people were drifting away, you know, you don't need aggro with the cops, do you? There was four or five people in the main room, dancing but really slow, like. The telly had been turned down low, but they'd got some music going on. It was loud, but smoochy stuff. I could see there was a bit of a mess in the big room and the kitchen and I could hear someone puking in the bathroom, but it wasn't my job to clear it up, was it?

'One of the men thrust a bottle in my face, said to drink up. Drunk as a skunk. It's disgusting when men get like that. He wanted to feel me up . . . ugh! So I pushed him off and went through into the big bedroom, and there was a couple on the bed . . . No, nobody I knew, I didn't know none of those people that was still there. I was looking for some jeans for Clay, and no one took any notice of me going through the drawers. I found some that I thought might fit Clay and I took them out to the garden, and tried to get him to change. I told him he must pull himself together and come away with me in case the cops came back. We could have walked back, easy, but he wouldn't. I don't know if he'd had some of his own pills, but he was, like, fighting mad, and talking a blue streak. I tried to pull him away but he wouldn't have it.'

'You were alone in the garden at that point?'

'The girl Kate was there, too. She was half-cut, hanging on Clay's arm, mad talk, saying she was going to teach someone a lesson. And Clay, honest, I wondered what he was on, because he didn't take no notice of me. He was all over her, telling her she should have some of his special pick-me-ups or some such, and I told him to shut it, that I didn't think he should push drugs on a girl who was in a bad state already, but he began to shout at me, and so did she, they both turned on me and . . .'

She drew the back of her hand across her nose. 'She pushed me! I was so surprised. But . . . it was so awful . . . he pushed me, too!'

'Clay pushed you?'

A nod. 'I stepped back and back and . . . I couldn't believe it! He kept pushing me one step back and then another, and they were both laughing and it was too much. I couldn't believe that this was Clay doing it to me. But he wasn't himself, you know?'

She rocked backwards and forwards. 'He called me names. He's never, before. Never! And so did she! Then he slapped me. Me! That was trying to help him! I couldn't believe it was happening. I wished I'd left him in the pond. I wished Gina and Big Scotty would come back but of course they didn't. They pushed me right back to the house. I couldn't go no further. So in the end I slapped him back. He's not such a big bloke. He fell on his backside, looking so amazed . . .! And she, that bitch, laughed and laughed and . . . I walked away. I was crying, I suppose. I looked through the big window into the big room as I passed, to see if anyone was still there and might give me a lift home, but by that time everyone else had gone, though they'd left the music on.'

'And the lights?'

'N-no. Dunno. Sort of. Not bright. Dimmed, like? I left. I didn't see anyone in the streets, all the way home. A couple of cars passed me, and that was it. And I did some crying, but then I told myself that he wasn't worth it, and what was I crying for, but there it was. So I got home and got out the vodka, and had a slug or two, and passed out in the chair. My flatmates were not amused, but . . . I had a terrible headache the next day. I used to get these headaches a lot but nowadays not so much. I went to bed, took some painkillers, turned my phone off, slept. I remembered later that Gina had talked about getting a takeaway but I wasn't up to it. I thought Clay might have rung me to apologize, but he never did. Then this morning I got up, ready to go to work, and that's when Milos came.'

Jess said, 'What am I going to do? He doesn't believe I left Clay there in the garden, and he doesn't believe that I don't know where he is now. I can't go to work, because he knows where I am, and I can't go to the police or he'll kill me.'

Ellie said, 'This doesn't make sense. You say you left Kate and Clay in the garden but everyone else had gone?'

'Well, I didn't see into the bedroom because that looks out on to the road and there was blinds there that we pulled down when we went in. But there was no one left in the big room at the back, no. Oh!' And she pressed the melting ice pack against her face.

Susan drew Ellie aside to where Rafael stood, leaning against the wall. 'I can't make sense of this. Do you think Clay killed Kate and then fled the scene?'

Ellie shook her head. 'If so, how did his stash of drugs end up in this house? Plus Kate's purse and necklace.'

Rafael clicked his fingers. 'Angelica has been telling us a pack of lies. I believe she left the party early but she must have gone back at some point, and picked the stuff up . . .' His voice trailed away. 'Only, if Kate and Clay were still there . . .? Why would Clay hand over his stuff to Angelica, of all people? And was Kate dead at that point in time? I can't see Angelica killing anyone, so Kate must have been dead by the time she got back. I mean, I can see Angelica robbing a body. But how did Kate come to die?'

'Angelica said Clay had got into a fight and gave her the stuff to keep for him.'

Rafael said, 'That's not true, is it? He still had his stash when he was in the garden with Gina and Jess, and I believe what they say. Their stories tally.'

'Timmy confirmed Angelica's story that she left early.'

'Did she go back after he'd dropped her off here? He wouldn't know anything about that. We can't believe anything that Angelica told us.'

Ellie agreed. 'One thing's for sure. There was no fight. Just a bit of horseplay. Nothing to make Clay want to hand over his stash to anyone else.' She turned back to Jess. 'You're sure, absolutely sure that Kate was still alive when you left?'

'She was screaming mad but very much alive. Mad as a box of frogs, if you ask me. Telling the whole world what she was going to do to Jake when she caught up with him. According to her, they'd been unofficially engaged for months till Angelica got her claws into him. Kate was saying that she was going to get Jake back, that Angelica was so kooky that he'd soon realise how stupid she was. Kate said Angelica was one of the wild oats Jake was sowing before he settled down to marriage. She said Angelica was Jake's bit on the side, like. Pretty enough to take around with him on occasions it didn't matter, but Kate swore it wouldn't last.'

'Do you think that's true? You've seen Jake with Angelica before?'

'Sure. Now and then. In the pub. Her all googly-eyed and him with his hand up her skirt. It don't take a genius to read that script.'

'Did you ever see him with Kate?'

'Mm. I think so. Once or twice. Some months back. Kate didn't speak to any of us, then. No, no. She was slumming and made it clear we weren't her cup of tea. A sharp voice. She tried to order him about and he . . . Well, frankly, if I'd been Jake and had Kate screaming at him about this and that, and she knew how to scream all right, and Angelica had come up, all sweetie-pie and said, "Aren't you a big, strong man," then I'd have had second or third thoughts about how good marriage was going to be with such a bully as Kate. She really was a bully, you know. All right, I know I shouldn't say such things about someone who's dead, but honest, I can understand why he preferred to spend party time with Angelica.'

'But Kate was alive when you left.'

'Absolutely. She wasn't making much sense, mind you. I reckon she must have been at the booze before she got there. I mean, one minute she was threatening to commit suicide and the next she was going to take a knife to Angelica, or to herself. Or to Jake. I stopped listening. All I wanted to do was to get Clay to come away with me, and he wouldn't. He seemed, I don't know, fascinated by Kate. Kept pawing her shoulder and saying he'd got just the thing to make her feel better. I lost it and shouted at him not to be so something stupid. And then he shouted and pushed me and . . . I should have handled it better.'

'What do you think has happened to Clay?'

'I don't know! *I don't know!*' They could all hear the anxiety and even dread in her voice.

Ellie said, 'You think he's run away?'

'I don't know.' Quieter, but with a sob. 'I've thought and thought, and I just don't understand where he could have gone. I've rung all the places where he hangs out, but no one's seen hide nor hair of him.'

'Wouldn't he normally report back to Milos? How often did he report, anyway?'

'I don't know. I've never wanted to know anything like that. Clay isn't that bright, you know? He got into drugs sort of by accident, and then . . . Well, no one's going to walk out on Milos, are they?' And more quietly, 'Clay isn't any threat to Milos. He isn't a leader. He's a follower. He's a sweet guy, who never hurt anyone.'

'You could see him running away if he'd lost his money and his stash?'

'Well, yes. Perhaps. But how could he lose it? When I left, he still had his moneybelt on him, under his T-shirt. And his pouch with the drugs in it. I saw them when I was trying to get him to change his jeans.'

'And you were the last ones left at the party?'

Jess's eyes grew larger than ever. 'You think I killed him? I wouldn't. Honest!'

'No, but . . .' Ellie didn't know what to think. 'Three of you were left in the garden. You, and Kate and Clay. What were they doing, the last you saw of them?'

'Clay was on the ground, where I'd pushed him. Kate was having hysterics. The noise from the radio . . . ugh. It got on my nerves. No wonder the neighbours complained.'

'The radio was still on inside the house? That's odd.'

'Why?'

'Andy and Lesley said that when the neighbours returned on Sunday evening, they didn't notice anything wrong at first, which means no noise or lights from the ground-floor flat. Now, I understand that their front door is on the street side of the house. Andy and Lesley's flat entrance is at the side of the house. When the neighbours returned they went straight upstairs as usual and it was only when they looked out of the back window that they spotted something in the garden that required investigation. They came down, went round the house and found Kate's body. It was only after that, that they found the front door open and went into the flat itself. It wasn't the noise which told them something was wrong. Jess, doesn't it look as if someone turned the sound off after you left?'

Ellie looked around at the others, who looked puzzled.

Rafael said, 'And the lights as well? But, who could that be?'

Susan said, 'Well, I suppose the police did, when they went round to complain about the noise?'

'No,' said Ellie. 'I don't think so. They only went round once, earlier in the evening. We know about that, because Jess was told about it when she went into the house to find some jeans for Clay.'

Rafael snapped his fingers again. 'So who was left to turn the sound off? Clay or Kate? I can't see either of them bothering.'

'Neither can I.'

'But who? There wasn't anyone else there. You didn't go into the house again, did you, Jess?'

'No. Catch me. I went round the side and out into the street and the noise followed me down the road.'

Ellie tried another tack. 'Can you remember if Kate had her purse with her in the garden?'

Jess thought. And nodded. 'Sure. A clutch purse. Expensive. Black, I think. Very dark, anyway. With a glittering initial on it. Yes. Her phone had a glitter case, as well. Pink. One of the new ones. Expensive. She was expensive, Kate. You could tell. Her shoes . . .' She whistled. 'And her dress. I wouldn't have minded that dress and shoes.'

'Was she wearing any jewellery?'

'Um, something round her neck. She liked glitter, didn't she? But I think, not sure . . . let me think . . . It was, like, ivy leaves in enamel, but with glitter bits. And diamond dangles in her ears. Not sure about rings. No . . . yes! A coupla modern ones, chunky chunks, you know? Knuckledusters. But, it was her shoes . . . Wow! They cost.'

Ellie thought about that. When she and Susan had searched, they'd found Kate's purse with the necklace and the diamond earrings in it but no mobile phone and no rings. So what had happened to them? And how had they come into Angelica's possession when she'd long since left the party?

This was a puzzle and a half.

Rafael said, 'Jess, are you sure about Kate's mobile phone?'

'She took it out, waved it about, trying to contact Jake, but he wasn't answering. Then she said she'd call a cab. Then she went back to trying to contact Jake. Then we got into a shoving match and I left.'

'After the visit from Milos, didn't you try to phone Clay?'

'Of course. Dozens of times. No reply. Goes to voicemail. I know he's been dossing down on people's sofas, here and there. I tried everyone I could think of but no one's seen him. He's made himself scarce and I can't blame him, really.'

A ring, short and sharp, at the front doorbell.

Ellie let Andy in. He looked hollow-eyed. His hair was all over the place, and his shoulders drooped. 'They threw me out. Lesley looks so ill. Oh, God! What am I going to do?'

Ellie set aside the problem of Kate and Clay, which was giving her a headache, and turned back into her usual practical self.

'Have you eaten, Andy? Come and sit down . . . No, in the kitchen. Then you can tell us all about it. Oh, you don't know Jess and Gina, do you? They were at the party at your place and have been telling us what they know about it.'

Andy looked at them. His eyes weren't focused and it was clear that he wasn't registering who or what the girls were. 'Er . . . right. Er . . . Sorry. Not quite . . .' He turned back to Ellie. 'What was that you said?'

Ellie beckoned to Susan. 'Take him into the kitchen, sit him down and feed him.' And to Rafael, 'Any ideas what to do with the girls? Will it be safe for them to go back to wherever they live, or shall we let them doss down here?'

Rafael was grim. 'Can you put them up? I'll stay, too. Sleep on the floor if necessary.'

Susan had Andy's arm over her shoulders, as he didn't seem capable of movement on his own accord. 'Rafael, one of them can sleep at the top with me, in the small bedroom next to mine. The other can sleep in Angelica's bedroom, right?'

Andy mumbled, 'I didn't want to leave Lesley, but they said . . . I shouldn't have left her. Suppose . . . suppose something happens tonight when I'm not there?'

Susan led him away, still talking.

Gina and Jess had got as far as the stairs and seated themselves on the lowest step. Stranded by the tide. Limp. All their bright youthfulness had disappeared and Ellie thought they were showing their true ages – they were probably both in their early thirties.

Gina was slightly more alive than Jess. Gina said, 'We can't expect you to take us in, Mrs Quicke. We really can't.' And waited for Ellie to say they were very welcome.

So Ellie did. 'I'm not turning you out at this time of night . . .' And what time was it, anyway? Coming up to nine o'clock? How time flies when you're enjoying yourself. 'So if you'd like to follow Susan into the kitchen, she'll look after you and show you where you can sleep afterwards.'

'And tomorrow?' That was Jess. 'What's going to happen tomorrow?'

'Tomorrow is another day,' said Ellie, who hadn't a clue what they were going to do tomorrow. Dump the whole caboodle on the police, probably. What else could they do? Ellie was not, definitely not, up to dealing with drug dealers. They broke the law and ought to be handed over to the police, and if they threatened her, then . . . tough. Well, probably tough. She was feeling brave at the moment but had a sneaking suspicion that tomorrow she'd be cowering in a corner, like Jess, whose bruises were spectacular.

Once the girls had disappeared along the corridor to the kitchen, Ellie heard the light patter of paws as Midge the cat descended the stairs. He rubbed at her ankles. Did he need feeding? Yes, probably. But he could wait a while for his food.

She picked him up and carried him through into the calm of her sitting room. The light was going. She drew the curtains with Midge over her shoulder, and then sat down in her chair to think. Midge curled round and round on her lap, and settled. She put her hand on his back, and her fingers rubbed his neck through his fur. He liked that, and would put up with it for some time.

Think, Ellie. Think.

Jess left Kate and Clay in the garden. One of them dies, and the other disappears. Surely the only reasonable scenario was that Clay gave Kate some drug or other which caused her to die. So let's think that through.

Clay wouldn't have expected Kate to die but he must have known that some people do have extreme reactions to the new combination drugs that have come on to the market. So, let us suppose that is what happened. When he discovered she was dead, he panicked. He realized he might be charged with her death, stole her things in a muddled attempt to delay police finding out her identity, and fled.

Well, that sounds all right. Sort of. Except . . . would a man like Clay rob a corpse for her jewellery? Her purse? Yes, maybe. But it took some nerve to remove earrings and a necklace from a dead body.

But, let's suppose that is what happened.

Very well, but where did Angelica come into the plot? It wasn't only Kate's possessions that Angelica hid in the house, but also the money and the drugs.

Well, Clay must have contacted Angelica, and asked her to hold the stuff for him while he made himself scarce.

No, that wouldn't work. It doesn't make sense that he'd give her the money *and* the drugs to keep for him. If he wanted to hire a car, or get on a train or a plane, he'd need money to pay for his fare. And when he got to wherever he was going, he'd need the drugs to sell, wouldn't he?

How much money was there? Perhaps there was a considerable

sum, enough to be worthwhile dividing up with Angelica? How can we find out?

Well, we're not asking Milos, that's for sure.

Now Angelica has disappeared, too. Why? And are they in this together?

An unlikely partnership. I mean, what has Clay got that Angelica needs?

Money, that's what. She's not interested in drugs, is she? No, there'd been no sign of that. But money, yes. She'd willingly accept the money. She was pretty desperate for money, wasn't she? But the drugs . . .

No, I don't believe she'd have been tempted to take them . . . only, apparently that's exactly what she did do.

She admitted she was given them, and that she then hid them in Thomas's Quiet Room. You can't get away from the facts.

Another thing: Kate's purse had ended up in this house but not her mobile phone and her rings. Could they still be here? Could Angelica have hidden them somewhere . . . but where? Haven't we searched the place already? Perhaps not thoroughly enough.

Perhaps we could find out where Angelica has hidden Kate's phone by ringing its number, which might lead us to where it's been hidden? But, how can we find out her number? Could we ring Jake to get it?

Ellie shuddered. If she asked Jake to give them Kate's phone number, he would want to know why they wanted it. He'd ask why they were interested, which would lead to his asking how Kate's purse had ended up in Ellie's house and he'd go straight to the police about it.

Which was probably what Ellie was going to have to do, anyway.

But . . . The chaos! The searches! The questioning! The suspicion!

Ellie sighed. The more she thought about it, the more she was inclined to think she didn't have any choice but to hand everything over to the police. She was way out of her depth. Only the police knew how to deal with drugs and stolen money and phones and disappearing people. It was not going to be fun, but that's what they must do.

Was that the phone ringing in the hall? It should have rung on the extension by her chair, but . . . bother! As she picked the receiver up, she heard a voice recording a message for her. Which ended as she said, 'Hello?'

She played back the message. Her dear husband Thomas had rung to say that things were pretty difficult and he proposed to stay overnight with his friends, if that was all right with her. Click off.

Well, it wasn't all right with her. She needed him back, that minute. But . . . those poor people were in such trouble, and it would be selfish of her to ask Thomas to return, and anyway, it would take him hours at this time of night, right across London.

In the morning, she would hand everything over to the police and be done with it. Meanwhile, she had guests who needed feeding and watering and put to bed with aspirins and hot milk.

And here came one of her guests.

Andy, hollow-eyed. The fact that he hadn't shaved that morning was now very apparent. Being fair, it hadn't looked too bad earlier, but now he was starting to look as if he'd been on a twenty-four-hour binge. A slight carelessness in his clothes was also apparent. The neck of his shirt open, one shirt tail untucked.

Ellie patted the arm of the settee beside her. 'Sit down. You look tired.'

He sat but he was not at ease. His eyes switched this way and that. He was arguing with himself? Castigating himself for his earlier neglect of his wife?

Or in need of comfort.

Ellie held back a sigh, and told herself to administer comfort. One of his hands wandered from pocket to forehead to neck. 'Tell me all about it.'

He sat on the edge of his seat. He might be physically present but Ellie had some doubt as to his mental whereabouts. Usually, when she asked someone to tell her all about it, they would pour out their life's history and, if not stopped, their mother's and father's as well. Every ailment they'd ever had, every wrong that had been done to them would be given the full treatment.

Andy breathed heavily and said . . . nothing.

Ellie said, 'She's going down to theatre tomorrow? Did they say when you could fetch her?'

His eyes came up to meet hers. He seemed to be listening to something but it probably wasn't what she'd said.

She tried again. 'Have you eaten?'

A slight frown. He was trying to remember, wasn't he?

She said, 'A cup of tea?'

He knew the word 'tea'. He nodded.

She got it. He was feeling guilty. If he would talk about it, she could help him. If he remained mum, the guilt was going to work inwards and poison his whole system. She said, 'Are you worried about Angelica? It seems to me that she knows how to look after herself.'

He nodded. He tried to twitch a smile. 'That's what Lesley used to say, but Angelica, as long as I can remember, she's called me her Big Brother and her Knight in Shining Armour. I called her my Little Princess. It was a very special relationship. When she was little, she'd come and sit on my knee and beg me for treats. She was everybody's pet.'

'Well, she's a pretty little thing and has probably always been spoiled.'

Another nod. 'I suppose so. That's not how it seemed at the time.'

Good. He might not be so ready to fall in with Angelica's every wish in future.

Ellie tried to be encouraging. 'Lesley is a great girl. She's strong, mentally and physically. She's going to be all right.'

'I think I've lost her.'

THIRTEEN

Monday evening

Ellie wasn't sure exactly what Andy meant by saying that he thought he'd lost his wife. Did he think Lesley no longer loved him? Had they really got to that point? Or did he think that Lesley might die?

Ellie chose the second option to say, 'No, no. It may take time but she'll pull through.'

He responded by looking away from her. Clearly, she hadn't got to the root of the problem yet.

She tried another tack. 'I understand that daughters bring out the protective instinct in men. Did you want a boy or a girl child?'

Head bowed. Hands clenched into fists. 'I didn't want to have children yet. She was supposed to be on the pill.'

He was angry with Lesley? Blamed her for getting pregnant before he was grown-up enough to want a child? Ellie said, 'Well, these things happen, despite our best intentions. I'm so sad for you both but, after a while, you can try again.'

'She'll never forgive me.' And that was a mere whisper. His face convulsed. He was going to weep. He put both his hands over his face and turned away, moving round in his seat as he did so.

What to do? She could leave him alone, which would be easy. Or she could comfort him.

She pulled him towards her. He dropped from his chair to the floor and she allowed him to cradle his head against her shoulder. He shook with great sobs of tears. Self-pity? Possibly there was some of that there, too.

'There, there,' said Ellie, rocking him as one would a child.

Susan tapped on the door and came in, looking as if she wanted to ask a question.

Ellie shook her head at Susan, miming for her to go away.

Susan cast her eyes upwards, and went. Susan was a darling. Susan was worth a dozen of this great lummox weeping in her arms.

He was going to be embarrassed when he recovered. And now, at long last, the words came limping out.

'I shouldn't have . . . she said she couldn't help it, but I . . . How was I to know that . . .? And in any case, she . . . It wasn't my fault!'

'No, of course not.' Well, actually, that was a lie, because it probably was all his fault. What exactly was it he was talking about, anyway?

'Lesley said . . . she shouldn't have said . . . but I admit I was perhaps too quick to . . . It was enough to drive anyone round the bend, wasn't it?'

Probably not, but I'm not saying anything.

She went on rocking him.

Finally, he made as if to withdraw from the comfort of Ellie's arms. He said, 'What am I going to do?'

'What about?' She found her hankie and gave it to him. He heaved himself back on to his seat, blew his nose and wiped his eyes. He gestured that she take back her hankie, but she waved it away.

His voice was thick. 'The flat. Everything. I was thinking. You've been very decent but we shouldn't have inflicted ourselves upon you. We should have gone to a hotel.'

'You were worried about Susan, remember? That's why you came here.'

Silence. He blew his nose again. Looked away.

Ellie said, in a gentle voice, 'You didn't want to think Angelica was responsible for the damage to the flat, even though you feared that she was. That upset you.' She was handing him an excuse for his bad behaviour.

He nodded, grateful for her understanding.

She said, 'You've been in touch with the insurance people about the damage?'

He washed his face in his hands, trying to straighten his spine. 'Lesley looked after everything like that. I did ring them. They'll send someone round but they say that if anyone else had access while we were away then we're not insured. I don't know what we're going to do, I really don't.'

'It's not the end of the world. Perhaps it might be a good idea to make a clean start somewhere else? You can get the flat cleaned up, the repairs done and sell it to someone else? Then you can move on, choose another place to make into your home.'

He sniffed, richly. 'I don't have the time to . . . Lesley always managed . . . Do you really think we can start again? When I was at the hospital, I tried to talk to her about it but she said she couldn't think about all that yet.'

I'll bet! You are an idiot, aren't you? She's lying there, facing a visit to the operating theatre, having lost her child, and you want to worry her with that!

Ellie managed to calm herself. 'A woman needs time to recover from a miscarriage.'

He attempted another smile. 'Ah, the weaker sex.'

Ellie nearly brained him. In fact, she did actually look around to see if there was anything she could hit him with. Hard.

He shuffled his feet, hands diving into his pockets. His brow creased then uncreased as he produced a mobile phone. 'I forgot. It had fallen off the bed. The nurse picked it up. Lesley said this was yours, that you'd asked Susan to give it back to you. Lesley's got her own now. I checked.'

Ellie's own phone! 'Thank you. Yes. That's good.'

He stood up, signalling that his period of womanish weakness was now over. 'You know what? I think I could fancy a bite to eat. I'll ask Susan what she can rustle up for me, shall I?' And off he went, perky as Pinky. Or whatever.

Ellie ground her teeth and told herself not to do so.

At least she had her own phone again.

She found her cleaner's details on it and pressed the right button. The phone rang and rang. Eventually a woman answered.

'Annie, is that you?'

A heavy sigh. 'Yes, Mrs Quicke. I've been expecting you to ring. I don't know what to say, I really don't. I'm that upset and so is Bob. I'd never, ever have thought of . . . Well, you know me. I wouldn't, would I?'

'No,' said Ellie, relieved to have her opinion confirmed that Annie was not a thief.

'After all these years! You could have knocked me down, you really could! I told her, I said, "Put it back." And she took the huff, honest! Told me it was all my fault and wanted to share it with me, which I couldn't! No, really I couldn't. When she told me what she'd done, I was that mad I could have done her an injury. I said, "What will happen when she misses it?" And she said . . . Well, pardon my French, but what she said I wouldn't sully my mouth with.'

Annie was referring to the woman she was currently paired with for work? What was her name? Ellie had only seen her a couple of times and then she'd been so busy she hadn't stopped to chat.

Annie continued, 'So I said she could find someone else to work with in future because I wasn't having it, no way! And she said was I going to tell on her to Maria, because that would make her lose her job, and I didn't want to put her out on the dole, did I? And I said if she returned it to you, all of it, I would just tell Maria that we'd had a difference of opinion and I'd prefer to work with someone else in future, but I wouldn't say anything about it.'

Ellie said, 'Thank you, Annie. You can imagine how worried I've been.'

'Yes.' Some reservation in her voice.

'Could you bring the package round this evening? Then I can get rid of it straight away.'

'Y-yes. The thing is . . .' Silence.

'What's wrong?'

'Well, you can have what I've got. Bob will bring me over. Right away?'

'Yes, thanks.'

Annie killed the call. Ellie put hers down, too. Thinking hard.

Annie was bringing over what she'd got. In other words, not everything that had been in the package?

Ellie found her house guests in the kitchen, looking subdued. She busied herself making sure they'd all been fed and knew where they were going to be sleeping that night. Then she fed the cat Midge, who didn't care to have his routine interrupted.

Andy and the two party girls were listless and inclined to droop. Susan set the dishwasher running and wiped down surfaces.

The light was fading so Ellie excused herself to draw the curtains on the ground floor. She came face-to-face with Rafael when she returned to the sitting room. 'You still here?'

'I'll sleep on the settee. That is, if you don't object?'

'Would it matter if I did?'

He grinned at her and punched her shoulder, lightly.

She grinned back. She said, 'You know what? You're growing on me. As you're being so useful, perhaps you'd like to sit in on a conversation I'm about to have with one of my cleaners. The old one, not the temporary one who's filling in.'

'Ah. So you've tracked down the missing package?'

'I'm not sure. And,' as the doorbell went, 'would you like to make sure this is a middle-aged blonde plus her somewhat solid husband, whose name is Bob? I'd hate to let Milos in under false pretences.'

'You wish is my command.'

It was Annie and Bob. Annie was fortyish, with dyed blonde hair and an ever-thickening figure. Bob had always been thick-set and was becoming more so. Between producing children, Annie had always worked, cleaning houses. Bob was one of the incredibly patient drivers who kept the buses moving. Neither of them looked happy to be there. Annie held a plastic shopping bag with the Morrisons logo on it. Bob hadn't been to the house before and looked around him with one quick glance before concentrating on Ellie.

Ellie said, 'You both came. I'm so glad. Come into the sitting room.'

They followed Ellie in. Annie started and put her hand to her heart when Rafael joined them. Of course, she didn't know who he was.

Ellie said, 'Don't worry. I've asked Rafael here to sit in on this conversation, as he is going to see that the stolen goods are returned to their owner this evening.'

'Yes. Well.' Annie seated herself on the settee and patted the seat beside her till Bob, rather stiffly, lowered himself on to it, too. 'Bob will tell you. You tell her, Bob.'

Bob said, 'The thing is, I don't hold with drugs.'

'Neither do I,' said Ellie. 'I was horrified when I heard that . . . that someone had hidden them in my house. So, if you'll hand them over, I'll see they get back where they belong.'

'The thing is,' repeated Bob, 'it's against the law.'

'I know that,' said Ellie. 'Don't think I haven't been through this already, because I have. I'm not happy about any of this. If I'd had the slightest idea that someone was going to bring drugs into the house, I'd have thrown her out straight away.'

Annie nudged her husband. 'Told you so. It wasn't anything to do with Mrs Quicke.'

Bob persisted. 'The thing is that they bring misery and homelessness with them. The law is right. They're wicked, and you shouldn't have anything to do with them.'

'Agreed,' said Ellie.

'I really am not happy about it,' said Bob, driving his point home with a sledgehammer.

'Neither am I,' said Ellie. And, turning to Annie, 'Tell me how you found out.'

'Well, I suppose, to be truthful, it was a bit my fault. You'd said "no" when I asked for the money for our daughter's surgery. I'd been sure you'd give it to me and I was choked when you said you wouldn't. I know, I know! It wasn't the kind of thing you usually give money for and you had every right to turn me down, but I was livid at the time and I shot my mouth off about it to Betty when we was having our tea break. I felt better, having got it off my chest, and we did the rest of the rooms as usual.'

Rafael asked, 'Who cleaned the Quiet Room?'

'Betty did. Then, when we was leaving, she said to me, "Why didn't we have a sandwich at the pub for a change?" We'd got an hour till the next job down the Avenue, and normally I don't, but she said as it was her treat, so I said "Why not?" And she showed me this wad of notes and some pills which she'd found and said I should have half, which would help us get the operation my daughter wants. I said, "Where did you get that?" And she said it was hidden in the cupboard in the Quiet Room, and that the reverend must have put it there, and that showed he was a hypocrite and a sinner and didn't deserve our respect. And I said, "No way would Thomas have brought drugs into the house." She said, "Why not?" because she doesn't know him like I do.'

Ellie agreed. 'No, Thomas wouldn't.'

'So I said to her, "I don't know who brought it in but it's not our Thomas and you've got to return it." And she said, "If it wasn't him, it must have been Mrs Quicke." And I said, "No way!" And then I thought a bit more and began to suspect who it could have been and I said, "I bet it's that uppity madam that Mrs Quicke has taken in, her being too soft for her own good sometimes." Betty said, "So what!" And I said it was stealing. Betty said it wasn't stealing because there was pills in the same package which must be illegal and you, Mrs Quicke, couldn't go to the police or you'd be done for pushing drugs yourself, and it was every citizen's right to arrest criminals and you ought to be put in jail and all your money taken away, and you were grinding the faces of the poor by not helping me out, and . . . and she went on like that until I grabbed the packet, but she held on to it and we had a right up-and-downer.'

'But you managed to get it. Thank you, Annie. I see her point of view, but the drugs were nothing to do with me and the money is not mine.'

'I know. I knew that when I stopped to think but just at first, just for a second or two, well . . . It did occur to me to keep some of it. Not that I did, you understand? Betty took a twenty out for herself, as she said you'd be willing to pay a reward for returning the money. And then we went on to our next job, only we didn't talk to one another again. I didn't feel right about it, any of it. And when we was ready to go home I said to her that I'd ask the agency to send someone else to work with me until my old mate gets back.'

'Betty took money out for a reward? Oh, dear. I don't know what to say. I suppose, under the circumstances . . . but you do understand, Annie, it's not my money so I can't really give a reward. Do you want one, too?'

Annie said, 'I asked Bob and he said not to ask for it. I did think you might offer but he said not even to think about it, and it's not your money anyhow, so I'm not asking, so there.'

Annie gave her husband a decided nod, at which he cast his eyes upwards, lifted his capable hands from his knees and replaced them there. He was out of it.

Annie handed Ellie a wodge of notes from her plastic bag. 'Here's what she found, less her twenty and what she paid for lunch. She said as you owed it to us. Which wasn't really true, but I wasn't thinking straight, like, till I'd talked it over with Bob.'

Ellie tried to think straight, too, but the rights and wrongs of this situation escaped her. It was right to restore stolen money to its owner, but if the owner had acquired it by illegal methods, then ought he to get it back?

It was all too much. The only thing she knew was that somehow she must protect those two valiant baristas, Jess and Gina, who'd come to her for help in dealing with Milos.

She said, 'I'll see the drugs and the money get back to the right person.'

Bob shifted. 'We-ell, you see. I'm agin drugs. I said, didn't I? So when Annie here told me what had happened, I said I didn't know how you had got involved, pillar of the community and all that, but that it had to stop there or the drugs would get back into circulation and do a lot more damage. So I flushed them down the loo.'

'What!' Ellie gaped.

'Yes,' Bob repeated, with a mixture of defiance and unease. 'I flushed the dratted things down the loo. And good riddance.'

So now Ellie couldn't give the drugs back to Milos.

Rafael groaned and put his head in his hands.

Ellie's heart thumped with fear. However was she to explain the loss to Milos? Would he descend on Bob and Annie to exact retribution? No, no! Surely not. But he might well do so, if he knew. Better not to say anything about them. She must pretend she'd found them in the house somewhere and . . . what then? If she told him what had happened, would he believe her? If she said that it was she who had flushed them down the loo, would he believe that? No, because she'd fed him another story earlier. Oh dear, oh dear. What a tangle!

On the other hand, her braver self insisted that Bob had done the right thing. He'd been more courageous than Ellie, who had learned of what Milos might do to anyone who crossed him. Bob knew what people like Milos might do, all right. He wasn't underestimating the probable consequences of his action but he'd done it all the same.

Annie's voice quavered, though she tried to control it. 'I told Bob what might happen because we all know what drug dealers can do to people who cross them, but he still did it. And I'm glad he did.' Though she wasn't, not really. Or anyway, only half glad.

Bob flexed his hands on beefy thighs and leaned forward. 'My father said that if you don't stand up to bullies, they'll walk all over you. He used to say to me, "What would our world be like now if we'd given in to Hitler? We'd be goose-stepping and not able to speak out when we saw something wrong, that's what!" My father fought in the Second World War and his father fought in the First, and I've got nearly all their medals except the one that got run over by the ice-cream van by mistake. Right?'

'Right!' said Ellie, wanting to clap and to scream. Both at once.

Bob leaned back and folded his arms. And nodded. 'I ain't got a lotta time for the police, mind. They're not like they used to be. But, to be fair, things ain't what they used to be, either. Drugs and that. Gangs with knives. That's new since I was a boy. We used'ta have gangs. The Kray brothers and their like, and yes, they was nasty. Yers. I stood at the side of the street to see the hearse with its black horses and the man in the silk hat walking in front of it when the first one of them died. But it was easy to decide then, right from wrong. You knew where you were. You had bobbies on the street, and we knew them, and they knew us, and we was taught right from wrong, and told what would happen to us if we did it again. Which some of us did, no messing, and then it was straight down the nick. Now it's all social workers and letting the lads off with a caution when they oughta have the fear of God put into them to teach them not to do it again. But knives! And drugs!' He shook his head. 'I don't hold with them.'

Rafael opened his mouth to speak, shook his head and closed his mouth again. Rafael had been brought up in the modern world which made excuses for anyone who committed a crime. Rafael was a child of today, who sought for compromise rather than challenged vice.

Ellie looked at the meagre bundle of notes in her hand. 'Is this all there was? I thought there'd be more.' She handed the money over to Rafael. 'What do you think?'

Rafael riffled through the wad. 'How would I know? I've never sold drugs or bought any. But I would say, at a guess, it's about half what I'd expect Clay to have taken at the party.'

Ellie felt very tired all of a sudden. 'You think that Angelica took a lot of it with her when she went on her shopping spree this morning?'

Rafael shrugged. 'You say she bought clothes. Her cards were maxed out, so maybe that's how she paid for them . . . But if so, why didn't she take the lot?'

Ellie remembered something Angelica had said. 'She told us that she was planning to pay you off with the money she got from letting drugs be sold at her party. She said that before witnesses. If that is so, this money is really meant for you, isn't it?'

Rafael shook his head. 'You'll think I'm being stupid but I don't want it. It's not mine. It belongs to Milos, not me.' And he held the wad out to Ellie.

Ellie stared at the money and didn't take it. 'It's beyond me, this whole thing. I can't think what happens next. I do not fancy ringing Milos up and telling him that his drugs have gone down the plughole, and let's just imagine me saying that yes, here's the money that your man took, but no, I have no idea how much it should be, but that's all we found, and we have no idea where the rest of it went.'

Bob was clear about what he thought. 'If it's money from drugs then it shouldn't be handed back to this man, no matter what. It's illegal.'

Ellie agreed. 'It's a grey area. If it weren't for dropping Angelica into the muck – and yes, she deserves it but I can't quite bring myself to do it – then it would probably be best to hand it over to the police. Only, if we tell them where we found it they'll think that we've been harbouring a drug addict or something.'

Rafael said, 'No police, or you'd have Milos invading your house as soon as the coast was clear. Look, I can see where you're coming from, but—'

'What I say is, you don't give in to bullies.' Bob heaved himself to his feet. 'You take it to the police, right? If you give this Milos the money, he'll buy more drugs and there'll be more kids lying in the gutter and taking overdoses, and you'll be responsible.' He lifted his wife to her feet. 'Come on, Annie. We've done what we set out to do; now we can go home with a clear conscience. Goodnight, Mrs Quicke. Good to have met you. Don't bother to come to the door. We'll see ourselves out.'

Bob ploughed on out to the hall but Annie hung back.

'Mrs Quicke, I understand where you're at, but you won't tell that man that Bob got rid of the drugs, will you? I mean, we haven't got much, but what we have got—'

'You don't want him busting up your house.'

'Nor my daughter, nor the grandkids.'

Bob bellowed from the hall. 'Annie! You coming?'

Annie sent a distracted look in Ellie's direction, said, 'I'm coming!' and obeyed the summons.

Ellie sat on her chair, trying to think. She looked at the thin bundle of notes which Rafael placed on the table at her side. She didn't want anything to do with it.

Her brain was in confusion. She thought of Lesley, lying in a hospital bed, and tried to pray for her. Only, her brain skittered off the idea of Lesley, and insisted on presenting other matters to her attention. Lesley's handbag: where was it? And there was something Lesley had said that she wanted Andy to know about, but what was it? Lesley had thought it was important, but . . .

Well, Lesley could have told Andy herself, couldn't she, when he was at the . . .

Jess. In trouble. Sharing a flat with others, who would by now have returned home and found the television broken. Who pays for . . .

Milos, the baddie. How to stop him from . . .

What time is it? Was it too late to ring Thomas, who might be able to calm her down and think of something sensible to . . .

A kaleidoscope of half-finished thoughts.

The clock in the hall struck the hour.

What hour? She looked at her watch . . . No, no. Why not take it off? It hadn't given her the right time for days.

Rafael stood up. 'It's getting late, Mrs Quicke. Any ideas about what we do next?'

She sighed. 'I'm right out of ideas. Lots of questions, no answers.'

'Do you want me to try to explain what's happened to Milos?'

She said, 'You're a brave lad. He might well turn on you.'

'I don't hold his money.' Rafael held her gaze. He knew very well that drawing Milos's attention to him might result in a visit from men who enjoyed stamping on people. He knew it and was still prepared to help.

She said, 'Give me ten minutes, all right?' She got to her feet with an effort – it had been a tiring day, hadn't it – and went down the corridor and into the Quiet Room.

FOURTEEN

Monday evening

The overhead light was too strong in the Quiet Room. She turned on a small side lamp which Thomas had imported to keep him company early and late on winter days, and switched the main light off.

She sat in Thomas's chair, which faced the picture worked in wools on the opposite wall. This showed Our Lord as a shepherd, who had left his flock to search for one lost lamb. When he had found it, he'd put it over his shoulders and taken it back to the fold.

Ellie had sometimes wondered what the woman was like who had worked that picture long ago. What sort of life had she led? Had she been an unmarried daughter who had stayed at home to look after her parents and who had had nothing much to do with her time except to embroider this picture and, perhaps, to read to her father and mother when their eyesight failed? She must have had decent eyesight herself, that long-ago woman. Had she also had faith in God? Surely she must have done so, or she wouldn't have spent so many hours on this picture of him.

I told Rafael I needed ten minutes. So, what should I pray for?
I suppose it doesn't really matter. God knows what I need.
I'm in such a muddle.
I'm not the lost sheep here. Am I? I'm not sure who is . . .
Rafael. Yes, I think I see that.
I can't pray. I don't know what words to use. I may be thinking with my heart instead of with my head. I probably am. If so, will you please straighten me out?

There was a knock on the door. The ten minutes were up, and she didn't think anything had been solved by her asking for ten minutes' grace.

Something was boring into her side. She fished out another of her grandson's toys; this time a piece of Lego which he'd left there.

She tried to keep his box of Lego bits all together in the sitting room behind the settee. This piece must have strayed.

Rafael opened the door. 'Are you all right?'

'Sure. My grandson could do with a personal minder. He must have left it here when I was on the phone earlier today, after the cleaners had left.' She held the piece up. Bright yellow. A window, complete with plastic glass panes.

Rafael twitched a contraction of his lips, which was meant to be a smile. 'Kids!' He was being polite. He wasn't interested.

Ellie glimmered a proper smile back at him. '"Out of the mouths of babes and sucklings." I prayed and thought my prayers were not being answered till, "Lo and behold!" I was told where to look for answers. Think about it, Rafael. We've all been waltzing round the problem and refusing to see what was under our noses. A window of opportunity. Right?'

No, he didn't get it. 'For whom?'

'How pleasant it is to hear someone say "for whom?" instead of "what?" Let's go and see what the others are doing.' She got up and led the way back to the kitchen, where Jess and Gina were sitting in a huddle, looking sorry for themselves. Susan was busying herself cooking, something which involved kneading dough.

Ellie smiled to herself. Was Susan fulfilling Rafael's wish to see her knead dough, because it caused her bosom to rise and fall in a delectable fashion, or was she teasing him?

Rafael's eyes were out like organ stops. Uh-oh, thought Ellie. Susan *is* teasing him. She could have used the food processor instead of kneading by hand. Good for Susan.

Now for the other girls.

Ellie said, in a brisk tone, 'Let's get one or two things sorted, shall we? Jess, have you been in touch with your flatmates to tell them what's happened?'

Jess looked hunted. 'I didn't dare. If I told them where I was, they might tell Milos. I know I ought to have warned them but I was frightened out of my life!'

'No, you weren't,' said Ellie. 'You're still alive. Yes, you've had a nasty experience, but sitting in a corner saying "poor little me" isn't going to get you anywhere. If you need our support, you have it, but now you must phone your flatmates and tell them what's happened. One or other of them might want to go with you to the police to report the incident.'

'I can't!' shrieked Jess. 'Milos will kill me.'

'Don't exaggerate,' said Ellie. 'He won't kill you. He relies on your having the backbone of a jellyfish not to report him, so you have to prove that you are a fine, upstanding, down-sitting young woman whom he can't mess about. Right?'

'Er . . .' Jess was visibly trembling.

'No, no!' said Gina. 'It's too much to ask.'

Ellie wasn't going to soften. Not now. There was too much at stake. 'If you don't report the damage to your television set, who do you think is going to pay for another one?'

Jess started to sob. 'I thought . . . I didn't think you'd . . .'

'You thought I would pay for it? Or Rafael? No. Why should we?'

'But I thought you'd let us stay here till the danger was over.'

'And how did you think that was going to happen? Was I to wave a magic wand and Milos would miraculously disappear? It's no good us sitting on our butts and hoping that someone else is going to straighten this mess out, because they're not going to do so. We have to take action ourselves. Some people might think that a houseful of women can be intimated without there being any consequences, that Milos can terrify us into behaving as if we were frightened little children. But we are not just a bunch of women. We are grown adults who have looked at the dangers of doing nothing and decided to do something about it. We are not going to be pummelled into submission and say nothing. We are not doormats. Repeat after me: We Are Not Doormats!'

Jess and Gina looked at one another with fear in their eyes.

Susan and Rafael said, 'WE ARE *NOT* DOORMATS!'

Ellie said, 'Repeat after me, '"We are not prepared to lie down and let a man walk all over us!"'

Susan thumped the dough on to the board with a flourish. 'No, no! We are not going to do that!'

Rafael clapped his hands. 'All together now! We are not victims!'

Ellie said, 'We are strong, independent women who can stand up for our rights!'

Susan said, 'Ditto, ditto!'

Gina and Jess looked only half convinced.

Ellie said, 'What you have to do, Jess, is to go down to the police station straight away to report Milos's assault on you. And, even more important, to report that Clay is missing.'

Dropped jaws all round. Except that Susan went on kneading dough and smiling to herself. Even Rafael's jaw had dropped.

'But—' said Gina.

'Well,' said Ellie, 'Clay has disappeared, hasn't he? No one's seen anything of him since Saturday night or early Sunday morning. You, Jess, you tried to contact him without success. Right?'

Jess nodded. 'Well, yes. But—'

'And,' said Ellie, 'Milos is also rampaging around, trying to find him. Also without success. Right?'

'Right,' said Gina, faint but persevering.

'So, what's happened to him?' Ellie asked. No one seemed to know. Susan paused in her task. A strand of hair had fallen over her eyes. She pushed it up with the back of her hand. Rafael's eyes followed her every movement.

Ellie nudged Rafael. 'I said what do you think has happened to Clay?'

Rafael started. 'He scarpered when . . .' A change of tone. 'Yes, why did he scarper?'

Susan threw her lump of dough into a basin and set it aside to prove. 'Well, I suppose he scarpered because Kate died.' She washed her hands, dived into the freezer and came up with a tub of some-thing which she proceeded to empty into a saucepan and heat up.

Ellie said, 'But we don't know how Kate came to die, do we? I mean, the police must have held an autopsy to find out but they may not have the result themselves yet. Ideas, anyone?'

Susan tried to work it out. 'Jess left Clay in the garden with Kate. By that time everyone else had departed. I suppose she might have fallen and cracked her head open on the edge of the pond. That is . . . Jess, did the pond have stone slabs around it or was it a plastic affair?'

Jess said, 'I think . . . yes, it was a really old pond which must have been there for yonks. It was made of concrete, with a sort of rolled-over effect round the edges. I suppose she could have fallen on it and hurt herself. But if that's how she died, then why didn't Clay call for help?'

Ellie said, 'Let's imagine the scene. She trips, falls and dies. If Clay called for help, he'd be found with the drugs and money on him and been arrested for pushing. So he fled. Or, on the other hand, if she died because of what he'd sold her, then ditto. So he ran away.'

Rafael said, 'Understandable.'

'Yes, but how come his stash and money ended up in this house?'

Everyone thought about that. Ellie said, 'Either way, if Kate died from the drugs or as a result of an accident, Clay was a witness to her death and the police need to know that he was there during the argument between Kate and Jess. And that he remained there when Jess left. Which is why Gina and Jess have to report Clay missing. Because he really does seem to have disappeared.'

'But—' Jess was not happy at the idea of going to the police.

'Trust me,' said Ellie, 'the police have to take notice when someone is reported to have been missing for over twenty-four hours. Clay has been missing for longer than that. It's now Monday evening and he hasn't been seen since the early hours of Sunday morning. When a formal complaint is lodged, the police start to ask questions. They'll check Clay's lodgings, and after that the first person they'll want to see is Milos. That should give Milos something to think about other than pursuing us for his money and, incidentally, it will take the heat off Jess with her flatmates who might otherwise want her to pay for the damage to their property. Right?'

Jess whimpered, 'They'll still expect me to pay.'

'Haven't you any household insurance?'

'I don't think so. Maybe our landlord . . . But why should he pay? Can't we just report Clay's disappearance on the phone?' She was not looking forward to going to the police, was she?

Ellie was bracing. 'Think of the publicity! The local papers will be falling over themselves to take pictures of you two beauties. It won't take you long to tidy yourselves up and present yourselves as the glamour girls that you are. I shouldn't wonder if you don't get a number of offers from men when the papers come out.'

Susan muttered, 'What sort of offers, I wonder?'

Ellie told herself not to giggle, which she very much wanted to do. So she ploughed on: 'Maybe you'll even be able to interest the tabloids in your story. I can see the headlines now: "Beauty queen puts her life on line for an old friend—'

Gina objected, 'But we've never gone in for beauty contests.'

'You could have. You've got the looks for it,' said Ellie, crossing her fingers. They really were too long in the tooth for beauty contests, weren't they?

Susan said, 'I've got another headline. How about, "All for love! Gina gave her all!"'

Rafael chimed in, '"Drug baron ruins beauty queen's looks!"'

Jess produced a mirror from her handbag, looked into it and gave a little scream. 'My hair! The bruise! I can't be seen like this!'

'You've got such a wonderful bone structure, it won't matter. That bruise is your evidence of assault. You have to go to the police before the evidence fades. And that means going now, tonight!'

'Oh, but I—'

'She's right, you know,' said Rafael. 'When you tell your story, the police will swing into action and you'll be famous overnight.'

Don't exaggerate, Rafael. We're very nearly there.

Gina said, 'But they'll ask us where we think he's gone. What are we to say to that?'

Ellie was soothing. 'You don't know, do you? So that's what you have to say.'

Rafael said, 'Ladies, I can only take one passenger at a time on the back of my bike. Shall I call a cab for you?'

Gina checked her handbag. 'Look, I've got a tenner. Let's spring a cab, shall we, Jess? You can ring your flatmates on the way, right? Otherwise we'll have them traipsing down to the nick to report you missing, too.'

Jess was teasing her hair out. She did in fact still look fabulous, even with a black eye. 'I'm still worried about Milos. What will he do when he hears that we've been to the police?'

Rafael was soothing. 'He's going to be too busy fending off the cops to worry about you any more. Let me phone for a cab for you.'

With many a chirrup, the girls were ushered out of the kitchen by Rafael to await the arrival of their transport.

Susan cleaned surfaces in silence. She checked that her dough had risen satisfactorily, which it had. She gave it a few more thumps, returned it to the basin and covered it with cling film. This she put into the fridge to prove overnight.

Opening the door of the oven, she drew out a tray of perfectly baked puff pastry rounds. The kitchen filled with delicious, buttery scents. Susan lifted the centre portions out of the puff pastry rounds.

'Vol-au-vents. Filled with chicken in a mild curry sauce. You'll be able to manage a couple, Mrs Quicke, or will they give you indigestion? I can freeze what we don't eat now.'

'I'd love a couple. What time is it? Have we missed a meal? Or two?'

'It's after ten. Will Thomas be able to get back tonight?'

'I'll ring him in a minute but I don't think so. Would you like a hot drink to take to bed with you?'

Rafael returned, having seen the girls off. 'Well, Mrs Quicke: I can tell you didn't want to say what you think has happened to Clay in front of the girls. Would you care to enlighten us? We won't faint. We can take it.'

'Oh, that's easy. According to what Jess and Gina have told us, Clay's a no-hoper. He's no money, no resources. If he's gone missing for all this time, then surely there's only one reason why. He's dead, isn't he?'

Tuesday morning

Ellie woke to the realization that all was not well. Something was wrong. But what?

Then she remembered that Thomas hadn't been able to come home last night. He'd felt unable to leave his friends and she'd understood that. She hoped he'd been able to get a few hours' sleep, but she knew that sleep doesn't come easily to the afflicted.

She lay there, thinking over what had happened the previous day and what she planned to do next. Midge the cat jumped up on to the bed and put his head under her hand. He wanted stroking. She stroked. He wasn't nudging her to get out of bed, so Susan must be up already and have fed him.

What of Rafael? He'd suggested sleeping on the settee in the sitting room, but with Jess and Gina returned to their respective homes, she'd offered him the small guest room that had been allocated to Angelina. The bed had been made up with clean sheets, so why not?

He'd accepted her offer but Ellie knew he hadn't slept well. She'd heard him move about a couple of times in the night. She'd wondered if he'd venture upstairs to Susan's domain, but no . . . He wouldn't risk another knee in the guts, would he?

Ellie grinned to herself, thinking that she hadn't needed to worry about Susan. Susan was very well able to take care of herself.

Midge the cat stretched himself out to double his length, then settled down for a quick wash and brush-up.

Ellie picked up her watch from the bedside table and checked her alarm clock. Her watch was half an hour slow. Why did she bother to wear it? Well, so that it would remind her to take it in for repair. That was logical, wasn't it?

She started upright. She'd forgotten that her daughter was going to bring little Evan for her to look after again that morning. Oh, dear! That wasn't going to work, was it? Not with drug lords menacing everyone in sight, dead bodies littering the landscape and Susan having to get off to an early start on Tuesday mornings.

Ellie shot out of bed. Well, crawled, actually. But she made it to the bathroom not much later than usual, showered and dressed in haste, and was on her way down the stairs while Susan was shrugging into her coat. And from behind Susan came the entrancing aroma of coffee. Proper coffee. Not something out of a jar.

Susan said, 'There's fresh rolls for breakfast. Do you still want me to take Kate's stuff in to the police station? I could do it on my way in.'

'Good idea. Yes, please. Perhaps they'll have the result of the autopsy by now, too.' Ellie turned into the corridor, nearly tipping over the stained mattress as she did so. 'I only hope I can remember the combination to the safe.'

Rafael appeared from the kitchen, coffee cup in hand. He was fully dressed, with a six o'clock shadow. He looked rested, handsome, and . . . amused. 'Do you want me to get a safe cracker in to open it for you?'

'How dare you! The very idea!' Ellie laughed. They all laughed. But they all three knew that it was quite possible Ellie hadn't remembered the combination. She sought for the numbers in her memory.

Dear Lord above! What is it? Don't let me down now!

It was . . . She had it. Her birthday and Thomas's. She hurried down the corridor to retrieve Kate's things, opened the safe without trouble and handed the bags of evidence over to Susan. 'Give me a ring when you've done it, right?'

Susan hesitated. 'Is it safe to leave you here by yourself?'

'She's not alone,' said Rafael, 'I promise I won't leave till Thomas gets back or we hear that Milos is under arrest.'

Ellie and Susan looked at him. Their trusty knight, defending the older generation. Was he indeed to be trusted? Yes, apparently he was.

He said, 'Mrs Quicke, come and have some breakfast. I've made proper coffee and Susan's rolls are a treat. The only thing is, I could do with borrowing an electric razor. The shops aren't open yet and I feel slightly grubby.'

Ellie apologized. 'I'm so sorry, Thomas has a beard and therefore no need of razors. Why not try Andy?'

'He's not back yet.'

'He's still at the hospital? I don't suppose you'd like to rummage through his luggage for a razor?'

'No, I wouldn't. If you can put up with it, I can.'

'Definitely,' said Ellie. 'I must ring my daughter before I do anything else. She wanted me to babysit for Evan this morning but I really don't think, not with everything that's going on, that it's appropriate.'

'I like kids,' said Rafael. 'I often watch my sister's. A great family man, that's me.'

Susan snorted and Ellie looked to see if he were joking. Apparently, he wasn't.

He noted their misgivings. 'Cross my heart and hope to die. Scout's honour.'

Susan was scornful. 'You were never a Boy Scout.'

'No. But I do like kids.'

Ellie said, 'Even so, I'll see if I can get her to find someone else to look after him this morning. Just in case.'

Just in time. Diana was about to step into her car when Ellie got through to her.

'Diana, I'm really sorry but I can't look after Evan this morning. I've got a house full of people who—'

'What? I'm dropping Evan off to you a little early because I have a meeting at half past eight.'

'Can't he go to the nursery for once? I know he enjoys it.'

'What? Surely you can manage to—'

'No, I can't. I really can't.' Ellie was surprised at herself for saying 'no' to Diana. Perhaps she was growing a backbone at long last.

'Oh, really! This is most inconvenient. The nursery doesn't like it if I turn up unannounced.'

'I know. I apologize.'

'Well, all right then. But you can have him this afternoon, can't you? If he's been to the nursery he'll be overexcited and then he'll want to have a nap. But if he does have a rest he won't sleep through the night tonight. So you'll have to keep him awake somehow.'

Now that wouldn't be easy. But what could she say? 'Thank you for understanding, Diana. I appreciate it.'

'Right. Oh, don't ring off. Didn't you say some friends of yours need a short-term lease on another flat? I'll bring some details with me when I come this afternoon.' And off went the phone.

Bother, thought Ellie.

Rafael hovered. 'Do you want your breakfast in here or in the sitting room?'

What luxury! To be served a meal in your own home, sitting in your favourite chair in the autumn sunshine, overlooking the garden which was looking colourful though it would soon be past its best and have to be shut down for the winter.

She couldn't prevent herself from thinking, fretting, worrying.

Halfway through her second cuppa, the phone rang.

It was Susan, unusually terse. 'I called at the police station and said I had some things belonging to the girl who'd died at the weekend. Some man came out and told me the case was closed, and if I had anything of Kate's I should give it to her family.'

'The case is closed?' Ellie repeated this for Rafael's information as he had suddenly appeared, hovering in the doorway to overhear what was happening. He'd probably been worrying that the phone call might be from Milos and was prepared to intercept it.

Ellie mouthed to him, 'Susan!'

He nodded but didn't remove himself.

Susan confirmed her statement. 'Closed. The post-mortem disclosed that Kate died of taking an illegal drug. There's a new one on the market, apparently, which mixes two or three earlier types and can be fatal. And this was. So the verdict at the inquest will be misadventure.'

'Misadventure.' Ellie didn't like the sound of that.

'Yes. They are not interested in her belongings, period. Their enquiries are continuing, the man said, but only to find who took drugs to the party. He asked me if I knew. I said I didn't know because I hadn't been there. He told me to go away and stop bothering him. Well, not in so many words but that is what he meant.'

Ellie tried to absorb the implications. 'But at least he'll ask Milos about it, won't he?'

'Dunno,' said Susan. 'I didn't take to the policeman, I must say. He as much as said that it was Kate's own fault that she died, it's made a lot of extra work for him when he's got enough on his plate already and why don't I go away and mind my own business.'

Ellie guessed, 'Did his ears go read when he got agitated?'

'Come to think of it, yes. Do you know him?'

'We've crossed swords in the past, yes.'

'I must go or I'll be late for my class. What shall I do with Kate's things?'

'I don't have any information about her parents or where they live. I do have Jake's phone number and he could tell her parents. Would you like to phone him or shall I do it?'

'Give me his number and I'll do it. You've got enough on your plate.'

'Hold on a mo and I'll get it for you.' Ellie tried to think where she'd written down Jake's phone number. Where had she been when Rafael had rung to give it to her? Had she been on this phone in the hall because, with any luck, she'd have scribbled a note on the pad there. She put the phone down and made her way to the hall. She really must get one of those new phones that you could carry around with you. It was ridiculous not to move with the times. No, there was nothing on the pad there. So, she must have written it down on something in the kitchen?

Yes, she had! She hurried back to the phone and gave Susan the number. Then she filled Rafael in on what had been happening. 'The autopsy on Kate reveals a drug overdose, so the verdict will be misadventure. The police told Susan to give Kate's things to her parents. She doesn't know them but will tell Jake that she's got them. The case is closed, except that the police will now be going after the drug pusher.'

Rafael said, 'How long is it going to be before Milos hears that the police are looking for him? Or, rather, for Clay? In other words, do you want me to tell Milos what's happened? Do you think we've done enough to keep him away from our door?'

'I don't know,' said Ellie. 'I hope so but I can't be sure, can I?'

He said, 'Look, I've got some phone calls to make and I expect you'd like me to get rid of that mattress, wouldn't you? Would you like me to source you a new one? I promise I won't leave the house but if I could have access to a computer I could deal with that for you and one or two business matters while you do whatever it is you usually do in the mornings.'

It was a decent offer. She said, 'First, I'll ring Thomas to see what his plans may be, then tidy the house. Unfortunately my part-time secretary is on holiday this week but I'll still have to deal with the post . . .' She went back to the hall to fish a big handful of mail out of the box behind the front door. 'You can use the computer in my study for now, but leave the door open so that I can yell for help if something nasty comes knocking at the front door, right?'

Rafael started off down the corridor, calling back, 'Password?'

'I never bother with one. And don't tell me I'm asking for trouble because I know it. I still don't use a password, right?'

Before she could reach the phone in the hall, it began to ring. She could hear Rafael was already on his phone to someone in her study, Oh, dear! She looked at the phone and enquired within herself whether or not she felt strong enough to deal with the call.

And, yes, it was Milos. 'Well?' No politeness necessary.

Ellie told herself not to panic. 'I have retrieved the package which Angelica dumped in this house. The drugs have been disposed of and—'

'What!'

'Yes. Flushed down the loo. Gone. Out of reach.'

A screech. 'What?'

'There's no point you getting aerated about it. Someone found them and flushed them down the toilet.'

'That's my property!'

'Well, that's a moot point since it's illegal to sell them.'

Fast breathing. 'Someone's going to have to pay me for them.'

Ellie said, 'I was going to say, try your insurance company, but I don't think they deal in drugs, do they?'

Another screech. 'What?'

'No, they probably don't. Anyway, the police say that the girl Kate died of drug abuse and they're actively looking for whoever gave her whatever it was that killed her. I suggest you have a rethink.'

'Where is Clay? You're hiding him.'

'Certainly not. I haven't seen hide or hair of him. I don't even know what he looks like.'

'I'll murder him!'

'I suspect . . . I may be mistaken, of course . . . but I think you should start looking for his body.'

FIFTEEN

Tuesday morning

'What?'

Ellie could imagine Milos jumping up and down with rage.

'I said to look for his body. As in corpse.'

'What the—'

'You must have wondered. No one's seen him since early Sunday morning. He must have left the garden at some point. Perhaps when he discovered that Kate had died from what he'd given her? But what did he do then? Who did he go to? No one admits having seen him after the party.'

And we won't talk about how the drugs and money ended up in Thomas's Quiet Room.

Ellie continued, 'The girl, Jess, whom you assaulted and whose property you damaged, hasn't seen him, either. And he's not in his usual haunts. Jess has taken her bruises to the police, by the way, so I suspect they'll be round asking for you any minute now and—'

Milos clicked his phone off.

Ellie looked at her receiver and said, 'Well, you did ask!' And cradled it . . .

It rang again. This time it was Thomas, concerned for her but distracted by his friends' problems. The wife was having panic attacks, they'd called out the locum doctor but he hadn't done much good, and they were trying to get her own doctor to call but he was booked solid and suggested they take her to A&E if she didn't improve. Thomas had got in touch with their daughter who lived some distance away, and who was going to have to get leave from work and get coverage for her two daughters in primary school and alert her husband, who was away on a business trip, before she could come over. Thomas was not going to be able to get away for some time.

'Ellie, you said there was some problem with Lesley. I've

been praying for her, and for you, too. What's the latest on her condition?'

Lesley! 'How awful! I'd quite forgotten her. Andy went to stay with her in the hospital last night and hasn't come back yet. I'll ring the hospital in a minute. No, wait! I can't ring him, can't I? No, I can't because they don't like people using mobiles in hospital. How awful of me not to have checked with the hospital this morning.'

She could hear the smile in his voice. 'Calm down, calm down. If he's at the hospital then that's where he should be. He's probably waiting for the ward rounds to be over before he can find out what happens next.'

She calmed down. 'You're right. Of course. There's been so much going on . . . but I'm all right, really I am. Rafael said he wouldn't leave while there was any—'

'Who's Rafael?'

'I forgot. You don't know about him. He's soft on Susan. Yes, I know she's got a boyfriend already, someone at uni, but Rafael is currently stuck on her. I rather like him, I must say, though I wouldn't go for him as a matrimonial prospect. Oh!' She saw Rafael leaning against the wall, arms folded, smiling at her.

Thomas said, 'Look, the moment you feel it's all too much for you, give me a ring and I'll get back as quickly as I can.'

'You can't leave your friends till their daughter arrives. I can manage.' She heard a cry of alarm at the other end.

Thomas said, 'I'll have to go!' and clicked off his phone.

A smile twitched at the corners of Rafael's mouth. 'So I'm not a good prospect, matrimonially?'

'Dreadful,' said Ellie. 'I wouldn't advise anyone to take you seriously.'

'Except that Susan is taking me seriously. She's no flirt. She would tell me to get lost if she wasn't interested.'

Ellie wondered if that were true. Perhaps it was. 'But you will lose interest as soon as she responds to you?' She heard the doubt in her voice.

And so did he. 'I can't promise. Somehow I don't think I will.'

She reflected that he was a man of many layers: there was the tough businessman on top, then the man who refused to take himself seriously, and then . . . a devoted husband and father? She said, 'Are you really a reformed rake?'

He treated her to his best, lopsided smile. 'I adore you, Mrs Quicke! What fun we could have had if we'd been of the same generation.'

She was amused. 'No chance! I go for the safe bet, not for rogues like you.' Then her smile faded. She had indeed gone for the safe bet in marrying her first husband, only to find out that he had a need to dominate everyone in sight. Yes, it had been a successful marriage in worldly terms, but only because she'd made herself into a doormat for him. After his early death, she'd learned to stand up for herself, with varying degrees of success. But she still quailed when her daughter Diana got on her high horse.

And then she'd met and married Thomas. She smiled, thinking of his loving care of her. She said, 'I suppose I must admit that Thomas is not a safe bet. He's thunder and lightning hidden behind a gentle frontage. He's a man for all seasons. At this moment he's supporting his friends through a bad patch like the rock that he is. When he comes home he'll be tired. He'll tell me what I need to know about what's happened. Perhaps he'll beat himself up a bit, saying that maybe he ought to have done even more to help his friends . . . which won't be true, and I shall tell him so. He'll spend a little while in his Quiet Room. Then he'll eat a hearty meal and we'll go to bed and hold one another and . . .' She blushed. 'Sorry. Too much information.'

He looked away from her. 'I have to confess, I have an uncle who was a minister. He used to give me piggyback rides when I was little and made me origami paper birds. He died last year. I miss him still.'

And so, another layer of his personality unfolds.

'You'll tell Susan that?'

'No need. She knows. She's been researching me.'

'She may not have found out everything she needs to know yet and she's not a person who can tolerate secrets.' Ellie shook herself back to the next task. 'I must ring the hospital and see what's happened to Lesley.'

'And I'll get back to work.' He disappeared down the corridor.

As Ellie dialled the hospital's number the front doorbell rang and someone used the knocker. 'Hello! Mrs Quicke? Are you there?'

Ellie knew that voice. *Andy! Well, at least he's surfaced.*

She let him in. He was unshaven, unkempt, short of sleep. But with a new focus. His chin seemed to have become more prominent overnight.

'Thanks,' he said to Ellie. He even sounded as if he meant it. 'I'm putting you to a lot of trouble, Mrs Quicke, expecting you to take me in. No key and no manners.' He twitched a smile.

For the first time, she caught an inkling of the charm Lesley had seen in him. She said, 'How is Lesley? They let you stay with her at the hospital? Did you get any sleep at all?'

'They say she's stable. They let me sleep in a chair beside her. I was glad to do so. We . . . er . . . held hands most of the night.' Almost, he blushed. But he was shyly proud of himself, too.

'Good for you,' said Ellie, meaning it. 'Now, when will they let her out?'

'She's going down to theatre any moment now.' He consulted his watch. 'She told me to go away and come back in three or four hours' time when she's on the recovery ward. If all goes well, they'll discharge her then.'

'And you'll bring her back here to be looked after?'

He grimaced. 'She says she can't impose on you any longer. She wants to go back home to the flat but that's impossible. I said I'd go round there, get some things she needs and see if it's possible for us to move back in. I can't imagine that it will be. She won't be able to do any cleaning or lifting for some time.'

'Of course not.' Why couldn't men clean up as well as women? Ah, well. If Andy hadn't been brought up to think that way it would be difficult to change him now. She said, 'You are both welcome to stay here.' She wouldn't tell him about Diana offering to get them another flat. They wouldn't have enough money to rent a second place. 'What do you need to get for her?'

'Some clothes and shampoo and stuff.' He braced himself. 'I'm not looking forward to it, but if that's what she wants I'll do it. I've checked with the police and they say that the girl they found in the garden died from an overdose, and I can go back into the flat and start clearing up if I wish. The only thing is . . .' He checked with Ellie. 'I must sound like a wimp but I'm dreading going in there by myself. And half the things Lesley wants, I won't even know where they are or what they look like. You wouldn't, you couldn't spare the time to come with me?'

Ellie thought she'd walked straight into that. Ugh. She'd got rid of her grandson for the moment, only to lumber herself with another man-child. 'I'd be glad to,' she said, trying to smile. 'You have a list?'

'I have.' He sought in his pockets and handed it over. 'I've been in touch with the insurance people again but there's no hope there. Of our own accord, we let Angelica and Susan have keys, and that invalidates our contract with them. It's a mess. We can't possibly live there at the moment. I think we'll have to move out, rent a flat somewhere else and then perhaps buy another place.'

There was another option, but until she saw the extent of the damage she wouldn't suggest it. On the other hand, 'My daughter is an estate agent. She's bringing round some details of places which might suit you this afternoon. She's a bit of a bully but she might be able to find you something. First, though, you'll want to shower, change your clothes and then have breakfast.' Hint, hint.

'You're an angel, Mrs Quicke.'

The way to a man's heart has always been through his stomach.

Ellie saw him off up the stairs, made various phone calls and sifted through the day's post before he came down, freshly shaved and in clean clothes. She sat him down in the kitchen with a substantial fry-up and some more coffee, and then went to update Rafael with Andy's news, ending . . . 'I reckon it'll take two or three hours to sort him out. If I leave the alarm on – I don't normally bother but we do have one for use when we go away on holidays, although I must admit that it's usually Thomas who sets it because I can't always remember which numbers to use – but if we set the alarm, you wouldn't have to stay here, would you? And can go off about your own business with a clear conscience?'

'Show me where you've written down the code for the alarm. You have written it down somewhere, haven't you? I'll follow you out and set the alarm. Then, when you're on your way back here, if you're uncertain about the code you can give me a ring and I'll be back before you to let you in. How does that sound?'

'You make me feel like a silly woman who needs a man to do everything for her.'

'I think you've a brain and a half, a heart bigger than London Town and that numbers are not your scene. That's fine by me.'

'Flatterer.' But she laughed. 'All right. It's a deal.'

Tuesday, mid-morning

Ellie told herself that the devastation at the flat could not possibly have rendered it uninhabitable. In her experience, men exaggerated the slightest disruption to the order of a household unless, of course, they'd created that disorder themselves, in which case they often swore that that was how they liked to live.

The first thing she noticed when they drew up outside the house was that the front window had been broken. That was the room which Lesley and Andy used as their main bedroom, wasn't it? Andy looked at it and winced.

He said, 'I've been trying to work out how much money we need to replace everything that's been broken or stolen. It's thousands! And I'd forgotten the window.'

Ellie got out of the car and made a beeline for the four large wheelie bins which the council had plonked on the tiny front garden. Two were marked for the upstairs flat and two for the ground floor one. She opened both. The upper flat's bins were half full. The ground floor ones were empty so they could tip a lot of broken stuff in those. Good.

Andy let them into the flat by the front door at the side of the house. At least the front door still closed and the lock still worked. There was a nasty smell of human waste.

Andy put his hand over his nose. 'I'll open some windows.' He hurried into the first room on the left – a tiny second bedroom – to do so.

Ellie stood in the hallway facing a big old upright piano, trying to remember what it was she ought to know about it. It took up so much space. It was an encumbrance. It had been wished upon Lesley by an aunt. Lesley hadn't known what to do with it, and it had ended up in the hallway. Before being taken to hospital, Lesley had told Ellie to get Andy to do something about the piano. Why?

Broken glass crunched under Ellie's feet as she stepped over to the piano and lifted the lid. Beer, or something stronger, had been spilt on the wood, removing the patina. The keys inside were yellowed and some had lost their ivory. She struck a note. Nothing. Dead.

There were some almost-empty beer glasses on the top of the piano, together with a lavatory roll and an electric kettle, for heaven's sake!

She called out, 'Andy!'

'Yes?' He'd moved on to the kitchen, banging open windows. 'What a pong! What is it?'

She removed the detritus from the top of the piano. 'Come here a sec.'

'What is it?' Andy appeared, looking harassed.

'Lesley was trying to tell me something about the piano and I can't remember what. Can you look inside it?'

'What? There's nothing.'

'No, not the keyboard. The top bit. I'm not tall enough to lift it up. You know, the bit the piano tuner takes off when he comes. He lifts up the top and puts it on the floor, then he takes off the whole front of the piano so that he can get at the wires. I don't have a piano but I remember that's what happened when he came to tune my mother's. There's quite a big space inside these old uprights. I think Lesley may have put some of your valuables in there before you left.'

'What?' But he obeyed her instructions. No sooner had he lifted off the lid than he exclaimed, 'What?' again, and withdrew first one and then two laptops, a jewellery box, a sheaf of papers and some bundles encased in bubble wrap. And then some wedding presents, still in their pretty containers.

'What?' he said yet again. He didn't seem to have a wide vocabulary, did he? 'My laptop, my grandfather's watch . . . the cup I got at school for . . . And her jewellery box! I was so angry with her for messing about in the flat when I was packing the car up. I suppose she had a last-minute panic about leaving these things out. But why didn't she tell me?'

Ellie didn't bother to reply to that.

Because you were busying yourself with the packing up of the car. Because you're an idiot. Because she was suffering from morning sickness and she didn't have the energy to explain.

He unwrapped some bubble wrap to show her a slightly tarnished cup engraved with his name. 'Irreplaceable,' he said.

'I'm so glad you've found it,' said Ellie. 'Perhaps you'd better put everything back for the time being? Or do you want to take them away with you now?'

'I've got an old suitcase under the bed. I'll put everything in that and lock them in the boot of the car. Thank God for my laptop. If only she'd told me! The trouble with her is that she doesn't think!'

Taking a small notepad and pencil from her handbag, Ellie tuned him out to survey what damage had been done to the rest of the flat.

Main bedroom: mucky bedding. Some drawers pulled out but nothing much seemed to be missing. Possibly this was where Gina – or was it Jess? – had been looking for a pair of jeans for Clay. Toiletries scattered. Broken window. Stains on the carpet.

The second, small bedroom. Hardly big enough to swing a cat. No wonder neither Angelica nor Susan had stayed long. It would be better to turn it into a study. Or a baby's room? Messed-up bed. Cupboards empty except for some winter bedding and coats wrapped in plastic. A beer bottle left on its side on the carpet . . . A stain on the carpet.

Bathroom. Ugh. A broken toilet which had leaked on to the floor. Sick in the bath. A foul smell. Carpet needs removing to the tip. Tiles would be better, anyway.

'Andy, can you get the bathroom window open?' Give the lad something to do and he might calm down.

Kitchen, partitioned off from the main sitting room by free-standing bookshelves. Vodka bottles, empty. Some broken. Beer and wine bottles, ditto. Crisp packets, empty. Cupboard doors left swinging open. Not a single unused glass to be seen. Or mug. Fridge door left open. Foul food inside. Floor needs a good clean. China and cutlery still in place. Pull-out larder fitment untouched. Oven, pristine. Microwave ditto. Water supply OK.

She went through to the sitting room which overlooked the garden. Stained carpet. Stained walls. Bottles, cups, glasses everywhere, some broken but some intact. Chairs overturned. One had its back snapped off. Cushions usually on the settee were piled in the corner for some reason. Not that much damage, really.

Andy gloomed his way into the sitting room. 'I've found the clothes she wants, I think. Can you help me with the toiletries?'

Ellie snapped her notepad shut. 'The damage is mostly superficial. A few hours with a team of cleaners and the place would look quite respectable. The carpets must be professionally cleaned. The window can be replaced within an hour. The chair can be repaired. The broken toilet is another matter. Shall I get on to my cleaning agency and see what they can do for you?'

'What! But . . . it's impossible!'

Ellie was beginning to get just the teeniest bit tired of this great clod of earth. She held on to her patience. 'I can have a team of cleaners and a plumber here within the hour. Do you want me to organize it or not?'

If he says 'What!' again, I'm going to clock him one.

He said, 'But . . .!'

'The cost? Nothing like the amount you'd have to pay to replace your two laptops.'

'But . . .!'

She pulled out her mobile and got hold of Maria at the cleaning agency. 'I'm sorry I interrupted your evening yesterday, Maria. There was an emergency. And now I have another one. A friend of mine and his wife have had their flat wrecked by an illegal rave or party or whatever they call them. She's in hospital after having a miscarriage and he doesn't know how to cope. Could you rustle up a good team to sort him out? Today. Yes, his wife will be coming out of hospital this afternoon with a bit of luck and I'll put them up overnight, but understandably she wants to get back home as soon as possible. Oh, and I'll need a plumber and someone to replace a pane of glass. If you can't get hold of someone . . . you can? Brilliant. I'll just run through what needs to be done, shall I?'

She signed to Andy to right a chair for her and used another to place her notepad on. He seemed unable to grasp the fact that things could be righted so quickly.

When she'd gone through her list, Ellie said, 'Send the bill to me and I'll sort it out later. Do you think you can get someone started on it this afternoon?'

Maria had a laugh in her voice. 'Well, Annie's free. She's refused to work with Betty any more. Neither would she tell me why, so I told them both to go home until they could work together again. Betty says she's not going to work for me any more but Annie will. I could pair her with . . . Yes, I'll have to ring round but I think I can find someone else. I know Annie will be glad of the extra hours if you can run to a spot of overtime. The plumber . . . Yes, can do. He may be able to do the window as well, but if not he'll know someone who can.'

'Brilliant! I'll hand you over to my friend who can tell you where his flat is and how you can get hold of a key.' She passed her phone over to Andy.

Fortunately Andy didn't respond with a 'What?' this time but managed to sound reasonably efficient while he gave Maria directions to the flat.

When he'd finished, Ellie said she wanted to look at the garden and asked if he would show her where Kate's body had been found.

'How should I know? She'd been taken away by the time we got here.' But he took Ellie outside and along past the sitting-room windows to a patio, which was also glittering with broken glass. Beyond that was a small lawn surrounded by shrubs, with a pond to one side. Dividing this property from the next was a tall fence partially disguised with a privet hedge. A small, rather dilapidated garden shed stood in one corner, the door ajar to show it sheltered a lawnmower and shelves of tools, empty plastic pots and so on.

A pair of jeans had been left by the tide, confirming Jess's story. Andy swooped on them. 'My best jeans! What are they doing here? Well, they'll have to be cleaned before I wear them again.'

The pond was small and kidney shaped. It probably measured five feet at its widest and wouldn't be very deep. It had been made by some long-ago gardener in the days before supermarkets sold plastic moulded in different shapes, or even before the time when you dug a hole, lined it with sand, placed a liner on top of that and hoped it wouldn't leak when filled with water. This pond had been made of concrete. There wasn't much water in it so it had probably sprung a leak in recent years.

Andy pointed to an area beyond the pond. 'They told me she was found there.' A trampled-down area of shrubs hinted at what had lain there but Ellie was more interested in the pond itself. There weren't any fish in it, nor plants. The level of the water was low and its colour was greenish to brown. Unappetizing. She imagined that any fish put in there would immediately express their disgust by dying.

The rim of the pond – as the party girls had said – was rounded. The grass of the lawn overlapped the edging here and there. Altogether, it was a depressing sight.

She said, 'You are no gardener, Andy?'

'I have better things to do with my time at weekends.'

'I remember. You play cricket.'

'Until Lesley cracked my knee.' He hadn't been limping up till that point, but now he remembered his ailments and rubbed the offending joint.

'What's that?' Ellie pointed to a dark stain on the side of the pond nearest the house. 'I'm told Clay got dumped in the pond at one point. Apparently he sat there with his knees up to his chin and they all had a good laugh, except for one of the girls, who is tender-hearted and helped him out.' She wouldn't mention that Jess had borrowed Andy's jeans for Clay. Andy had got them back, hadn't he? Clay had never got as far as changing into them.

She said, 'That dark stain on the edge of the pond – what do you think it is? Blood?'

'What? Why should there be any blood there? The police didn't say anything about the girl shedding blood. And anyway, she was way over on the other side of the pond, a good six feet or more.'

If only Rafael were here. He'd understand the importance of that stain, wouldn't he? But this man is . . . ugh!

She made her voice calm. 'Yes, I can see where she was found.' She bent over, licked her finger and rubbed at the dark stain. And tasted it. It tasted of dirt. Perhaps a little metallic? She didn't really know what it should taste like. In her opinion, the police had been remiss in not testing that stain. Although, to be fair, if Kate had been found lying in the shrubs and there was no sign on her of blunt force trauma, the police wouldn't have seen the significance of that stain on the pond. If there'd been a second body, however . . . But there hadn't, had there?

She said, 'Can you taste this stain for me?'

'Why on earth should I?'

She refrained – just – from rolling her eyes.

He really is a boor. I can't think why Lesley wanted to marry him.

She turned back to the house. 'Well, let's get the toiletries Lesley has asked for, shall we? And then perhaps you can make a list of what's been destroyed. The glasses, mainly. Do you know how many you had before?'

'Lesley deals with all that.'

She tried not to bite her tongue, which would only hurt. 'Well, perhaps if you buy half a dozen to start with, that would plug the gap. And some more toilet paper. The food that's left in the fridge will have to be thrown away. Perhaps we should start on that now and, before you know it, Annie and her new partner will be here and will sweep through the place in no time.'

'You think you can wave a fairy wand and everything will be back to normal in a trice?'

I think you're the most selfish man I've met in a long time. If Lesley sticks with you for any length of time I'll be extremely surprised. What's more, I shall cheer her on when she leaves you. Or pushes you out. It's a nice thought that the flat is in her name.

She said, 'Let's look at the toiletries, then, and make a shopping list for later. After all, you can't expect Lesley to come back from hospital to face an empty fridge and nothing to drink out of.'

'Do as you please. I wash my hands of it.'

I am seriously going to clock you one! No, I won't. I really don't want to be had up for murder. Or would it be justifiable homicide? I need Thomas to tell me which it would be. And he'd calm me down, too.

She managed to force a smile. 'Then let me have the list of things Lesley's asked for and I'll check it over, shall I? You can drop me back home as soon as Annie and her new partner arrives.'

'You're not going to leave me alone to deal with all this? I thought I could rely on you to help me.'

'Didn't I come with you? Haven't I arranged a clean-up for you? Now I have to go back home as I'm looking after my grandson this afternoon.'

'Well, you can't expect me to drive you if I have to wait here for your cleaners to arrive.'

'Very well. I shall ring for a taxi. Now, you know what to do next? Find a dustpan and brush, and some thick gloves to protect your hands, and start dealing with the broken glass. Fortunately your wheelie bin is empty and you can dump everything in there. And then . . .'

He wasn't listening.

She gave up on him and phoned for a cab.

SIXTEEN

On the way home, Ellie told herself she ought to be more patient in her dealings with Andy. The poor man was under considerable stress. On the other hand, she didn't have to stay at his side and hold his hand one minute more than was necessary, did she?

Perhaps he felt she was being difficult, too.

Anyway, she wanted to be home when her grandson arrived. She'd never hear the end of it if Diana arrived to find the house empty.

Passing through the Avenue, she found she was hungry and asked the cab driver to stop outside the Village Bakery. She bought some of their spinach and cheese pastries, a soft scone for Evan, some more bread and one of the bakery's egg and bacon rolls, which were far too much for her to eat but which she thought Rafael could manage. And, remembering his offer to return if needed, she dialled his number to say she was on the way home with some lunch but had remembered the code for the alarm, if he was busy. And if not, did he fancy a bite to eat with her?

She really didn't want to be alone in the house at the moment. Milos might have been diverted but, on the other hand, he might not.

Rafael arrived at the house before her. He'd showered and shaved. He was wearing a dark-green silk shirt and matching waistcoat with tailored black trousers. Very fetching. Instead of a motor bike, a discreet but expensive Audi had been parked in her driveway.

She said, 'Just in time for lunch. I hope you're hungry. And I've got lots to tell you.'

She'd thought Rafael would be interested in that stain on the side of the pond, and indeed he was.

'Can you describe the stain? What colour was it?'

'Black. About eight inches across? Blob-shaped. I did wet my finger to see if I could taste it, but that wasn't much good as I don't really know what blood tastes like.'

'Metallic.' He stared off into the distance.

When Ellie got up to make them a pot of tea, he said, 'Kate didn't bang her head in the garden, did she? So whose blood is it on the side of the pond. I wonder if—'

'Clay. Yes, I think so. He wasn't in any of the wheelie bins outside the house, though.'

'What? You have a weird imagination.'

'I know.' She was cheerful about it.

The front doorbell rang.

Ellie shot to her feet. 'Diana! How could I forget? I'm babysitting for my grandson this afternoon.'

Diana was beating a tattoo on the bell. Impatient as always. 'Come on, Mother! You know how busy I am. Hurry up! Evan's been complaining about feeling sick and I really can't be doing with that in my car. Here, take these!'

She handed Ellie a clutch of papers advertising flats to rent and for sale. Ellie nearly let them slip as she helped Evan out of his car seat. He was clutching Hippo, his favourite soft toy, but his colour wasn't good.

Before Ellie could get the little boy into the house, Diana had driven off with a spurt of gravel.

'Evan dear, do you really feel sick?'

Evan shook his head. He was languid and heavy-eyed. He made heavy weather of mounting the step into the porch and was brought up short by seeing a strange man in the hall.

Rafael and Evan stared at one another. Sizing one another up. Which was the alpha male in these circumstances?

Evan took one wobbly step forward and . . . uh-oh! . . . up it all came.

Evan wailed his discomfort and dropped his favourite toy, the velvety soft pink hippopotamus.

Ellie dumped the fliers Diana had given her on the shelf in the hall and took Evan off to the cloakroom to wash him and the toy down.

Rafael – good for him – got a mop from the kitchen and cleaned up the mess on the floor.

Ellie sat Evan on her lap in the kitchen and gave him tiny sips of water to drink. He wasn't really hot. He hadn't got a fever. He wasn't ill. He'd had an overloaded stomach and he'd unloaded it.

He began to revive.

Rafael washed his hands at the sink. 'So, little one, what have you been eating?'

Evan turned his head away from Rafael. No answer.

Rafael sat down near Ellie and said, again, 'You've been stuffing your face with something you hadn't oughta?'

Evan whispered something. Ellie bent down to hear him.

He whispered again, still ignoring Rafael.

Ellie hid a smile. 'Oh, dear. You shouldn't have done that, Evan. Just look what's happened.'

Evan pushed himself off her lap and landed on the floor with a thump. Then he made for the sitting room, where he emptied his big box of Lego out on to the floor.

Ellie said, 'Thank you, Rafael. Someone at the nursery didn't fancy his lunch, so Evan ate his share as well as his own. No wonder he was sick. I'd better keep an eye on him.'

Rafael followed her into the sitting room. 'My nephew, aged four, ate not only his own Easter egg but also his sister's. She was furious and he chucked up the lot. Do you suppose everyone has to overeat before they discover the consequences? I don't think I did. But then, I haven't got a sweet tooth.'

Evan was happily stirring Lego pieces around on the floor. Ellie dithered. 'He seems settled now and I really ought to clean up in the kitchen.'

'What you mean is, can I be trusted to watch the lad while you go about your business?'

He'd got that right. She took a step towards the door. Evan paused in his play but didn't scream for her return. She left the room, walking slowly so that he could call her back if he weren't happy at being left with Rafael. But Evan didn't call her back, and Rafael seemed happy to sit and watch the lad, so she left them to it.

What to do first? She checked to see if there were any messages on the phone in the hall. Nothing. Good. She hadn't finished dealing with the morning's post. Did she have time to do that before anything else happened? And, she must ring the hospital to see how Lesley was doing. She lifted the receiver on the phone in the hall, only to put it down again as Evan came out of the sitting room and toddled off down the corridor with Hippo clutched under his arm. Followed at a distance by Rafael. Evan was going for a nap in the Quiet Room? Oh, dear.

Yes, he turned in there, leaving the door ajar.

She told Rafael, 'Diana really doesn't like him taking a nap in the afternoons because he doesn't sleep through the night afterwards. But after having had an upset stomach, I expect he needs it. Hopefully he won't be out for long. He'll be safe in the Quiet Room. He'll pull a couple of cushions off the chairs and doss down on the floor for maybe half an hour. I'll have to wake him after that, if he's not woken of his own accord.'

Someone rang the doorbell. Sharply. Insistently.

Ellie sighed. 'No peace for the wicked. Who can that be?'

A woman's voice. 'Let me in!'

Angelica? Surely not!

'Please, please, please. You won't regret it, I promise!'

Rafael rubbed his chin. He was doubtful about trusting the girl, and who could blame him?

Ellie hesitated. 'I suppose . . . she does hold the answer to a number of important questions. I'll let her in. But don't let's leave her alone at any time, right?' Ellie swung the door open.

Angelica was on the doorstep. 'Surprise!' she cried, thrusting her left hand in Ellie's face.

A diamond ring sparkled. 'Oh, I'm so happy! You must congratulate me!' Angelica enveloped Ellie in a bear hug, rocking her to and fro. 'Where's Andy? I've got to tell Andy and that cow he's married. Won't she half be cross! Yes, Rafael – I'm getting married and I've got your money, and some for Mrs Quicke, too. So champagne is in order, right?'

Angelica danced around the hall, leaving a trace of expensive scent behind her. She'd been shopping again. Her outfit was brand new and right up to the minute: an apology for a skirt, a fitted bodice-style top and high heels. 'I can stay here till the wedding, can't I, Mrs Quicke? It's going to be soon, soon, soon! Oh, let me give you your money. I told you I'd repay you, didn't I? Aren't I a good girl? And do you think I should ask our desperate wallflower, Susan, to be my one and only bridesmaid? What do you think?'

She opened a brand-new handbag – Ellie could smell the leather from where she stood – and brought out an envelope. From this she extracted a cheque which she handed to Rafael. 'There! For you, my good, kind friend, who helped me out when I was in such trouble! Payment in full. And for you, Mrs Quicke, although we never really worked out how much I should pay you in rent, I've got a cheque for you, too, which should cover it and leave some over for the gas and all the other nasty household bills, right?'

Ellie gaped at the cheque put into her hand. Made out to her. Six hundred pounds, which was more than enough.

Except that she didn't feel like taking it.

'Don't look so cross, dear Mrs Quicke, it's a perfectly valid cheque. And I've got some more money to pay off all my credit cards. Isn't that brilliant?'

Rafael looked dazed. 'How did you come by this money?'

Angelica was airy. 'I asked Jake and he gave it to me, the dear love that he is! I assure you that the cheque won't bounce.'

Rafael said, 'It's drawn on his father's business account.'

Angelica said, 'Jake says nothing is too good for his little sweetie pie. From now on it's caviar and champagne all the way for his little wife-to-be.'

Ellie removed her thumb from the bottom right-hand corner of the cheque. It was indeed a business account but the name printed on the cheque meant nothing to her. There were two signatures, as is often the case for business accounts. One was illegible. The other was . . . she held it closer to her eyes to make sure . . . that of Jake Hartley Summers.

Jake had bailed Angelica out? And given her a ring?

Rafael had doubts, too. 'You mean that you and Jake—?'

Angelica dimpled. 'Isn't this fun? I should take you both out for lunch, I suppose, but really, you're both looking too sad and dreary for that. This is the happiest day of my life. I must ring my mother and tell her to get herself a decent outfit for the wedding.'

Rafael said, 'How did you get Jake to raid the company's coffers for you?'

A tiny shrug. 'He wants me to have everything I need to make me happy. He hadn't enough in his personal account, or not till the end of the month, and of course his father trusts him with paying certain bills.'

'Not to this amount, I'm sure.'

'Oh, you're such a killjoy! I tell you, Jake can make it right at the end of the month. So stop being such a grouch and cash it. I owe you that much, don't I?'

'Yes, you do. But . . .' Rafael made as if to tear the cheque in two but stopped himself and looked at Ellie. 'What do you think, Mrs Quicke? I have a feeling Jake misused his position in the family business to pay us off.'

Ellie was still looking at her cheque. 'I agree. It raises some other interesting questions, doesn't it? Angelica, I'm not accepting this cheque because, if I do, it means you've paid me for renting a room and that would make you a tenant. I don't want that. I don't want you in my house. So I'm tearing up this cheque . . .' And she did so, into tiny pieces. 'And now, once again, I'm asking you to leave my house. Go back to your mother's. Move in with Jake if you wish.'

Angelica pouted. 'Oh, dear Mrs Quicke, I know you don't mean that. And I'm far too happy to let you upset me. I suppose I did behave badly in the past, but that is all behind me and the future is golden. I know you won't grudge me my good fortune. I want to get married from this house. Don't you think that's a splendid idea? We can have the reception here in the hall and eat in the dining room, spilling over into the sitting room at the back, and even into the garden if we have a marquee, which I'm not sure about, but that would be fab, wouldn't it?'

Ellie's brain went into shock.

Angelica waltzed around the hall. 'We can have the wedding cake here at the bottom of the stairs. I shall throw my bridal bouquet into the air but not in darling Susan's direction as I really don't think she's likely, being the dumpling that she is, ever to have men asking her to marry her.'

Rafael said, 'I wouldn't mind.'

Angelica couldn't stop spinning her fantasy. 'I shall wear a white gown with a low back and a small train. I'm thinking a sort of Grecian robe and flowers in my hair but not a veil. Veils do get in the way, don't they?'

Ellie grabbed at her composure and nearly missed. For two pins she would have taken hold of Angelica and shaken some sense into her. Fortunately she managed to damp down her outrage and forced herself to speak calmly. Or almost calmly. 'Angelica, come into the sitting room. We need to talk.'

Angelica dimpled. 'Mrs Quicke wants to haul naughty little me over the coals for causing so much trouble, and I must take my scolding in the spirit in which it is intended, right? Oh, and darling Mrs Quicke, is that good coffee that I can smell? Would it be possible for me to have a cup? Not in a mug, but in a bone china cup and saucer. When I'm married I'm going to ban mugs in the house. Soooo ordinary.'

She bounced into the sitting room and, confronted by the pile of Lego pieces which Evan had strewn on the floor earlier, walked carefully around them to arrange herself prettily on the settee.

Ellie muttered to herself, 'This has got to stop!'

And then, *I need to think.*

Giving herself time to think meant that she acceded to Angelica's request for a cup of coffee. By the time she'd made another cafetière and carried a tray of coffee cups and saucers back into the sitting room, she knew what she should try to do.

She poured coffee.

Angelica was peering out of the window. 'The lawn is big enough for a marquee, isn't it?'

'Yes,' said Ellie. She took a cup over to Rafael and, as she put it on the side table, leaned over to say, 'You've got one of those new phones, haven't you? That can record conversations?'

He nodded, narrowing his eyes, and took his phone out of his pocket.

Ellie put a second cup down on the coffee table beside the settee. 'Here's your coffee, Angelica. Come and sit down. I need to ask you a few questions.'

'Oh, must I?' A pretty pout. But she did as requested.

Ellie took her own seat, noting out of the corner of her eye that Rafael had placed his phone on a cushion beside him. Not far from Angelica.

'First,' said Ellie, 'I need to get the timings for Saturday night straight in my mind. Angelica, you went to Lesley's flat to start the party off. Clay was there, selling drugs—'

'I didn't know that!' Perfect innocence shone in her blue eyes.

'Oh, yes, you did. And, by the way, have you a cheque for Milos as well?'

She smiled. A catlike, satisfied little smile. 'Oh, no. What he did was illegal so I don't have to pay him.'

Ellie gaped. The stupidity of the girl made Ellie feel giddy. 'I dare say you are correct in law, but you will have to face him sometime.'

'That's all right.' A shining smile. 'You can tell the police all about him. They'll arrest him for selling drugs and put him in jail, and serve him right.'

'I see what you mean,' said Ellie, feeling rather faint. 'But as I have no first-hand knowledge of the party, I doubt if the police will act on my say-so. You will have to tell the police yourself.'

'Oh, no. I'd be much too frightened to do that!'

Ellie took a deep breath. 'Well, let's leave that aside for the moment. Let's return to the party. Everything was going well, perhaps a little too noisy, but no one had called the police yet. Jake arrived and didn't care for what he saw. Then Kate arrived looking for Jake. You managed to prevent their meeting. You went outside with Jake, who refused to stay and drove away. Timmy Lee came out to console you. You and Timmy went off with the intention of going to a nightclub. On the way there, you changed your mind and asked Timmy to drop you off here. Have I got all that right?'

'Yes, of course. I came straight back here and went to bed.'

'What time would that have been?'

A pretty shrug. 'I'm not sure. Midnight? One o'clock?'

'So when did the fight occur?'

'Just before I left. Just before Jake left. Clay was bleeding. Someone had bopped him on the nose. So he thrust his bag at me and left to go to hospital.'

'You forgot to put that bit in your timetable just now.'

'I was so distracted, I didn't know what I was doing.'

'Other partygoers tell me there was no fight, that Clay wasn't hit on the nose, that he didn't bleed and wasn't taken off to hospital.'

'Really? I assure you that's exactly what happened. How else could I have got hold of his stash?'

'Indeed. And how did you get hold of Kate's purse and jewellery?'

Angelica hardly missed a beat. 'Oh, Susan took that. Didn't we find it in her rooms?'

'Susan didn't go to the party and can prove it. Also, there were two important things missing from Kate's purse: her money and her mobile phone.'

'I expect Susan has made use of them.'

Ellie leaned forward and picked up Angelica's brand-new handbag. Angelica made a furious swipe but missed. 'Give me that back!'

'In a minute.' Ellie opened the bag and retrieved a pink, sparkly phone. Kate's phone? Ellie said, 'You gave your own phone to Rafael yesterday in part payment of your debt to him, so whose is this? It's Kate's, isn't it? If I give it to the police they'll be able to trace all the calls she made on it.'

Angelica flapped her eyelashes as she thought how to counter this. 'Oh, well. I forgot to say that Timmy Lee came round to see me on Sunday morning, after you'd all been so terribly pious and gone to church. He asked me to look after a bag of his girlfriend's things for him. I didn't look inside. Why should I? I just popped it into the safest place I could think of.'

'Nonsense. Your fingerprints were on that purse, or you wouldn't have tried to stop me putting it in a plastic bag for the police to look at.'

'I was just curious to see whose it was, that's all. Was it really Kate's? How very odd. I suppose Timmy went back to . . .' Her eyes switched from side to side. 'He must have gone back to the flat on Sunday morning for some reason. Perhaps he'd dropped his watch or something. And found Kate dead and . . .' She shuddered deliciously. 'Do you think he really might have found her dead and . . . and robbed her?' Eyes enormous, mouth quivering.

She really was some actress.

Ellie said, 'Timmy Lee came to see me. I couldn't understand why at the time. Now I suppose he came to make sure that you and he were using the same script. I don't think he trusts you, Angelica. With reason, don't you think?'

'Timmy isn't a great friend of mine. I've only known him for a short time. I really don't know whether or not I could trust him with something important.' Huge eyes.

'I don't think you can trust him as far as you can throw him. Not when you're going to drop him in it for murdering Kate.'

'Oh, oh! How could you say that! He didn't murder anyone!'

That sounded like the truth. 'How do you know that?'

'Well, he said.' A delicious little wriggle. 'Kate was dead when he found her. He was worried that I might be involved in her death so he took her things to delay identification.'

'His family aren't going to be pleased if he's arrested for stealing from a corpse. There is a law against doing that, you know.'

Angelica pouted. 'Really? Are you sure? Well, I had no idea what he was up to.'

Rafael leaned forward. 'Milos is looking for Clay's body.'

Angelica started, and her colour faded. 'What! What did you say?'

'Did you kill him? Or did Timmy Lee?'

Angelica scrambled to her feet. 'No, neither of us! I swear it! I swear!'

Incredibly, it sounded like the truth.

Rafael said, 'Then who did?'

'No one!' She wrung her hands. 'Oh, how could you say such a thing? I thought you were my friends! How could you even think of . . . Oh, Oh, Oh!' Tears ready to fall. She began to pace up and down. 'I'm innocent, I am! I wouldn't hurt a fly! I didn't kill Kate—'

'No, of course you didn't. She died of a drug which Clay had given her.'

'There you are then! She did it to herself! I said so all along!'

'Said to who?'

'To . . . to Timmy, of course.'

'No. You said it to Jake.'

'He wasn't there!'

'Sit down again, Angelica. Let's go through your timetable again. Jake came to the party. Kate arrived but didn't see him. Jake left. You went off with Timmy. You were not there for the next act in the tragedy.'

'Of course I wasn't there. I've said so, all along. I don't know how you can think I was responsible for anything else that happened.'

'Let's go over what we know. Kate was stranded in the garden with the party girls, Jess and Gina, the photographer Big Scotty, their driver Wilf . . . and Clay. And that was when the fight occurred, if you could call it that. Big Scotty dumped Clay in the pond. Gina, Big Scotty and Wilf departed. The party in the flat was winding down. Clay, Jess and Kate were left in the garden. Kate was hysterical, wanting to get Jake back. Jess also departed, leaving Kate and Clay alone. The last thing Jess saw was Kate on the phone to Jake, begging him to return.'

'I have no idea what went on,' said Angelica, listening hard. 'I wasn't there.'

'No, you'd gone clubbing with Timmy Lee. You really had. But while you were at the club you got a phone call from Jake, who'd gone home. He'd had a hysterical phone call from Kate, saying she'd taken some drug or other, possibly intimating that she was going to commit suicide unless he got back to her. Jake thought that you, Angelica, would still be at the party, so he phoned you, not realizing you'd left straight after him. He wanted you to deal with the situation, to get Kate to hospital or whatever. He told you he was on his way back to the flat himself. You agreed to get back yourself, as quickly as you could. You asked Timmy Lee to give you a lift. The two of you got there to find Kate dying and Clay trying to resuscitate her, without success. I don't know whether or not Kate could have been saved if you'd got her straight to hospital, but it didn't happen.'

'She was already dead. Still warm, but not breathing.'

'So which of you killed Clay?'

Angelica licked her lips. 'No one. I went inside. I was upset. I didn't see anything. They came and told me, afterwards, that Clay was dead.'

'Was it Timmy who killed him, or Jake?'

A toss of the head. 'I have no idea. Neither of them. Jake wasn't there. How could you think that I'd get mixed up in anything like that?'

Rafael sighed. 'It must have been Jake. He'd grown up with Kate. They'd dated for years. It was assumed by both their families that one day they'd marry. Jake wasn't head over heels in love with Kate but he was comfortable with her. Then he met you, Angelica, and he sidelined Kate. When he heard that Kate had gone to the party looking for him, and that she was threatening to take some drug or other, he realized how much a part of his life she was. He didn't want her to die. If he'd got there in time he might have saved her, but he didn't. He would have felt guilt and anger. He would want to lash out at somebody.'

'No, no. Jake didn't do anything. It was Timmy!'

'Why should Timmy want to do Clay an injury? He wasn't attached to Kate in any way. All he'd done was chauffeur you around, Angelica. I think Jake did respond to Kate's frantic telephone calls.

He got back to the flat only to realize Kate had been as good as her word and had taken the drug which Clay had offered her. And died. Then, out of guilt and remembrance of all the years he and Kate had known one another, he killed Clay. How did he do it, Angelica?'

She wailed, 'I don't know! I didn't see. I went to the loo when I saw what happened to Kate. Jake said, afterwards, that he hadn't meant it. He knocked Clay for six. Clay fell back and hit his head on the edge of the pond, and he never moved again. And none of it was my fault!'

SEVENTEEN

'So, at long last, you admit that Jake was there.'

Angelica sniffed and looked away.

Ellie tried to work out what had happened. 'If what you say is true, then Kate's death was misadventure, which is why the police have closed the case except for looking for her supplier. If Jake had refrained from taking out his anger and loss on Clay but had rung the police when he saw that Kate was dead, then they would have arrested Clay for supplying the drug and Jake would have been in the clear.'

'Clay would have faced a prison sentence,' said Rafael.

'True. But not perhaps a very long one. Only, Jake hit Clay and killed him. Could he be charged with murder?'

Rafael shook his head. 'It wasn't murder. There was no premeditation. His action is understandable in a way. Jake lashed out at Clay in his distress, not meaning to kill him. His solicitor will probably tell him to plead that it was an accident. If the jury believe him, he might get off with a slap on the wrist. If they don't, he'll go down for manslaughter.'

'Noooo,' wailed Angelica. 'He can't go to prison. It was an accident.'

'Yes, if you'd reported it to the police straight away,' said Ellie. 'But you didn't. Jake and Timmy between them disposed of the body, didn't they?'

'How should I know?'

'Come on, you were there. You saw everything. How did they manage it?'

'I don't know!' Tears flowed. 'I said they shouldn't tell me. They took Clay off for a ride in the boot of Jake's car.'

'While you robbed Kate's body?'

'No, no! That was . . . you see . . . I wanted to keep it all a secret till I had time to think. I thought it would be a good idea if I took her things so no one would know who she was.'

'You also took Clay's stash and his money?'

'Yes, but I gave half the money to—'

'Timmy Lee. For his trouble. Ugh!' Rafael looked sick.

Ellie said, 'How long did Jake and Timmy take to get rid of the body?'

'Not long. They said they'd only had to go round the block. I don't know what they did with the body.'

'What was Clay wearing?'

'How should I know? I don't notice such things.'

'Think!'

'Well, I think maybe a black, zip-up hoodie over a black T-shirt. Jeans. Trainers. The usual.'

'The men didn't tell you where they'd dumped him?'

Angelica shook her head.

Ellie said, 'They only went around the block? Now, where . . .?'

Rafael interrupted her, addressing Angelica, 'So that's why Jake has given you a ring and stolen money from his firm. You're black-mailing him into marrying you.'

'No, no!' screamed Angelica. 'He loves me, he really does!'

Rafael was remorseless. 'You've overlooked the fact that you and Jake have saddled yourselves with an accomplice in the person of Timmy Lee. What has he asked you to do for him? He has been on to you, hasn't he? What did he want?'

'Nothing! You're frightening me!'

Rafael made a sound of disgust. 'You do realize you're going to have him on your back for evermore, bleeding you white? So, what is the price of his silence?'

'Nothing! He's been wonderful! I won't hear a word against him. I gave him nearly all the money from Clay's belt and he said that was enough.'

Rafael followed this up. 'But he came round to see Mrs Quicke to find out what she knew. He doesn't trust you, Angelica. And quite right, too. So how are you going to keep his mouth shut in future?'

'Jake will . . . I'm sure that—'

'You think Jake will kill him, too?'

Angelica took refuge in noisy sobs. 'Oh, you're being horrible to me! How could you even think such a thing?'

'I'm reading your mind, my dear. Don't tell me you haven't

thought this through, because I wouldn't believe you. Have you discussed killing Timmy Lee with Jake yet?'

Angelica squealed, 'Oh, how could you! I wouldn't! You're being beastly!'

The phone rang. Ellie drifted out to answer it. She was thinking hard. Where would those two men have stashed a corpse in the middle of the night?'

She picked up the phone.

'Well?' It was Milos again. 'You think someone killed Clay – if so, where did they put the corpse and why?'

'Why? To delay it being found. And to stop you from jumping on them.'

'But where?'

'Somewhere in the block where the party was held,' said Ellie. 'My first thought was that you should look for a house which has got scaffolding up or the builders in. They could dump the body inside that, away from the road. But then I thought the builders would have discovered a corpse when they returned to work yesterday, and there's been no indication of that, no flashing lights or police cars. Then I thought that, if there was a house for sale, they might have put the body there.'

'The estate agent might have been showing people round yesterday.'

'I don't think it's inside the house. I think . . . it's a horrid thought . . . we all have these big wheelie bins for rubbish nowadays, don't we? They're really big. I heard someone's aunt actually fell inside one when she was trying to clean it out. Her cries for help were heard by a neighbour but she couldn't get out by herself. Clay wasn't a very big man, was he?'

'Jesus, Mary and Joseph!' He clicked off.

Indeed. We need all the help we can get on this one. But, goodness gracious, is Milos a Catholic? How can a drug dealer be a Catholic? Maybe he was brought up in the Catholic Church and has forgotten what being a Christian means until now, when he's brought face-to-face with the death of one of his employees?

A bitter wail brought Ellie back to the present as little Evan came staggering down the corridor towards her, dragging his pink hippo by one of its ears behind him. 'Ganny, Ganny, Ganny!' It was his version of 'Granny'.

Ellie picked him up and gave him a cuddle. One cheek was flushed and he felt slightly hot. Was he teething? Uh-oh. If so, he wouldn't be his usual happy self until the tooth broke through the gum.

Evan buried his face in her shoulder and snuffled. Then raised his head and wailed again. 'Hurts!'

'Teething?' said Rafael, who had followed her into the hall. 'My sister rubs their gums with something which knocks them out for a while. It's probably against doctor's advice but it works.'

Ellie rocked from one foot to the other. 'Poor little boy. Teeth are a pain, coming and going, aren't they? Your mum refuses to let me use anything which I can buy over the counter . . .' She met Rafael's disbelieving eyes and grinned. 'But yes, I do have a bottle of something which I bought at the chemist's and it does seem to help. Come along, little man.' Halfway to the kitchen, she called back, 'Rafael, you haven't left your phone in the sitting room, have you?'

In other words, could Angelica have spotted he was recording her words and have taken advantage of his momentary absence to snaffle his phone?

He lifted it in his hand to show her he still had it. 'Teach your grandmother.'

She smiled. No, he wouldn't have let that happen, would he? Ellie sat Evan in the big chair in the kitchen. Once his gum had been rubbed, he relaxed. Instant relief. Instant happiness . . . so long as Diana didn't find out. A cup of milk in a short while would disguise the distinctive aroma of the medicine.

She switched on the light. A sudden rainstorm rattled at the windows and the sky had turned dark grey. Ellie had hoped to take Evan out in the garden, or for a walk around the block, but she wouldn't do that in the rain. She was washing the tears off his face when the doorbell rang.

Now what? She didn't want to leave Evan alone in the kitchen, knowing what havoc he might create. She would have to take him with her, whether he wanted to be moved or not.

He didn't want to be moved. He expressed his disapproval by hitting her with Hippo, and throwing himself backwards as she picked him up.

Well, tough! Someone was at the door and . . .

What was that? Someone had opened the front door with a key?

But who had a key? Not Andy, no. Susan had one, of course, but Susan wouldn't leave her class at this time of day, would she?

'Hulloa!'

Ellie struggled along the corridor with Evan in her arms, trying to hurry but, oh, Evan was getting far too large for her to carry . . . And there was Jake Hartley Summers, Angelica's fiancé, standing in the hall. Surprise!

The light in the hall was dim. Raindrops shimmered on the shoulders of his coat. Ellie hardly recognized the man. His skin was sallow. He looked as if he'd aged ten years overnight. He was wearing business gear but his tie was awry and his shirt was not pristine.

Perhaps that was what being blackmailed into marriage did for you?

Or was it guilt at having murdered Clay?

Evan filled his lungs and roared into her ear. She put him down on the floor, holding on to him with a hand on the back of his blue dungarees. He tried to pull away. She held on but had to take a couple of steps as he threw all his weight against her. If she let go, he'd crash on to the floor . . . and then he'd raise the roof, wouldn't he just!

Angelica appeared in the doorway. 'Oh, darling Jake! I'm so glad you came. I just don't know how I'm to get through the hours till we're married. Come here and give me a kiss.'

He ignored Angelica to greet Ellie with a smile that flashed on and off without warmth. 'Good afternoon, Mrs Quicke. Forgive the intrusion. I did ring the bell, but when there was no reply I used the key Angelica gave me.'

How many keys had Angelica had made? And she'd given one to Jake? Well, at least that one could be retrieved without too much aggro. Still holding on to Evan, who was panting to get away, Ellie held out her free hand. 'Thank you for bringing the key back. I'm grateful.'

He hesitated, but finally drew a key out of his pocket and handed it over.

Evan swiped at Ellie's leg with his hippo. It didn't hurt, but she was caught unawares and relaxed her hold on him enough to let

him slide out of her grasp and away into the sitting room. He
ignored Angelica, making a beeline for the pieces of Lego which
he'd emptied on to the floor earlier. At least he'd stopped yelling.

Angelica, dimpling, stepped coyly to Jake's side and presented
her cheek for a kiss. 'My sweetie, lovey-pie. Who's my darling for
evermore, mm?'

Jake took his hands out of his pockets – he was definitely ill at
ease – and put his arm around her shoulder in a sketch of a hug.
He didn't kiss her but said, 'Your cousin Susan rang me. Said she
had some things of Kate's. She wanted to know if I wanted them,
or if I would like to hand them on to Kate's parents. She said she'd
meet me here, so I took time off work although it's very . . . It's
not exactly convenient for me to . . . My father is on the warpath,
actually.'

Angelica deployed her eyelashes at him. 'Your father is a darling.
I love him to bits. Did he jump up and down with joy when you
told him his only son is getting married at last?'

'Yes. Of course.' The lines of strain on his face told a different
tale.

Another key turned in the lock of the front door and Susan let
herself into the hall. What was she doing home at this time of day?
She was wearing her usual outfit for uni, consisting of a black
T-shirt and jeans over trainers. She had her tote bag over her
shoulder. Pure student. So far, so scruffy. But she had allowed her
guinea-gold hair to curl around her head and her complexion was
peaches and cream. Perhaps she had even swiped at her eyelashes
with mascara for a change?

Angelica wasn't about to be upstaged. She advanced on Susan,
waving her left hand with its engagement ring on it. 'Congratulate
me, Susan. Jake has finally got round to proposing. Isn't he just too
sweet for words, giving me this wonderful ring?'

Susan blinked. She looked at the ring, at Angelica's face and then
at Jake. And lastly at Ellie. There was a question in her eyes. *Isn't
this a bit soon? What about his feelings for Kate?* Nevertheless,
Susan managed to make the correct response. 'Congratulations. I
hope you'll be very happy.'

This was not enough for Angelica. 'I realize that an engagement
ring is not something likely to come your way, but you might at
least pretend to be pleased for me.'

Rafael was leaning against the doorframe. He said, 'She can have a ring from me any time she wants.'

Susan blushed and looked down at the floor. Yes, her eyelashes had definitely been treated with mascara.

Angelica didn't smile. Her voice became sharp. 'Oh, we can't possibly take anything Rafael says seriously, can we? Jake, are you taking me out to lunch somewhere nice?'

'I . . .' Jake didn't know where to look, or where to put his hands.

Ellie diagnosed a man on the verge of disintegration. Interesting. If she were to put pressure on him now, would he crack open like a nut? She said, 'Jake, I've just had yet another phone call from Milos, looking for Clay. I told him to see if there was an empty house nearby, and if there was, to look in the wheelie bins stored in the front garden.'

Jake turned a strange greenish colour and reached out for the newel post of the staircase. They all heard him try to work moisture into his mouth. He tried to lick his lips, which were dry. He let himself down on to the bottom step. He said, 'Sorry. It's very close in here.' He pulled his tie down and fumbled to undo the top button of his shirt.

'Jake!' Angelica's voice rose. 'Pull yourself together.' And then, bemused, 'You didn't put him in a wheelie bin, did you?'

Rafael unstuck himself from the doorframe. 'Clearly, that's exactly what he did do. I wonder how soon the body will begin to smell. You want a glass of water, mate?'

Jake didn't reply. He let his head hang low. His city shoes were scuffed. A lock of hair hung over his forehead. Not romantically.

Ellie was almost sorry for him. 'That is where you put him, isn't it?'

A nod. A snuffle.

Angelica didn't know whether to support her fiancé or take to the hills. 'You mean, you really . . .? Ugh! How could you? I can see it was a good idea in one way, but . . .'

Ellie said, 'Jake, you loved Kate, didn't you? Maybe not enough to marry her, but you had a kindness for her?'

He jerked his head, up and down. But didn't speak.

Susan took the plastic bag containing Kate's purse out of her tote bag and put it down beside him. And stood back. She didn't want to touch him.

He put his hand over the purse. His throat worked but he made no sound.

Ellie said, 'At least her body was found and has been properly looked after. Did she look peaceful when she died?'

This time he lifted his eyes to hers before he shook his head. Tears welled.

Ellie pressed him further. 'How did it happen that she took the drug that killed her?'

He spoke to Ellie as if they were alone together. 'I'd gone home. I was in bed when she phoned. She said that as I'd stopped loving her, she wanted to end it all. She said she'd taken a lethal dose of something. She said she was giving me one last chance. If I'd ever had any feelings for her, I would get her to hospital to be pumped out. I begged her to hold on, to get an ambulance. She refused. She was hysterical. I was afraid she meant what she said but I knew she liked to play games and I wasn't sure whether she was serious or not.

'I didn't know what to do. If she had indeed taken a drug, I didn't know how long it would be before she was past saving. On the other hand, if she were playing games, the ambulance people would be furious if I got them to go there and it was all a laugh. Who could I contact? I rang Angelica because I thought she'd still be at the party. I told her what Kate had said and begged her to check. It turned out that Angelica wasn't at the flat. She was out clubbing but she did say she'd get back there as soon as she could.

'I got there by breaking the speed limits; luckily there wasn't much on the roads. Angelica and Timmy pulled up behind me as I arrived. We found Kate dancing around in the garden with Clay, laughing. Both of them. Laughing! So it was a try-on, she hadn't meant to commit suicide at all! I was so angry! I think I swore at her. Yes, I think . . . to my shame. She began to cry. She said she really did mean to commit suicide if I had stopped loving her. She put something in her mouth, lay down on the ground and closed her eyes. I thought she was dead!'

He rocked to and fro. 'I tried to rouse her. No good. And Clay . . . Clay laughed! He actually laughed! So I clocked him one. He fell and hit his head on the edge of the pool. I was so surprised! I couldn't believe it! I shook him and he went all floppy on me. I'd killed him! And then . . . And then, Kate sat up. She started to laugh. She said she'd held the pill under her tongue to fool me and look what I'd done to Clay! She said I'd killed him for nothing because she'd only been play-acting!

'I could have throttled her! And then she started to choke and . . . there I was, trying to give Clay the kiss of life, and Kate clutching her throat . . . I thought she was pretending again, but no, she'd actually swallowed the pill! By mistake! And there was I, trying to get my phone out to call the police and the ambulance people . . . and . . .'

Ellie said, very softly, 'Angelica and Timmy prevented you from calling for help. How did they manage that?'

He writhed, remembering. 'Angelica tried to get my phone out of my hand but I hung on to it and tried to push her away. And then Timmy hit me. At least, I think he did. From behind. Suddenly I was flat on my back looking up at the sky and the music had stopped and it was all quiet and—'

'What music?'

He looked bewildered. 'I don't know. There was music coming from inside the house when I got there. Kate and Clay were dancing to it in the garden. When I woke up again, the music had stopped and I was lying on the ground. Shivering. I was so cold. I couldn't think what I was doing there at first. My head hurt. It still does, a bit.' He rubbed the back of his head. 'I suppose Timmy must have knocked me out. Then I remembered. I thought it must have been a dream. I hoped it was a dream. But I got up and Kate was lying there, looking somehow not like herself any more. I touched her and she was getting cold. Clay had gone.'

Ellie said, still speaking in the soft voice that seemed to work on Jake, 'Timmy and Angelica moved him?'

'They'd dragged him as far as round to the side of the house but they needed me to help them get him into the boot of my car. I'd been knocked silly. I wasn't thinking straight. They told me to take hold of Clay's legs, and I did. They told me to lift him and carry him, and I did. They told me to put him in the boot of my car and I did. I was like a zombie.'

He wailed, 'I'm so ashamed! I killed Clay. For nothing. She'd taken the pill to frighten me. It was all play-acting. She hadn't meant to die. And he was dead and she was dead and I hadn't meant any of it to happen.'

'But you drove your car round to find somewhere to put Clay?'

'Timmy said to drive. And I did. He said to stop. And I did. He told me to get out and help him. We tipped Clay head first into a wheelie bin. Timmy said that was good riddance of bad rubbish. I got back into my car and went home.'

Ellie said, 'Leaving Timmy and Angelica to get back in their own time. And you didn't phone Angelica the following day?'

He shuddered. 'No. How could I? And I had to pretend I didn't know what had happened to Kate all that day and the next.'

'But you took Angelica in yesterday with all her luggage? And agreed to her terms?'

Jake turned to look at Angelica, who was on her phone . . . or rather, on Kate's phone. He said in a dead voice, 'Angelica has given me a life sentence. My father's found out that I've stolen money from the firm. I can't cope. I've tried to tell her that I can't marry her but she won't listen. She says everything will be all right if I just keep quiet and behave normally.'

'Of course it will,' said Angelica, interrupting her phone call to give him a bright smile.

Jake shook his head. 'I can't stop thinking about what I've done. I'll keep you out of it, Angelica. I'll say I went back alone to the flat and found Kate dead. I'll say I killed Clay because he laughed at my distress. I didn't mean to, but I did. I'll say that I panicked and hid his body all by myself. I won't mention you were there, or Timmy. I'll say it was all my fault. I'm sorry if this upsets your plans for us to marry but you must see I can't carry on as if nothing has happened. I'm going to go to the police. I understand I'll have to go to prison. I killed two people but I didn't mean to hurt either of them. Maybe they'll understand and let me off with manslaughter. But I can't let this lie go on and on.'

The front door clicked open . . . How many keys had Angelica handed out? Susan was right: Ellie would have to get the locks changed.

Timmy Lee walked in warily, his eyes everywhere. He was wearing a waterproof poncho, black and shiny with raindrops. So it was still raining outside. His hair was also black and shiny but his face was white in the shadowy hall. He stripped off his poncho and tossed it on the floor.

'Timmy, darling!' Angelica greeted him with a big smile. 'You're just in time. Jake here has gone all suicidal. Wants to go to prison or to kill himself, or both. Would you like to take him outside and reason with him?'

Ellie gasped. What did Angelica mean by that? It sounded as if . . . No, surely she didn't mean that she wanted Timmy Lee to take care of Jake, did she? To silence him? Or to kill him?

EIGHTEEN

Tuesday teatime

Timmy ignored everyone to concentrate on Angelica. He smiled. A small, tight smile. 'I told you, Angel. Jake is the weak link in your plans for the future. You should have let me deal with him when Kate died. I could have constructed a romantic double suicide for you and then we'd have been in the clear.'

Angelica pouted. 'But *you* wouldn't marry me, Timmy. Jake is my own true love and can give me everything I want in life. He just needs to keep his nerve and we'll be home and dry.'

Jake's body sagged. He shook his head, over and over. 'It's no good, Angelica. I'm through with pretending.'

Angelica said, 'Timmy, you know how to stop him, don't you?'

Timmy said, 'Why should I?'

'Because . . .' Angelica's eyes shone with a wicked innocence. 'Because if you don't, I'll have to tell the authorities that your papers were originally drawn up for another member of your family, someone who hasn't got a police record.'

Narrow eyes almost closed. 'That's not true.'

Eyes wider than ever, she smiled. 'It's close enough. You carry a knife. I've heard you threaten another student with it when you couldn't get your own way about something, and you get ants in your pants every time your papers are mentioned.'

Ellie's brain went into overtime, trying to work out why Timmy had helped Angelica in her schemes.

Yes, he didn't want anyone looking at his papers, so he'd do anything to avoid the attentions of the police.

He had gone to the party, stayed for a short while and left with Angelica for the club. Then had come the phone call from Jake to Angelica asking her to return to the flat to help him with Kate. Angelica had asked Timmy to give her a lift back to the flat and he'd agreed. Why not? He would think that he'd be earning brownie points by helping Angelica out.

Only, the problem back at the flat was far more serious than he'd expected. Jake, Angelica and Timmy were faced with a hysterical Kate, threatening all sorts in an effort to get Jake back. Clay had been no help at all.

None of them had known how to handle the situation. There had been a lot of shouting and screaming. Suddenly the situation had turned from tragi-comic to tragic. Kate had pretended to commit suicide. Jake had hit the drug supplier, who'd died. It had been an accident, but yes, he'd died, and that didn't half complicate matters!

Then Kate 'woke up' and by mistake had swallowed the drug. She might have been saved if someone had called for an ambulance. Jake had tried to do so.

Angelica hadn't for several reasons; foremost of those was probably panic. Yes, of course she would panic! Kate was dying . . . well and good. But Jake had killed Clay! At all costs, Jake had to be prevented from alerting the authorities or the future she'd planned for herself would be lost for good.

Timmy wouldn't have wanted to call an ambulance because he couldn't afford to be found at the scene of a double death.

Jake had tried to call the police and . . .

What had happened then? Angelica would have screeched to Timmy to stop Jake . . . and at that moment Timmy would also have seen that he had to stop Jake. So he'd hit Jake from behind and knocked him out.

One blow. That's all it would have taken. Timmy didn't look as if he'd ever been much of a boxer, but he'd panicked and lashed out. Luckily Jake was only stunned, not killed.

Ellie could understand Timmy's reasoning. He was not, repeat not, going to let his future go down the drain because some idiot girl had killed herself by mistake, and her even more idiotic friend had taken his revenge on a drug dealer, of all people. Drug dealers were the lowest of the low.

So then Angelica and Timmy were faced with the problem of two bodies to dispose of. Who had decided what they should do next? Angelica or Timmy? That would be for the police to decide. Kate's body could be left in the garden, to be found by someone else later. Her death would not be regarded as suspicious. But the evidence of blunt force trauma on Clay's body could land all three of them in jail, so his body had had to disappear.

Timmy had acted to save his own skin as well as Angelica's. From his point of view, he was wise to back Angelica. No doubt she promised him the earth in exchange for his silence. She had no money herself but her fiancé had enough for both her and Timmy. Timmy didn't need the money, but he did need her silence and that of Jake . . . and that's why he'd been sniffing around, trying to ensure that neither Angelica nor Jake would betray him to the authorities.

In Angelica he had met his match. She might appear to be a fragile beauty, but she had a tongue that could weave a spell to ensnare unwary souls. Her fragility was deceptive, but Timmy had known her for a while and he understood that she'd have no compunction in giving him up to the police if her future were endangered.

Timmy Lee had not intended to become her partner in crime, but circumstances had pushed him into making a couple of wrong decisions. He would not break under pressure, as Jake had done, or as Angelica would probably do.

Ellie could see that if Jake planned to go to the police then Timmy would need to deal with him.

Timmy said, 'Come along now, Jake. I'll take you somewhere quiet and we'll talk things over.'

It was an invitation to death on a rainy afternoon.

Angelica had mentioned that Timmy carried a knife . . .

'Yes, Jake,' said Angelica. 'Go along with Timmy. He'll help to get you sorted out.'

Did Angelica think that Jake was no longer any good to her? Did she fear that he might fail to keep her out of the picture and that she might be sent to prison as an accomplice? Was Angelica ditching her hopes of marriage into a wealthy family?

Could she really be that cold?

Um, yes. She was switching sides. Angelica now wanted Jake dead. And so did Timmy Lee.

Jake gathered himself together. 'Where are we going?' Like a child.

'We'll take your car, shall we? For a little drive. To somewhere quiet, where we can talk everything through. You'll like that, won't you?'

'I'd like that. Somewhere quiet. Far away. Sort it all out. And then we can go to the police together.'

Susan said, 'No, don't go!' In a frightened voice.

Rafael took out his wallet. 'Look, Jake! That cheque. I don't want it. Here, take it and tear it up. That should put you right with your father again.'

Jake wavered, frowning. 'My cheque . . .? Well, yes. I suppose . . . But . . .' His eyes lost contact with Timmy's. He stood still, unsure of his next move.

Ellie heard a click as a knife appeared in Timmy Lee's hand, a sharp blade that caught the light. The knife added another dimension to the situation.

'Come along, then,' said Timmy. The knife flickered in his hand. His eyes locked on to Jake's.

Rafael said, 'Hold on, now!' And started for Jake.

Timmy slashed the air with his knife, indicating that Rafael keep his distance. All without taking his eyes off Jake.

Susan lashed out at Timmy with her tote bag. He sidestepped and backhanded her. She yelped as she fell.

Rafael shouted, 'No!'

Timmy smiled, the knife flickering in his hand this way and that but his eyes never leaving Jake. 'Come along, Jake. These people are no use to you now. Let's get out of here. Get it over and done with.'

Jake nodded agreement. 'Yes, it's the right thing to do. We'll sort it out, together. I haven't had a minute's peace since I killed that man. It'll all be over soon, won't it?'

Timmy took a step back on silent feet. His left hand reached backwards for the door.

Jake was within his reach.

Timmy's hand found the latch on the door.

Rafael dived for Jake and took him to the floor in a rugby tackle.

Timmy lunged forward. He seized Rafael's hair and put the knife to his throat. 'You shouldn't interfere! Release him or I'll dig a hole in your eye!'

Something ginger shot across the hall from the sitting room. Midge the cat?

A wail, and little Evan blundered into the hall, making straight for Ellie. 'Ganny, Ganny! Midge bit me!'

He held up his arms to her to pick him up but, as quick as Ellie was, Timmy Lee was quicker. Timmy scooped up the boy and held him high. Evan hit out at him but he might as well have been hitting the wall.

Evan wailed, 'Put me down! Bad man!'

Timmy said, 'Get up, Jake. You're not hurt. And I know you want to come with me. And anyone else . . .' The knife flashed. 'Anyone else moves and the boy gets cut. Understood?'

Evan screamed with fury. 'Bad man!'

Everyone else froze.

And the doorbell rang.

No one moved, except for Evan. Bright red with rage, he screamed at Timmy, 'Put me down!'

The bell rang again. And again. The knocker went *tap, tap, tap!*

'Delivery, missus!'

Two voices. Male.

Rafael got to his feet. He was laughing. 'The new mattress for your bed, Mrs Quicke.'

Timmy backed away to the wall, still carrying Evan, who went on screaming and beating at his captor's neck.

Timmy's eyes darted everywhere, his arm firmly around Evan. 'Don't answer it. They'll go away.'

'No, they won't,' said Ellie. 'They can hear Evan scream so they know there's someone here. Timmy, give me the boy. He's no use to you and he'll burst your eardrums if he keeps screaming like that.'

Slowly, Timmy relaxed his hold, letting Ellie take Evan from him.

Rafael opened the door to the delivery men with their plastic-wrapped mattress, saying, 'Come on in.'

Timmy Lee clicked the knife shut and tried to slide out of the door past the delivery men, who hadn't caught on to what was happening, and halted, half in and out of the hall.

'Stop him!' cried Rafael.

The delivery men gaped, the mattress between them. 'What?'

Timmy screamed at them, 'Let me through, you stupid—'

The delivery men might not be quick on the uptake in appre-hending a criminal but they weren't going to put up with being called names. That raised hackles. The foremost man said, 'Who you calling stupid?'

Rafael grabbed Timmy from behind and swung him round.

Timmy tried to shake him off.

Ellie, one-handed, hampered by a screaming child, tried to dial for the police.

Rafael was thrown off and . . . the delivery men blocked Timmy's exit by standing foursquare in the doorway with the bulky mattress between them.

Timmy gibbered, and then . . . and then . . .

Timmy drove his knife into himself.

In and up.

Blood seeped out over his hands as he folded inwards and let himself down on to the floor. He was out of it.

'What the . . .!' The delivery men.

Oh, dear! A bloodstain is so hard to get out of a wood floor.

Ellie pulled herself out of shock and said into the phone, 'Police and ambulance, please. And hurry!'

Angelica made a dive for the front door. She was getting away . . .

Susan swung her tote bag round, catching Angelica at the back of her knees so that she stumbled and fell, hands scrabbling the floor. And squawked.

Susan sat on Angelica, driving the air out of her lungs.

The delivery men froze.

Ellie jiggled Evan, speaking to the phone. 'Yes, yes. That's the address. Do hurry. I think that a young man has done himself an injury.' And then, to Evan, 'Milk, Evan? Tea?'

Evan stopped mid-scream, inspected her face to see if she really meant to give him some food and sighed. 'Biccy and milk.' He laid his head against her neck, and one of his chubby hands reached up to clutch at her neckline. 'Hippo. Where's Hippo?'

Rafael retrieved Hippo from where Evan had dropped the toy and handed it to the boy, who clutched it, hard.

Ellie prompted him, 'Say thank you, Rafael.'

A long, sweet sigh. 'Thank you.' And then, unexpectedly, 'Love you, Ganny.'

Ah, the sweet little one. He could be very affectionate, at times. Far more so than his mother had ever been.

Ellie shifted from foot to foot in the age-old manner of a woman soothing a child.

The foremost delivery man said, 'Well, blow me! Is this a stunt for the telly, like?'

Rafael took charge. He said, 'I wish it were. Attagirl, Susan. Can you keep Angelica there for a moment?' He helped Jake up off the floor and made him sit on the hall chair. 'Now, mate. Keep in mind, killing Clay was an accident. And here.' He stuffed Jake's cheque into his pocket. 'I don't want this. Give it to your father. He'll need it to get you bail.'

The delivery men were lost. This sort of thing simply didn't happen, and therefore it was not taking place. The larger of the two recovered first. 'Look, do you want this mattress or do we take it back?'

'Yes, please,' said Rafael. 'Can you bring it inside?'

'Where you want it put?'

'Would you carry it up the stairs for me?' asked Rafael. 'And take the old one away and dump it.'

The larger of the delivery men looked hard at Timmy, groaning on the floor, and looked away, making it clear that if people chose to push knives into themselves it was nothing to do with him. 'We deliver to the ground floor of the house, not further, and we don't take the old one away, mister.'

'Surely . . .?' Rafael fluttered some notes into their hands. 'An exception?'

Again, the delivery man glanced at the figure of Timmy. And again decided it was nothing to do with him. 'Well, if you put it like that! Where you want it?'

'Leave it at the top of the stairs and I'll do the rest.' Rafael ushered them up the stairs as yet another visitor arrived.

Andy, with his arms full of packages. 'Hello? I need to dump these things before I get back to the hospital. Lesley's out of surgery but they're keeping her in tonight. What's going on here? What's Angelica doing on the floor?'

'Angelica is wanted for murder and mayhem,' said Ellie. 'Leave her be. She's going down to the police station to make a statement and then she's on her own. I suggest you let her get on with it, for once. She and the man on the floor are the ones who wrecked your flat, helped Kate to die, murdered the drug dealer and disposed of his body. We're waiting for the police and an ambulance to remove them.'

Andy was going to say, 'What?' any minute now, so she forestalled him. 'So, that's good news about Lesley. She'll be out tomorrow?'

Andy's mouth dropped open and stayed that way. 'Why is Susan sitting on Angelica?'

'Because Angelica is finally learning that crime doesn't pay. Susan, you can let Angelica get up but first take away her shoes and her handbag. She won't run far without them.'

'What . . .?' said Andy. 'I don't understand. That man is bleeding!'

'So he is,' said Ellie. 'And I wish he weren't. But if people will carry knives then such things do happen.'

'Shouldn't we be doing first aid or something?' He dropped his packages to kneel by Timmy, who seemed to have drifted off into another world.

Ellie said, 'Don't touch him, Andy. If you pull that knife out, he'll die. Wait for the paramedics, who will know how to staunch the bleeding. And,' hearing the ambulance siren impatiently requiring entry into the drive, 'here they come. Will someone please see to it that they can park in the drive? Also the police, when they come. Thank you, Rafael. Thank you, Susan. You're both stars. Now, if anyone needs me I'll be in the kitchen, feeding Evan.' She went down the corridor to the kitchen.

The kitchen was nice and quiet. The clock on the wall announced it was time for tea. Good. She'd get Evan settled first, and then she'd feed the others and ring Thomas and oh, dear! She'd forgotten to ask if Andy needed feeding tonight.

There was a ring at the doorbell, heavy footsteps and raised voices. The police and the ambulance people had arrived. Good-oh.

'What shall we have to eat, little one? Not just biscuits. You must be hungry, after all that's happened today.'

'Hippo wants food, too.'

First things first. Food for the little one.

Tuesday evening

Evan was cranky. He walked around, trailing Hippo but could settle to nothing. He wailed softly to himself, but when picked up he wanted to be put down. And when on the floor, he wanted to be picked up. Ellie didn't dare let him go to sleep or he'd be waking Diana up every hour in the night. Meanwhile, she had something else to worry about. Thomas would surely be making every effort to get home this evening so how many more people would be needing supper?

Would she need to give a statement to the police?

Listening hard, she heard Rafael's voice, followed by miscellaneous rumbles from, presumably, the paramedics and police. Then she heard Susan's voice, steady and calm. And, finally, Jake's.

The ambulance drove away. More chat in the hall. The police car drove away.

Finally, she and Evan were alone. All was quiet. An uneasy, waiting quiet.

Ellie ensconced herself in the big chair in the kitchen. She took Evan on her knee and tried to interest him in the picture books she kept for him to tear up or throw around . . . which he duly did.

Ellie cuddled Evan, who cuddled Hippo. He was warm but not too warm. And heavy. It was a relief when Diana swept in to collect the boy, scolding as she went. 'Come here, look at you, what have you been doing? Mother, I did think I could trust you to . . .' Diana tossed Evan into her car, buckled him in and drove off, spurting gravel.

And then the house was quiet again . . . until her phone rang. It was her cleaner, Annie, ringing to report on progress at the flat. The bathroom and kitchen had been scoured clean, the carpets spot-cleaned and the bed linen had been laundered, dried and replaced on the beds. The broken glasses and empty bottles and cans had been removed and the place was now spotless. The new toilet and replacement pane of glass would be fitted on the morrow, which meant that Lesley could indeed return to the flat then, if she wished to do so.

'Well done, Annie. And thank you.'

'I have to warn you,' said Annie, 'that sir was not satisfied. He said we had oughta got through quicker.'

Ellie sighed. 'Yes, Annie, I'm afraid some men will never learn how much it takes to clean a house properly. But I know, and I'm thanking you for what you've done. It was a nasty job and I think you've done brilliantly. I'll see you get a bonus.'

Ellie sat on in the kitchen, thinking that she ought to stir herself to get supper ready. And lacked the energy to move.

Finally Rafael and Susan returned. They came straight into the kitchen and sank into different chairs.

'It's over,' said Susan.

'Jake confessed,' said Rafael. 'I'm almost sorry for him.'

'Angelica cried,' said Susan, 'but she'd banged her nose somehow and her tears didn't have the usual effect.'

Susan allowed herself five seconds rest and got to her feet. 'You look worn out, Mrs Quicke. Don't you worry about supper; I'll do it.'

'Thank you, my dear. I must say, I am feeling rather tired tonight. Can you work out how many there's going to be?' Ellie resorted to counting on her fingers. Thomas, Susan, Rafael, Andy . . .?

Rafael said, 'Andy's gone back to the hospital for visiting hours, so at least he's out of the way, though he said he'd be back to sleep here. He's complaining about the cleaning team you arranged to deal with the flat. Says they're a noisy lot. He wonders why they can't work without putting the telly and the radio on.'

Ellie managed a smile. 'Can you imagine what would have happened if he'd been left to clear up by himself?'

'I can,' said Rafael. He imitated Andy's slightly whining tone of voice. 'Mrs Quicke, you won't believe this but I found them making tea for the plumber instead of getting on with the job that they were being paid to do!'

Ellie grinned. 'Completely overlooking the fact that it is I who arranged to pay for the cleaning up of the flat.'

She wasn't sure what she hoped for in Lesley's marriage. Lesley and Andy had had a bad start but maybe they could work things out.

What of Jake and Angelica? She rather hoped Jake's family would stand by him, get him bail and a good solicitor. In her opinion, he was weak rather than wicked.

As for Angelica! Ellie didn't envy the police in trying to extract the truth from that little beauty. Perhaps, if Angelica were fortunate and managed to get a good solicitor, she might get away with probation. In which case, Ellie would be sorry for whichever probation officer took the girl on.

Ellie was annoyed that Timmy had tried to kill himself on her premises. Blood is so difficult to get out of parquet flooring. On the other hand, she didn't want him to die. She decided to ask Annie to see if she could get the stain out.

Later – perhaps tomorrow – she'd call the hospital to see if Timmy had survived. If he had, she supposed he would be barred from taking his degree. Presumably he would also be out of favour with his family, who had hoped for so much for him.

A key turned in the lock and Thomas returned, at last! Ellie's world had righted itself. Yes, he was very tired, but he'd done what he could to help his friends until their daughter had arrived to look after them. Now he let go of the stresses of the day, gave Ellie a big hug and wondered whether he should have a beer with his supper.

At that very moment, Susan sang out that supper was ready. Hurrah!

Thomas went straight to the kitchen, sniffing the aroma of cooking. 'What is it? Chicken and . . .?'

Susan elbowed him out of the way. 'Go on! Sit down! Chicken pieces in a herb sauce, with new potatoes and fresh greens. I don't need telling you'll eat twice as much as anyone else. Oh, and this is my friend Rafael.'

'Rafael?' Thomas looked blank. He hadn't met Rafael yet, had he? And there was Rafael, perfectly at his ease, giving some clean glasses an extra polish.

Ellie introduced them. 'Rafael's been most helpful today. I don't know what we'd have done without him.'

Thomas registered that a place had been set at the table for Rafael as well as for Susan, and acted on the hint. 'Rafael, is it? You're welcome. I fancy a beer. Would you like one, too?'

Everyone ate. And calmed themselves down after the tensions of the day.

After his second helping had disappeared Thomas pushed back his plate and leaned back in his chair. 'Thank you, Susan. I feel half human again.'

Ellie wondered, without caring very greatly, what Susan might produce for afters. Cheese and fruit? She could leave it to Susan to provide. Ellie relaxed, letting her arm and shoulder rest against Thomas's. He patted her hand and shifted his chair to be even closer to her.

Rafael sifted through the pile of papers Diana had left for Andy to see. 'Do you fancy a million-pound waterfront property, Susan? Nice big kitchen.'

Susan stirred something in a pan on the stove. 'I haven't finished college yet.'

'How's about I set you up in a restaurant of your own?'

'With my old friend Angus as my sous-chef?' She tasted the mix and nodded approval.

Rafael grinned. 'Certainly not.'

'Jealous?' Susan dug some of her home-made ice cream out of the freezer, ran a metal scoop under the hot water tap and dished out four portions.

'Yes. And sensible,' said Rafael. 'It wouldn't work.'

'I have to finish my course before I can think of the future.' Susan poured a luscious toffee and cream mix over the helpings of the frozen pudding.

'Then we can get married in six months' time?'

'What are you offering?'

'What do you know?' Rafael half closed his eyes, studying Susan.

She picked up two of the plates and paused. 'I know all about your father, the solicitor, who is on the verge of retirement. I know about your mother, who runs the local WI and everything else in sight. I know about your sister, who married a loser but has got shot of him and lives near you with her two small children. I know you've a first-class degree in maths and super maths and all that jazz. As for the money lending business, I know you inherited money from an aunt and don't have to work but that you like to keep your hand in doing this and that. The moneylending is just a sideline which amuses you, but I know you've invested in a rundown block of flats and are doing them up to rent out. I know you're doing most of the work yourself, not because you can't afford to employ others but because you like to keep busy.'

Rafael said, 'You wouldn't want a husband under your feet all day long, would you?'

She smiled. 'I know you have a penthouse flat in the centre of town but I don't want to live high in the sky without a garden, and I'm not going to marry you just to provide you with a housekeeper and cook.'

Rafael pushed the details on the flats to let towards Susan. 'Take your pick.'

She put two of the puddings down in front of Ellie and Rafael. 'It doesn't matter where but it has to be a home, not an advert for *Homes and Gardens*. I want there to be trust between us, and laughter, and thinking about what's best for the other person. For it to work we must want the same things out of life. I want children, and I think you do, too . . .'

'I'm fond of my little nephew and niece, who aren't much older than your Evan. But I didn't want any of my own until I met you.'

Susan went on, 'I know you want me, and I will admit I fancy you something rotten, too. But there has to be more than that. A loving kindness. Courage for when bad things happen. I wasn't looking for marriage so soon, and when you came on to me too quickly, I reacted too sharply.' And here she blushed. As did he.

'But,' she said, 'when I got to know you . . .'

Her voice faded.

Rafael said, 'Your terms are accepted.'

Susan leaned over to kiss Rafael.

Thomas peered a query at Ellie. Rafael was a stranger to him, so did Ellie approve? Ellie nodded. Yes, those two would be all right together.

Thomas said, 'Bless you, my children, and now, may I please have my dessert, too?'

That evening, a bright eight-year-old asked his mother, 'Why is that man looking in our wheelie bins?'

His mother peered out of the window in time to see a large man slamming out of their garden gate only to turn into the one next door, which was currently occupied by a builders' skip plus the usual wheelie bins.

'What's he doing, mum?'

His mother reached for her mobile phone and reported to the police that a man was trying to extricate a corpse from next door's wheelie bin. It might have been easy to dump a limp body into the bin but it was proving difficult to extract. The police car arrived just as Milos attempted to turn the wheelie bin over in an effort to dislodge the body. This led to a number of difficult questions being asked and, eventually, to charges being laid. So in the end, both the bodies were accounted for and laid to rest.